I0536162

Truth or Consequences

Sharon C. Cooper

Amaris Publishing LLC

Truth or Consequences

By: Sharon C. Cooper

Copyright © 2014 by Sharon C. Cooper all rights reserved.
No part of this book may be used or reproduced in any manner without written permission except in the case of brief quotations embodied in critical articles and reviews. For permission, contact the author at www.sharoncooper.net

ISBN: 978-0-9903505-1-4
Book Cover: Selestiele Designs
Published by: Amaris Publishing LLC in the United States

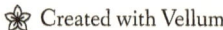 Created with Vellum

Disclaimers

This story is a work of fiction. Names, characters, and incidents are either products of the author's imagination or are used fictitiously. Any resemblance to actual events, locales, organizations or persons, living or dead, is entirely coincidental.

Please be advised that this story has adult and sensitive content not recommended for those under the age of 18.

Acknowledgments

Special thanks to one of my dearest friends and writing bud, Claire Fadden.
Claire, you **ROCK**!

Victoria, congrats again on winning the contest! I hope you enjoy the story!

Nasi, what can I say but, girrrl you're something else! Thank you for everything. You're truly a godsend!

Chapter One

Malik Lewis ambled through the halls of Supreme Security Agency, his Stacey Adams clicking rhythmically against the marble floor. He spoke and nodded as his employees hustled through the hallways, greeting him while they hurried off to their designated areas. Sometimes he found it hard to believe how much the agency had grown over the years. With a staff of seventy-five—which included security experts, IT specialists, and a host of support staff—his organization was one of the largest private security agencies in Illinois.

"Good afternoon, Malik."

"Hey Malik. We missed you at the meeting this morning."

"What's up, boss?" Stan, one his most reliable armed security supervisors, greeted and fell in step alongside him. "I heard a vicious rumor that you might be facilitating the morning huddles for the next four weeks."

"Yeah, don't remind me." They turned down the hallway that led to Malik's office. "I didn't know Ted was going to be out of the office that long." As owner and CEO of the agency, Malik wore many hats, even if it meant facilitating meetings, which he hated. Normally Ted, the Executive Protection Director, would oversee morning huddle, but not for the next few weeks. Ted was home with his wife, busy playing new daddy to one of the cutest baby girls Malik had ever seen … it even had him thinking about having a kid or two one day.

Pushing open the double glass doors, the men walked into the large suite that opened into a receptionist area and two offices, one being Malik's.

"Hey, no Vicky today?" Stan asked, referring to Malik's executive assistant.

Malik glanced at his watch, surprised it was already four-thirty in the afternoon. "She should be back shortly. She's making a couple of runs for me."

"All right, I'll catch her later." Stan followed Malik into his office, but stayed near the door. "I'm going to have your mini-me on the Fontaine assignment for the rest of the week."

Malik set his briefcase down and regarded Stan with a smirk. "A regular comedian, huh? Mini-me?" Stan had been giving him the business about Travis Kincaid, the kid Malik had hired a few weeks earlier.

"Hey, what can I say? Besides being a little rough around the edges, he reminds me of you, just younger."

Seeing potential in him, Malik had personally hired Travis. The young man started with the Chicago police academy, but thanks to his temper, got himself kicked out before graduating. CPD didn't care that his skills were like those of a master shooter. He had excelled at the physical agility tests, and had great detecting instincts. They wanted someone with Travis's leadership ability, but it was equally important that he could follow instructions without coming across as a know-it-all. Malik had to admit that he'd hired the kid because he reminded Malik a little of himself. A smartass, fearless, and intimidating force with quick thinking ability as well as physical prowess.

With a little guidance, those qualities could definitely come in handy.

"So are you okay with him being on the Fontaine assignment?" Stan asked, cutting into Malik's thoughts.

"Hey, if you think he's ready, go for it. Just keep an eye on him. Dealing with his big mouth and cocky attitude might pose a challenge for you."

Stan shrugged his linebacker-size shoulders. "Eh, I think he'll be all right. If not, by the time I'm done training him he'll be one of your best bodyguards." He turned toward the door. "Catch you later."

Like a trusted advisor, Stan was one of Malik's most valued assets and had been with the company since the beginning. He played a part in the solid relationship the agency had with local law enforcement, as well as the state and federal government. Malik tried for years to give Stan a role worthy of his importance in the company, but being a security specialist was all he wanted to do, and he was damn good at it.

Malik released an exhausted sigh. He stood at the large window in his office behind the desk and gazed at the busy downtown traffic below. It felt good to be back at the agency. By the second meeting that morning, his patience had worn thin, his meeting tolerance depleted. It didn't help that throughout the day his mind kept straying to thoughts of a beautiful, curvy goddess who he hadn't seen in months. How a one-night-stand could rock his world the way she had was a mystery to him.

"For Christ sake, why don't you just call the woman already?"

Malik turned from the window and narrowed his eyes at Wiz, who walked into his office, closing the door behind him. Known for his ability to hack into any computer system and manipulate anything remotely technological, Cameron received his nickname, Wiz, honestly. They'd first met years ago during

3

their Navy days and went through SEAL training, serving on the same team together. Other than Quinn Hamilton, Malik's best friend, Wiz was one of few men Malik could count on for anything.

"Call who?" Malik finally asked.

"Man, don't play dumb with me. You know damn well who ... Natasha Lockham, Alandra's sister. That *is* who you're thinking about, isn't it?"

"Wiz, don't start," Malik grumbled. Not in the mood for any ribbing, he pulled out his desk chair and plopped down in it.

"What do you mean don't start? I'm sure I wasn't the only one who noticed how distracted you were in that meeting this morning." Wiz sat on the edge of the oversized mahogany desk and folded his thick arms across his broad chest. "As a matter of fact, your attitude has been shitty for the past few months and we both know why."

Wiz knew about his one-night-stand with Quinn's sister-in-law and took every opportunity to rag him about it. And then there was Alandra, Quinn's wife. Malik was pretty sure that when she told him to take care of her sister, she didn't mean for him to seduce Natasha into giving him the most amazing sex he'd ever experienced.

"I'm counting on you to look after my sister," Alandra said *just above a whisper. "Promise me." When he didn't respond, she moved closer. "Promise me."*

"There you go again, staring off into space. Now tell me again. Why haven't you called Natasha?"

Malik sighed loudly and rested his head against the back of his leather chair. Closing his eyes, he rubbed his forehead. *I am not having this conversation.* There was something to be said for hanging around people who knew you almost better than you knew yourself. Before retiring from the Navy, he and Wiz spent practically every day together, raiding terrorist compounds, traipsing through jungles, and bouncing from one op to another. It was almost impossible for them not to know what the other was thinking, honing in on each other's attitudes, knowing in a heartbeat when something was off.

"I can't call her, man." Malik stood abruptly, sending his chair slamming into the wall. He reclaimed his spot at the window and braced his hands against the windowsill, as if staring out at nothing in particular would provide him with the answer to his problem.

"Why the hell not? I've never known you to shy away from any woman, especially one as hot as Natasha. Mr.-I-Can-Pull-Any-Woman-I-Want is punkin' out," Wiz scoffed, his patronizing tone clawed down Malik's spine. "So what's the problem?"

"The problem?" Malik turned and glared at his friend. "Wiz, your IQ is higher than anyone I know and you have to ask me what the problem is?" Malik's voice boomed. "She's a damn surgeon! No, actually, she's the fucking Chief of Staff at one of the largest hospitals in Chicago. I can't ask her out!"

Wiz stood a few inches shorter than Malik, but that didn't stop him from stepping to Malik and getting in his face. "Why not?" he asked, his voice raised to match Malik's forceful tone. "You've beaten some of this country's most vicious advisories. Hell, you've even been shot at pointblank range and left for dead. And you expect me to believe that your punk-ass is afraid to step to a woman?" Wiz shook his head. "Unbelievable!"

Malik clenched and unclenched his fist; anger churned in his gut as he stayed rooted in place. No one pushed his buttons the way Wiz could and Wiz knew it. "Man, fuck you!" Malik spat out, unable to think of anything more brilliant to say.

He turned and paced across the lush, carpeted floor. He ran his sweaty palm over his clean-shaven head, breathing in and out slowly to get his anger under control. It wasn't Wiz's fault that he was letting thoughts of some woman affect his usual laid-back life. Problem was, she wasn't just any woman. She was the only woman he had ever met who had garnered a second, third, and hundreds of thoughts thereafter. Since their passionate night in Los Angeles, Malik hadn't been able to think of much else.

He peeked over his shoulder at his friend. Wiz's comments wouldn't have stung had they not been true.

"What the hell would we talk about?" Malik asked. "Sure, I can tell her anything she wants to know about taking apart and cleaning a M4 assault rifle, or show her how to use just the right amount of C4 to blow-up a small section of a building without the whole damn thing tumbling down. Heck, I can even teach her how to take out a tango target at 2000 yards, but after that," he shrugged, "I've got nothing. We come from two very different worlds and have absolutely nothing in common."

Wiz stared at him; his green eyes boring into him like a high-beam laser zoning in on its target. Malik rarely flinched, but damn if Wiz wasn't making him squirm.

What the hell is happening to me?

Wiz threw his head back and a bark of laughter erupted, bouncing off the light blue walls and filling the large space.

"Damn! I wish Quinn could see you now," Wiz said, still laughing when he collapsed into one of the leather chairs facing Malik's desk. "How many times did you give us a hard time about our women? Talking about our noses being wide open and how the mighty had fallen. Now who's whipped? Yeah, it's probably good you're not calling Natasha. If she messed you up with just one night, you probably can't handle anything more."

Your day is coming. There is a woman out there who is going to bring your crazy ass to your knees. Quinn's words from a few months earlier invaded Malik's thoughts. He remembered teasing Quinn mercilessly after watching him fall under Alandra's spell.

"Shit! I'm fucking screwed," Malik mumbled and dropped down in the chair next to Wiz.

"Maybe not totally screwed, but you're definitely going to have to clean up your language." Wiz crossed his legs, lifting one ankle to rest on the opposite knee. "I'm pretty sure Natasha won't tolerate your incessant cursing. Man, just ask her out. I don't understand why that's so hard."

"I don't want to ask her out! Don't you get it?"

Wiz's eyebrows knitted together. "Apparently I don't."

"Despite what happened that night, Tasha is not the type of woman you just hit it and quit it. She's ... she's different, special. You know me. I'm out to have a good time. I'm not looking for forever, and she's a forever kind of woman."

"Tasha, huh? Well," Wiz stood and shoved his hands deep into the front pockets of his jeans and braced his weight on one leg, "all I have to say is that if you're interested in Natasha, go for it. If you don't someone else will."

Malik cursed under his breath. He hadn't thought of Natasha seeing anyone. He gripped the arms of his seat and pushed up to a standing position, irritation twisting in his gut.

"Sometimes you get on my last fuc—"

Two light taps against his office door, followed by a bark, halted Malik's words.

"Sorry to interrupt guys," Victoria Bracero said, stepping inside of the office. Tank, Malik's Rottweiler, was at her heels, and trotted over to him, his tongue wagging.

"What's up, boy?" Malik bent down and ruffled the dog's short fur. Tank had been his constant companion since Malik retired from the military almost two years earlier.

"Hey Vicky," Wiz said.

Victoria, Malik's executive assistant and right-hand woman, strolled across the room. Her blonde curls bounced with each long step. She wasn't only Malik's assistant. Her sexy looks, physical strength, and street-smarts converted easily into a standby bodyguard when he needed her in a pinch. Few would believe that she knew twenty different ways to kill a man with an ink pen as her only weapon.

"What's up, Wiz? I haven't seen you in a while." She stepped into his waiting arms and smiled a salacious smile that seemed to be reserved for him. "Where you been hidin'?"

"I've been around." They hugged and Wiz planted a kiss on her cheek. "You're never here when I stop by."

"I know. My boss," she jerked her head toward Malik and quirked her eyebrows, "treats me more like a personal assistant than an executive assistant."

"I'm sure. He's a regular slave driver."

"I don't appreciate you two talking about me like I'm not here." Malik walked around his desk, with Tank following close behind. "Vicky, thanks for picking up Tank from daycare. How did he do this morning?"

"They said he had a good day, but you know they love him there." Victoria headed toward the door. Malik had no idea how she moved around so seamlessly in four-inch heels, but she strutted in them as if they were tennis shoes. "Considering how large he is, I think most people are surprised by his laid-back demeanor."

Malik bent down and ran his hand along Tank's strong back. The dog's shiny black coat glistened under the office lights as he patted Tank's side. "Yeah, my boy here is just like me: cool, calm, and collected until someone steps out of line."

"Uh, yeah, I guess." Victoria smirked at Wiz. "All right, fellas, I have a little more work to do before I head out. Let me know if you guys need anything."

"Now getting back to what we were talking about," Wiz said after Victoria closed the door. "Apparently you and Tasha had enough in common to spend the night with each other, and most of the next day together. You even cooked for her. I think that speaks volumes. Ask her out and see what happens."

Another knock sounded at the door and Victoria walked in, closing the door behind her.

"Hey, Malik, there's a lady in the waiting area." She glanced down at the small yellow pad of paper in her hands. "Her name is Rosalyn Lee. I told her that since she didn't have an appointment and you were in a meeting, you might not be able to see her this late, but she said it's urgent. It's about her sister. I guess she was a friend of yours. Do you have time to speak with her?"

"Actually, I have to get out of here anyway," Wiz said and handed Malik a flash drive. "That's the info you requested." Then he turned to Victoria. "Vicky, baby, take care of yourself and don't let this big lug of a boss work you too hard." He kissed her hand and headed for the door.

"Okay, Wiz, hope to see you soon," she said, her grin huge and her tone flirtatious. "You know you can come by even if Malik isn't here."

Wiz laughed, but kept walking. Malik didn't know why she bothered flirting with him when she knew what everyone else knew: Wiz was still in love with his ex-wife, Olivia. Even a woman as fine as Victoria couldn't distract him from his plans of reuniting with his ex.

"Now who did you say she was again?" Malik asked, bringing Victoria's attention back to her reason for being in his office. Dropping the flash drive into his pants pocket, he moved to his desk.

"Rosalyn Lee. She said you knew her sister. Maybe you should meet with her, she looks pretty distraught."

Malik shrugged. "All right." He followed Victoria to the door. Tank stood and trailed behind him, but Malik snapped his finger and pointed to the padding in the corner on the other side of his desk. "Stay."

"Ms. Lee? I'm Malik Lewis," he said, stepping outside his office. He assessed the short, middle-age woman who reared her head back to look up at him. He stood six-foot-eight and people were often caught off-guard when meeting him for the first time. She pushed her red-rimmed glasses up on her nose and extended her hand.

"Hi Mr. Lewis, I'm sorry to stop by without calling first, but I really needed to speak with you." Her voice was raspy, as if she'd been crying.

"Sure, come on in." Malik tilted his head toward his office. "I have a few minutes before I need to leave." He followed behind her, taking in her attire. Considering she was probably in her early forties, she dressed as if she were much older. Her long, straight gray skirt that stopped mid-calf appeared to be two sizes too big, and the black, thread-bare sweater looked as if it had seen better days.

"Why don't you have a seat on the sofa," he said and closed the door. "What can I do for you, Ms. Lee?" He sat down in a paisley upholstered chair across from her.

Rosalyn ran thin fingers through her thick black curls before dropping her hands to her lap, toying with the hem of her sweater.

"Mr. Lewis, I've been on a mission's trip for the past eight months, returning a couple of weeks ago. I found out my sister, Susan, died five months ago ... during child birth." She sniffled, swiping at her sudden tears. "I didn't know," she sobbed. "She was all alone. Besides some very distant cousins, we don't have any other family."

Malik stood, grabbed a box of Kleenex, and handed it to her. A flicker of anxiousness curled in his gut. He didn't do well with women crying.

Upon closer perusal, he had to admit that there was something familiar about this woman. *Susan, Susan,* he tossed the name around in his head, trying to connect the name of Rosalyn's sister with a face. *Oh crap!* He suddenly knew whom she was referring to. *Sue died during child birth?* He hadn't seen her in well over a year and even then they had only hooked up on occasion.

"Ms. Lee, I'm sorry to hear about your sister, but—"

"Please, call me Rosalyn." She wiped her face and crumbled the tissue in her hands. "I'm sorry. Of course you're probably wondering what this has to do with you."

The thought had crossed my mind.

"When I returned and found out my sister had passed away, I obtained her death certificate. This past week, while going through her things, I ran across one of her journals. Inside, she mentioned her pregnancy." Rosalyn wiped at her eyes again. "Mind you, I didn't even know she was pregnant. After more digging, I went in search of a fetus death certificate for the baby, but came up empty handed." She stopped and stared at Malik expectantly.

He tilted his head, wondering why she stopped. "Go on."

"I'm told that the baby didn't die, but was taken into foster care. When I contacted the state, they have no record of the child."

Malik shrugged, totally not understanding what this had to do with him. "I'm sorry, Ms. Le— I mean Rosalyn, but missing persons is not my expertise. I can give you the name and contact information of a good P.I.," Wiz immediately came to mind, "but there's nothing I can do for you."

She straightened and cocked her head, her gaze studying him intently. "What if I told you the baby was yours?"

"I think Dr. Halsey is killing new mothers."

Hospital Chief of Staff, Natasha Lockham, glanced up from

the document she was reading and stared at her head nurse. There was no way Natasha heard her correctly. Apparently, her migraine was affecting her hearing.

"Layla, I think I misunderstood you." Natasha closed her eyes and rubbed her temples, praying the throbbing in her head would cease. Especially since she needed to ensure the document in front of her was perfect for the finance department. "I thought I heard you say that Bob was killing women."

Silence filled the office space and Natasha slowly opened her eyes and lifted her head. Unspoken agony was evident and glowing in Layla's light-brown eyes. *Oh God.* Dread spread through Natasha's body like a California wild fire, scorching every nerve ending along the way. The youngest chief of staff in the hospital's history, Natasha had been in her new position for six months and felt like a firefighter at times. She put out more fires than she cared to admit.

She gripped the edge of her mahogany desk, using it as a brace to keep herself steady as she slowly pulled herself into a standing position. Feeling like crap for the majority of the day, she really should have left and gone home hours ago. Now she wished she had.

Natasha and Layla had been friends for years. Layla was by far one of the most skilled nurses she had ever worked with, so there was no way her friend would come to her with an accusation without just cause.

"I assume your comment is based on fact." Natasha leaned forward, palms down on her desk. "Because I don't have to tell you ... that's a serious charge." Her voice trailed off. She prayed that Layla would tell her that she had misunderstood, but she remained silent.

Layla glimpsed back to ensure the door was closed and then stepped closer. "You know I wouldn't come to you with something this serious without a good reason." The quiver in her voice matched the erratic rhythm of Natasha's heartbeat.

"Risk management hasn't said anything to me," Natasha said, her voice just as low as Layla's, despite the closed door. The fact that her admin assistant had already left for the day, and none of the other offices were near hers, didn't make her feel any more comfortable discussing this particular topic. "Surely if risk management suspected anything they would have started a root cause analysis of questionable deaths."

Layla ran her hands down her face and released a ragged breath. "Tasha, risk management might not know. I don't know if anyone knows. You're the first person I've mentioned this to."

Seconds ticked by. They stared at each other, neither saying a word. Natasha could hear her father's words ring in her head. *Don't ask a question unless you're prepared for the answer.* Though she would hate the response to any questions asked, there was no way she could ignore this damaging allegation.

"Maybe you need to start at the beginning." Natasha reclaimed her seat, staggering a bit in the process from the pressure in her skull and now the anxious butterflies knocking around in her stomach. She pointed to the upholstered chair in front of her desk. "Sit. Tell me what happened?"

"There's a baby missing."

Chapter Two

Natasha sat in her office, the overhead lights dimmed and her desk lamp providing a sliver of illumination. *Why would five of Dr. Halsey's patients die after giving birth?* She rested her head against her forearms on top of the desk, the constant throbbing and light-headedness taking its toll. She had temporarily forgotten how bad her migraines could get. The afternoon conference calls and the conversation with Layla hadn't helped.

Natasha couldn't wrap her brain around Layla's suspicions of Dr. Halsey, a well-respected doctor, not just in Illinois, but also in New York and Texas where he'd worked years earlier. Why would he intentionally take the lives of his patients? *None of the women had preexisting conditions.*

Natasha slowly lifted her head and opened her eyes, glad the nausea had passed. Standing, she gathered her purse, briefcase, and jacket. She had contacted risk management and filled them in on her conversation with Layla. The fact that five of Dr. Halsey's patients died within the last two months from pregnancy related complications was enough to raise concern. Layla didn't have solid proof of any wrong doing. The baby boy she thought was missing had been officially signed out. However, the relationship of the person who he was released to wasn't clear.

Thankfully, today was Dr. Halsey's last day of work before he left for a two-week vacation to Acapulco. That would give Natasha enough time to do some digging of her own.

She clicked off the desk lamp and eased toward the door, having second thoughts on whether or not she was in any shape to drive. After doing a mental catalog of everything she'd eaten that day, she hadn't come up with anything that might have triggered the ache in her head. All she knew was that she couldn't wait to get home and take something.

Her cell phone rang.

That was all she needed—an excuse to sit back down and close her eyes for a minute before leaving.

"Hello," she answered, her voice barely a whisper. She sat on the sofa in the far corner of the office, placing her bags and coat down next to her.

"Tasha, what's wrong?" her ex-husband, Martin Lockham, asked, concern evident in his voice. "You don't sound too good. Are you okay?"

Divorced for nearly ten years, she and Martin were still good friends. They had first met in grade school and started dating in high school, only to marry during her residency. Turns out it wasn't the best decision, considering they were divorced a year later. Her eighteen hour workdays, and the desire to be the best surgeon ever, didn't help in nurturing her marriage. It also didn't help that Martin had cheated on her.

"Hey Marty. I'm all right, just suffering from a migraine." She leaned back against the sofa and rested her head, her eyes still closed. She fiddled with the diamond charm hanging from a platinum chain around her neck. It was the last gift from her father before he was killed during his combat tour in Kuwait. "To what do I owe the pleasure of your phone call?"

"Sorry to hear about the migraine. I know how debilitating they can be. Well, I'm not going to hold you long. I don't know if you remember, but this Saturday would've been our tenth year anniversary."

Natasha had remembered, though the thought fleeting.

"I called to invite you to dinner. Maybe we can also go dancing or to a show afterwards."

She would always love Martin, but she wasn't in love with him and wondered if she had ever been truly in love. Since their divorce, birthday presents from him arrived every year, and he invited her to dinner on their would-be wedding anniversary. Her family and friends couldn't understand how she could forgive him for cheating on her, but they didn't understand the friendship they'd established well before saying 'I do'. Besides, he claimed loneliness from her absence for his reason for cheating. Although it was no excuse, she understood. Things were different now. For the first time since their divorce, she wanted more.

Thoughts of Malik Lewis and their one night of incredible sex came to mind. Her cheeks heated reliving the number of times he'd made her come. Until that evening, she had no idea she was capable of such passion and wanton behavior. The icing on the cake was when he cooked for her the next morning ... well, technically that next afternoon. She hated cooking. To have a man whip up a brunch with little or no effort had earned him huge points.

"Tasha?"

Her eyes flew open and she bolted upright, only to groan and grab her head when the room started spinning. Pushing her long tresses away from her face, she fought to keep the bile that rose to her throat down and steadied herself.

"Tasha, where are you?" Martin's anxious voice rang out. "Are you still at the hospital? Do you need me to come and get you?"

"No, no I'm fine. I moved a little too quick is all. I'm still at the hospital, but I'll be heading out soon."

"I don't think it's a good idea for you to drive. If your migraine is as bad as the ones you used to have, then I think you should stay put. I'll pick you up."

"No. That's not necessary." Sometime she hated that she wasn't in love with Martin. The short time they were married, he was a good husband. Until he cheated. Now, as good friends, they talked at least a couple of times a week and for the most part, she enjoyed spending time with him. *Then why am I trying to think of an excuse so that I don't have to go out with him Saturday night?*

Natasha stood and began gathering her things again. She knew why she didn't want to go out with him. She wanted more. At thirty-five, it was way past time that she started thinking about remarrying and having a family. With no prospects, if her Mr. Right didn't come along soon, she would miss her window of opportunity to have a couple of kids before she was too old.

"Marty, I'm getting ready to leave."

"Are you sure you don't need me to pick you up?"

"I'm sure, but thanks. As for Saturday, I think I already have something planned. Let me double check and get back to you."

After a slight hesitation he spoke. "All right. Well, let me know. And I'll check on you this evening to make sure you made it home okay."

There is no getting rid of him. "Okay."

Natasha left the wing of the hospital where most of the offices were located, finally making it to the lower level that would lead to the parking lot. She blinked several times to focus, the pressure behind her eyes causing blurriness.

Maybe driving isn't such a good idea.

She switched her Michael Kors bag to her opposite shoulder and headed for the doors that would lead her out of the hospital personnel only area. Apprehension swept through her and she stifled a groan as the busy sounds of the hospital grew louder the closer she got to the main area. The evenings were the most hectic and she really didn't feel like dealing with crowds, but she needed to stop by the nurses station before heading out.

A wave of dizziness assaulted Natasha. She reached for one of the double door handles and the door flew open.

"Whoa!" A tall man grabbed her by the elbow, keeping her from falling into a heap on the floor. "Are you okay?" He led her to a bank of chairs and helped her sit down. "Should I get a nurse or a doctor for you?"

The stranger's heady scent—a mixture of sandalwood and leather—was the first thing that caught Natasha's attention, but it was his deep, sexy voice that caused her to look up at his face. The constant pounding in her head and her unfocused sight didn't detract from his handsomeness.

When he cracked a smile, revealing perfectly straight teeth, she realized she'd been staring. "*Lo siento. Muchas Gracias.*" She adjusted her handbag and briefcase, planning to stand, but wobbled on the way up.

He smiled. "I see you speak Spanish." He extended his hand and pulled her up.

She frowned. "Huh?"

"Spanish. You said I'm sorry and thank you in Spanish."

Natasha didn't know what she said. All she knew is that she needed to lie down before she passed out. "My father was Hispanic." She cast a glance at him again, feeling more comfortable than she should considering he was a stranger. "Every now and then Spanish slips out. What about you? I take it you speak the language."

He shrugged. "I have some Mexican friends. I've picked up a few words here and there."

Natasha swayed again and he grabbed her around the waist. "Maybe you should sit for a moment. You don't seem too steady on your feet. Are you sure I can't get someone from the hospital staff, Ms. ..."

"Natasha. Natasha Lockham."

"Nice to meet you. I'm Ray Newton."

Malik hadn't planned on stopping by the hospital to see Natasha, but after his visit from Rosalyn, he had an excuse. There was no way he was the father of Susan's baby. The timing might have said otherwise, but he believed in practicing safe sex. There were no slip-ups. Besides, he knew they weren't exclusive. The only reason he was still thinking about the conversation was that he had promised Rosalyn that he would look into the situation. Maybe Natasha could give him more information regarding Susan's death and the whereabouts of her baby. Assuming there was a baby.

"May I help you?" the receptionist asked when he approached the hospital's help desk. She looked up at him in silent awe, which happened a lot because of his height.

"I hope so. I'd like to speak with Dr. Natasha Lockham. Do you know if she's here?"

"I can check for you. Your name?"

"Malik Lewis."

While she dialed the number, Malik glanced around the sitting area. A doctor approached the waiting room and a group of family members leapt from their seats and surrounded him, tossing out questions faster than the doctor could answer. When one of the women burst into tears, Malik knew he had seen enough. He turned back to the receptionist, but his attention diverted to the nurse standing near the copy machine, who openly stared at him as if she knew him.

He might forget a name, but rarely did he forget a face, and she didn't look familiar. Shorter than the average woman, her heart-shaped face displayed very little makeup, except for her cherry-colored lips. Her light-brown eyes held his attention, bright and friendly.

"I'm sorry, sir, but Dr. Lockham is not answering," the receptionist said, reclaiming his attention. "She might be—"

"Is there something I can help you with?" the woman previously staring at him asked, moving closer to the desk.

"This is Malik Lewis," the receptionist said. "He's looking for Dr. Lockham, but she isn't answering. Normally I see her when she leaves."

"I'm pretty sure she's still here." The nurse peeked at her watch and then back at Malik. "She actually should be on her way down. We were supposed to meet here five minutes ago." She walked around the counter and approached Malik, her hand extended. "I'm Layla."

"Nice to meet you." Malik shook her small hand.

"Let's head toward her office. We might run into her."

"Thanks." Malik strolled along side of her. "Have we met before?" he asked, his curiosity getting the best of him.

She laughed, taking four steps to every one step he took. "Not exactly, but Natasha has mentioned you."

Malik's brows drew together. Something in his gut fluttered at the thought that maybe Natasha had thought of him as much as he'd been thinking of her.

He pointed at himself. "She mentioned me?" He tried, but failed to keep the surprise out of his voice.

A smile slid across Layla's glossy lips. "Yep, she mentioned you." They walked around a corner and Layla's steps slowed. "Hey, it looks like you're in luck. There she is now."

Malik followed her gaze until it landed on the woman who had featured in many of his dreams, whether it be day or night. What he hadn't expected to see was a man with his hands on her, helping her to a chair.

"What the hell," he mumbled and hurried in her direction, not liking how pale she looked nor how close the guy was standing next to her. Layla jogged alongside him to keep up.

"Malik," Natasha said when she glanced up. "What are you doing ... oh God, did Quinn send you? Did something happen to my sister?" She leapt up, stopped abruptly, and grabbed her head, stumbling forward.

"Oh shit." He reached out and grabbed her around the waist to keep her from going head first to the floor. "I've got you." He squinted at the man who had a hold of her arm. "I said I have her."

Seconds passed and the guy didn't let go. Instead, he glared into Malik's eyes as if challenging him to a duel.

"Take your hands off of her or so help me—"

"Malik, please ... don't." Natasha held onto his arm as if it were a life preserver. She was clearly too weak to stand on her own.

The stranger finally released her. Outside of his mother, Malik couldn't ever remember feeling so protective of a woman. He didn't know who the man was, but if he had to guess, he'd say he was military. The immaculate dress shoes, straight-back posture, and conservative haircut screamed military. However, it was the lethalness in his eyes when he stared Malik down that made him think the guy might even be special-forces.

"Here, sit her down," Layla said from behind him.

"What's wrong with her?" Malik sat next to Natasha, her eyes closed and her skin getting paler by the minute as she slumped in the chair.

"She's been suffering from a migraine for most of the day,"

Layla explained, the back of her hand against Natasha's fore-head and then her cheek.

"A migraine?" Malik repeated. "You mean to tell me a headache can take her out like this."

"Malik, why are you here? Is it ... Alandra?" Natasha's voice hitched. "Please don't tell me—"

"She's fine. I just came to see you," he said, deciding to delay telling her about the conversation that he'd had with Rosalyn. Well, part of the conversation anyway. There's no way he would tell her about what the woman read in her sister's journal.

"Natasha, have you taken anything?" Layla asked.

"No," she mumbled. If Malik hadn't been practically sitting on her he wouldn't have heard her. "Waiting ... until I get home."

Malik looped his arm around her and Natasha rested her head against his shoulder, surprising the hell out him. His heart leapt inside of his chest at the feel of her in his arms, recalling their naked bodies doing the horizontal tango. The memory throttled him like a lion on its prey, sending blood straight to his groin. They didn't know each other well, but that night there was a connection between them that he had never felt with any other woman. His feelings for her weren't just about the sex; he and Natasha connected on all levels. Now, holding her close brought the memories all back.

"This is her second dizzy spell in the last ten minutes," Ray said. "She slammed into me coming through the door and I had to catch her before she fell."

"Who are you anyway?" Malik asked.

"This is Ray Newton. He's a health records technician here at the hospital," Layla said absently, now checking Natasha's pulse. Malik glared at Ray. Unease gnawed inside his gut, twisting and churning like it used to do when he was on an op and something bad was about to happen.

"Layla." Natasha opened her eyes, barely, and lifted her head from his shoulder. "Can you contact Dr. Johnson? Find out when's a good time to meet with him Monday regarding what we discussed earlier."

"I'll take care of it. Are you sure you're okay? You're not looking too good and your pulse is racing."

"Can't you give her something?" Malik asked, his arm still around her. It felt surreal to have her so close, thinking that he would never see her again. Her familiar scent—cinnamon with a hint of vanilla—drifted through the air around him each time she moved.

"I could, but it would probably knock her out."

"Go ahead and give it to her if it's going to make her feel better. I'll get her home."

"No," Natasha protested. "I can get home. Then I'll take something."

"I don't think it's a good idea for you to drive," Layla said cautiously, as if expecting a battle.

"She's not driving." Malik stood and scooped Natasha up into his arms, ignoring her protests. "If you can hand me her bags, I'll head out now."

Layla grabbed the bags. "I'll carry them."

"Malik, I can walk," Natasha mumbled against his chest, her words contradicting the limpness of her body.

"I know, baby," he kissed her forehead, "but I would prefer to carry you." Malik hurled a parting glare at Ray before heading for the exit.

Chapter Three

Malik drove through the Lincoln Square neighborhood, glancing at a sleeping Natasha curled on the passenger seat of his Chevy Tahoe. He hadn't been to her place in months and was going by memory. A quick glance at her driver's license revealed the address.

He found it hard to believe that she was sitting next to him, even if she was barely conscious. How many times had he dreamt about seeing her again? It seemed longer than three months since Quinn and Alandra fled the country, running away from trouble that started years ago when Alandra was kidnapped by a Mexican drug cartel. He hated that his friends had to endure that nightmare, but had they not, he wouldn't have met Natasha.

Malik pulled up to the small bungalow and cut his engine. He sat back and perused the front of her house, glad to see that she had left a few lights on. Taking his gaze away from the house, he savored the beautiful woman sitting next to him. There was still something about her that stirred a longing within him.

He exited his truck and patted his pocket for her keys as he went around to the passenger side. Natasha hadn't stirred the whole trip. After opening her door, he reached over to unhook her seatbelt. Her subtle, yet enticing fragrance gave him pause. It was the same perfume she wore that night. That night that had ruined him for any other woman.

Malik stared at her. He ran his hand through her brownish-red hair that hung just passed her shoulders, wanting to touch more than her long tresses. He took in the delicate features of her light-toffee complexion, a combination of her African American and Hispanic heritage. Malik's gaze traveled lower to her mouth, longing to kiss those lips of hers again. Add those features and her perfect curvy body, combined with brains and a sweet disposition, and you had the woman he couldn't stop thinking about.

Okay, get it together, Malik. He straightened and adjusted himself, not surprised by how easily his body reacted to her.

"Natasha." He gently shook her. Her soft snores were the only sound in the cabin of his truck. "Natasha. Come on, baby, wake up. You're home." He shook her again and her eyes lifted half-mast, but he could tell she was still out of it. Something inside of him softened, hating to have to wake her, knowing she wasn't feeling well.

"All right, let's get you in the house." He would just take her in, get her settled, and leave.

Gathering her in his arms, he nudged the truck door closed and walked the short distance to the front of her house. Suddenly, the door swung open and he instinctively pulled her closer.

"What happened?" a tall, thin man with wire-rimmed glasses and a book in his hand asked. "And who are you?"

"Malik. I'm a friend of her sister, Alandra." Malik quickly went through the mental catalog of what he knew about

Natasha, trying to remember if she had a brother. He knew there was another younger sister, but couldn't remember if there was a brother. "Who are you?" he finally asked.

The man looked him up and down before responding. "Her husband."

The shock of his words hit Malik full force. He thought back. If he wasn't mistaken, Natasha had told him she'd been divorced for ten years. No way could she have given herself to him the way she had that night if she were married. Or maybe she'd just gotten married. It had only been three months since their time together, but while in the military, he'd known people to fall in love and marry in less time than that.

"Where can I lay her?"

"Tasha, sweetheart. Tasha?" The guy grabbed hold of her upper arm and started shaking her. "What have you done to her? Natasha!" He shook her harder and Natasha stirred in Malik's arms, snuggling closer to his chest.

Malik wasn't known for being a patient man and this dude was pushing his luck. "Listen, she got sick at the hospital and I offered to bring her home. Now you can move your ass out the way so I can lay her down somewhere, or she goes home with me."

"Like hell! I'm not letting you take her anywhere."

"Then move."

He stepped out of the doorway. Malik followed the man to the back of the house and down a narrow hallway. They stopped at the second door on the right, and the guy turned on one of the lamps. Malik took a quick glance around as he approached the queen-sized wrought iron bed covered with a white comforter and a mound of colorful pillows. The room screamed feminine touch, and from what he could see, there was no sign that a man shared the room.

Malik went to lay Natasha on the bed, but stopped when

26

she curled into him, snuggling closer, her small hand on his chest. She felt so right in his arms, but one thing he definitely didn't do was another man's woman.

He laid her on the bed and stepped back, noticing the photo of her and Alandra on the nightstand. If she were married, why wouldn't she have a photo of her and her husband? As a matter of fact, when he walked through the house, he didn't see any sign that a man lived there.

His gaze swept the intimate space again before he returned his attention to the man who was now slipping off Natasha's shoes.

"So who are you again?" Malik asked, his gut telling him that this so-called 'husband' was lying.

The man dropped the last shoe to the floor and stood to his full height. Though tall, Malik still had him by at least seven or eight inches.

Malik didn't miss the way the man's features darkened, his light-colored complexion slowly turning red.

"Who I am is none of your da—"

"Oh but it is." Malik stepped to him and the man took a step back. "Since I promised Alandra I'd keep an eye on Tasha, I sure as hell am not leaving her here with someone I don't know. Now who the hell are you?" Natasha mumbled something and turned on her side, still not waking. Layla had warned that the medication she'd given her would knock her out.

Malik turned his attention back to the man standing before him. "I asked, who are you?"

The guy sighed, threw up his arms, and let them drop to his side. "Dr. Martin Lockham, Natasha's ... ex-husband."

Malik stared at him for a moment, deciding on whether or not he was telling the truth. "So if you're an ex-husband, what are you doing here?"

He met Malik's gaze with a smirk. "Tasha and I are trying to work things out, get back together." He shoved his hands into the front pockets of his pants and rocked on the balls of his feet. "So if Alandra really *did* ask you to look after my wife, your services aren't needed. I'm surprised my sister-in-law didn't tell you about me."

Malik folded his arms across his chest and glared at Martin, not missing the way the guy kept licking his lips and clearing his throat. *He's lying.*

"Actually, I'm surprised your *ex-wife* didn't tell me about you when I was with her last night."

Martin's cocky smile slipped, telling Malik everything he needed to know.

"Why you sonofa—" He charged toward Malik, but stopped suddenly when Malik dropped his arms and expanded his stance. All Malik needed was a reason to kick his ass.

"Man, you don't want none of this." His voice was a low rumble as he approached Martin, who didn't back down. "I don't know what type of game you're playing or why the hell you're here, but don't ever fuck with me."

"Malik ... Marty, what's going on?"

Malik turned at the sound of Natasha's voice. She was laying on her side, her tired, glossed-over eyes zoned in on them. "Malik, thanks for bringing me home. Good night." Her voice was weak, but her words and her stare were solid.

He stared at her without speaking. Just like that, he'd been dismissed. *Ain't this some shit.*

"I'll show you to the door," Martin said, humor in his tone. "And yeah, thanks for bringing her home. I can take it from here."

The next morning Natasha laid in her queen-sized bed, with pillows all around her, feeling out of sorts. She hated taking medication, especially for her migraines. They always knocked her out, leaving her feeling loopy and exhausted the next day.

She must have fallen asleep immediately because she couldn't remember anything after sending Malik home. A sweet sensation flowed over her body and her eyelids drifted shut at the thought of Malik. No one would ever believe how gentle and thoughtful he could be considering how intimidating and dangerous he appeared. She was probably one of the few who had seen his other side. When he had flown from D.C. in the middle of the night, to pick her up from Chicago and then fly to L.A to see Alandra, she saw the man he hid from others.

Three months earlier:

Natasha stared out at the moonlight shining over the Pacific Ocean. Arriving in Huntington Beach, California in the middle of the night, she hadn't had the pleasure of seeing one of its famous sunsets. Instead, she spent her time saying good-bye to her sister, Alandra, and brother-in-law, Quinn Hamilton.

She turned from the window and dabbed at her eyes with the tissue, which was balled up in her hands. She had mourned for Alandra years ago when she thought she'd died after being gunned down. Her sister had returned from the dead, only to have to turn around and disappear again. It didn't seem fair that Natasha was losing her a second time, and she still didn't understand why they had to leave the country.

"Someone so beautiful should never have tears in her eyes."

Natasha jerked her head toward the doorway, surprised to see Malik Lewis. Tall enough to be a pro basketball player, with a strong, solid body and broad shoulders, he easily filled the doorway of the bedroom. The intensity of his dark eyes and his steady gaze sent a wave of awareness through her body, rooting her in place. She usually leaned more toward the preppy, white-collar, serves on numerous non-profit boards type of man. Yet, there was something mysterious and dangerous about the man standing before her. Something that stirred a longing inside of her that she hadn't felt in years.

"Alandra told me you were a tea drinker." He lifted the mug, steam billowing above it. "I thought you might like a cup ... to help you relax," he said, but didn't step into the room.

Natasha studied him holding the mug that was dwarfed within his large hand. Right now, she could use more than a cup of tea, unless the one he held had a big dash of hard liquor in it. Something to dull the pain in her heart is what she really wanted.

"I personally prefer a shot of tequila when I need a pick me up," Malik shrugged, "but that's just me."

Natasha couldn't stop the smile from spreading across her lips. Being around him was the one thing that had made the unexpected trip bearable. On the flight to L.A. he had kept the conversation light, except for when he gave her a hint of the trouble that had led him, Quinn, Alandra, and Wiz to Washing-ton, D.C. Still, she wasn't sure what had taken place, but she knew it was bad. Not just because of a few bruises Alandra had obtained since she'd last seen her, but because the three former SEALs were sticking to her sister like a second skin. Something traumatic had happened. Her sister was jumpy and Quinn's behavior was no better. She understood it was his natural instinct to be protective of his wife, but Alandra could barely go to the bathroom without him following close behind her.

Malik stepped into the room and handed her the tea. "If you would prefer something stronger, just say the word. Quinn has a full bar downstairs."

"Thanks," Natasha took a timid sip from the mug, "I'll keep that in mind. Before the night is over, I might take you up on that offer."

Setting the cup on the bedside table, she dropped down on the bed. Her heart hadn't felt this heavy in years and part of her wanted to cry. The other part of her wanted to throw something. She didn't associate with a lot of people due partly to her work schedule. Mostly she didn't have a lot of friends thanks to all of the moving around they did as kids, her father being in the military and all. Alandra was more than her sister, she was her best friend.

"I guess they're gone, huh?" she asked of Alandra and Quinn.

"Wiz just left to take them to the airport. There's a private jet waiting for them." Malik stood against the wall in front of her, studying her with those intense eyes of his. She could only imagine the fear he had instilled in enemies he confronted when he served in the Navy and on special ops.

"Are you ever going to tell me where they are going? Where they'll be living?"

He shook his head. "No," he said simply, as if she didn't have a right to know. As if she was some child who couldn't be trusted with the truth. He pushed away from the wall and sat on the bed next to her. His huge thigh grazed her leg and the nearness sent a blast of heat shooting through her body. "It's not safe for them, nor is it safe for you to know where they're going."

Natasha turned to him. "But you know."

"That's different."

"How? How is that different?" Anger simmered in her gut, slowly working its way up. She wanted to punch him in the arm to release some of her frustration and she would have if she didn't fear her hand would break upon contact. "I may never see my sister again and you're acting as if it's no big deal." Her voice cracked and she was afraid her frustration would soon give way to tears.

"Listen," he said, his voice low and gentle, "you're going to see her again. Right now, we just have to take precautions to

ensure there are no backlashes to some things that have transpired over the last few weeks."

Natasha couldn't hold back any longer. Tears filled her eyes, blurring her vision. She hated feeling so weak and needy. In her line of work, rarely did she let her emotions get the best of her, but tonight was different. Tonight she was losing her best friend.

"Outside of my youngest sister, who I haven't seen in years because she's trying to find herself by traipsing around Europe, I'm all alone." A tear slid down her cheek and Malik cursed under his breath. "I mourned Alandra's death once and it feels as if I'm doing it all over again."

Malik wrapped his arm around her and pulled her close, placing a kiss on top of her head. "You're not alone. I'm here if you need me."

"Yeah, you're here until you deliver me back to Chicago. Then you'll disappear, too." She tried to push away from him, but he didn't loosen his grip.

"I'm not going to disappear. If ever you need me, just hit me up." He patted the cell phone clipped to his side. "I'll only be a phone call away." He pushed her long hair away from her face, the back of his knuckles sliding down her cheek. He lifted her chin forcing her to look at him. "Only a phone call away."

She swiped at her tears, his soothing tone sending wicked coils of desire flowing through her veins. Her gaze stayed on his lips. Lips so tempting that it was taking everything within her not to cover them with hers. She'd never been attracted to the bad-boy type, but she was seriously drawn to Malik, and it wasn't just physical. He was a walking contradiction. On the outside, he was this big, strong, fighting machine who looked as if he would kick ass first and ask questions later. Yet, there was more to him. He was kind, gentle, loyal to his friends, and he made her feel safe. She would normally feel on edge sitting that close to a man she barely knew, especially considering they were sitting on a bed.

"So ... what, you drew the short straw and have to be the designated babysitter?" she asked, trying to lighten the mood.

Amusement flickered in his eyes. "No straws were drawn, and for the record, I don't see spending time with you as babysitting. If anything, I lucked out. I get to spend the next twenty-four hours with a very beautiful woman."

Heat rose to Natasha's face, sending her hormones into a tailspin. She lowered her eyes, hoping he didn't see need in her gaze, because right now all she wanted was for him to kiss her. The wanton thought surprised her. Never had she wanted a man the way she desired Malik at that very moment.

She glanced back up at him. Desire loomed in his eyes. Were they thinking the same thing? Craving to taste each other? Her gaze lowered to his mouth and her heart rate kicked up a notch when his tongue swept across his lower lip. She wasn't sure who moved in first, but before she knew it, their lips were touching. An engulfing flame swept through her and all common sense flew out the window.

The intensity of their kiss went from zero to ten in a heartbeat. One minute they were exploring each other's mouth, and the next their tongues tangled to a rhythmic beat that had her pulse pounding to the same cadence. All thoughts of Alandra and Quinn were forgotten when Malik eased her back on the bed. One of his hands cradled the back of her head, while the other gently traveled down the length of her body, tracing along every curve.

He moved from her mouth, trailing soft kisses along her jawline down to the hollow of her neck. Natasha hadn't been with a man in over a year, and even then she didn't feel the tiny prickles of delight nipping at her nerve endings the way they were now.

With nimble fingers, Malik quickly undid the buttons on her blouse, allowing the light-weight garment to fall open. He raised up on his elbow and stared down at the pink lace covering her breasts. Natasha swallowed hard when he dragged the back of his hand down between her breasts, slowly over her flat stomach, not stopping until he had her out of her denim shorts.

He moved back up her body and released the front clasp of her bra. A moan rattled against the back of her throat when her breasts spilled out into his hands.

"You're even more enticing than I imagined." His voice was raspy with desire as his gaze scanned every inch of her body, hunger brewing in his eyes. His large hands covered her breasts, caressing and stroking, Natasha squirmed under his touch, barely holding on. "I want you," he murmured before he lowered his mouth to a taut nipple, slowly chipping away at Natasha's control. Sucking. Teasing. Licking.

"Malik," she said breathlessly, her head thrashing back and forth against the sheets. Her hands clawed frantically at his strong shoulders, and down his muscular arms as he continued the sweet torture to her body. "Malik." She couldn't seem to get any other word out, too caught up in the sensual torment of his demanding lips against her heated skin. Tired of grappling at his clothes, wanting to feel him skin to skin, she tried her words again. She squirmed beneath him until she was able to place her hands on each side of his face. "One of us," she panted staring into his eyes, "has on too many clothes."

His left eyebrow rose a fraction and he regarded her. The beginning of a smile tipped the corners of his mouth, and had Natasha been standing, she would have puddled to the floor. The man was too sexy for his own good.

He turned his head and kissed the inside of her palm. "I guess we should do something about that, huh?"

He removed his T-shirt in one swift move and Natasha lifted to her elbows, unable to pull her gaze from his body. His pecs and six-pack, clearly carved by a master sculptor, glistened under the bedroom lights. She didn't think she had ever seen a more perfectly fit man in her life. *Good Lord* were the only words that came to mind; her mouth watered and she sat frozen in place.

With his intense gaze glued on her, Malik backed off the bed to his full height. He retrieved a condom from his wallet, placing it on the bedside table. A bout of nerves rattled inside Natasha's stomach when he went for his belt buckle and kicked off his shoes. She couldn't believe what she was about to do, but she had no intention of letting her mind talk her out of something she wanted. Something her body craved.

Malik's jeans slid down his long legs, followed by his underwear. Her mouth dropped open. *Oh ... my.* His erection stood at attention and Natasha wondered how he'd been able to pack his length inside his briefs. Everything about the man was huge.

Rays of ecstasy shot through her as he approached the bed, anticipation threatening to make her lose control.

"Now, where were we?" Malik asked when he climbed back onto the bed and hovered above her. His mouth lowered over hers and she wrapped her arms around his neck, giving herself fully to his kiss. She savored every swirl of his tongue, the sweet, juicy feel of his lips. Suddenly, her reasons for being in L.A. didn't matter. All that mattered was that moment. That moment with Malik.

He slid his hands between their bodies and Natasha bucked against his touch.

"If you want me to stop," he mumbled against her mouth, "say so now or—"

"*No te detengas*," *don't stop* she rasped, her breaths coming in short spurts as his hand slid slowly to the V of her thighs and into her wet panties. "*Por favor, no te detengas.*" *Please don't stop.*

· · ·

Natasha heard herself moan. Malik slipped two fingers inside of her and the passion burning within threatened to explode. She pushed her hips against his hand, heaving with need as he teased and fondled.

"Malik, please. I need—"

"Natasha?"

Natasha's moans grew more erratic as Malik picked up the pace, his fingers moving in and out of her faster ... deeper ... harder. Her nails dug into his arms. "Malik," she cried, her control teetering on the edge as she rocked against his hand. One last thrust and everything within her exploded. His mouth crashed over hers at the same time she screamed his name, her thighs locking his hand in place.

"Tasha?"

"Tasha!

Natasha's eyes flew open. She froze. Her heart pounded in her chest as she squeezed the pillow between her thighs. *Wh ... what?* Her mind raced as she tried to figure out what was going on. That wasn't Malik's voice. *I must have been dreaming.*

"Tasha?"

Her gaze shot to the door. *¡Dios mio! Oh my God! How long has he been standing there?* Seeing Martin standing across the room, embarrassment hit her like a two-by-four upside her head. Mortified by what her ex-husband might have witnessed, she closed her eyes and concentrated on getting her breathing under control. Seconds passed. Her heart dropped and disappointment settled in when she realized it was only a dream. *It seemed so real.*

"You okay?" Martin asked.

"Uh, yeah. I'm fine." She moved the pillow to the other side of the bed, suddenly realizing she only had on underwear. She quickly covered herself and glared at her ex. "Marty, why are you here?" It was bad enough that he stopped by unannounced last night, but to still be in her house, and in her bedroom, was not okay.

"I stuck around. You were so out of it last night and I didn't want to leave you alone." He folded his arms across his chest. "Looks like that was a pretty erotic dream you were having. Care to tell me about it?"

Heat rose to Natasha's face and she looked away. That dream was her reality a few months ago and apparently her subconscious couldn't let the memory of her night with Malik go. She dreamt about him almost every other day, each time a different snippet of her time in L.A. She turned back to her ex-husband.

"My dreams are none of your business." She eased up into a seated position, the sheet covering her semi-nudity, her head still feeling a little loopy. "I appreciate your concern, but you can't just show up at my house whenever you want. That house key is for emergencies only."

"My being here hasn't been a problem before. Does this have anything to do with the guy that brought you home last night?"

"No. This has nothing to do with Malik. This is about you and me."

"I see." He stared down at his shoes and then back at her. "Well, I just came to check on you and let you know there's breakfast in the kitchen for you."

Natasha's mouth dropped open. She couldn't remember Martin ever preparing breakfast. Since Malik had made brunch for her while in L.A, she realized how much she enjoyed having a man cook for her.

"I can't believe you cooked."

"Well, I didn't actually. I went out and picked up some

bagels, cream cheese, and stuff like that. You know, like what we used to have on Saturday mornings."

"Oh." Her shoulders drooped. She didn't know why she expected more. "Let me shower and I'll be right there."

Twenty minutes later, Natasha was showered and dressed. Quickly changing the linen on the bed, flashes of the night before popped into her mind. She didn't like how territorial Marty had been with Malik. It was past time for her and her ex to have a talk. He needed a reminder that they were no longer a couple.

Marty could have gotten himself killed last night, she thought with a smirk. It wasn't funny, but her ex-husband had no idea who he was dealing with. From what she knew of Malik, he fought first and asked questions later. Marty trying to be tough probably wasn't a good idea. Natasha remembered some of the stories Alandra had told her about the type of missions Navy SEALs took on and Natasha had no doubt that Malik was one of the Navy's best. Everything about him screamed danger, take charge, and don't mess with me. She didn't like being bullied into doing something she didn't want to do, but she appreciated how Malik took control of the situation the night before, getting her home safely. Just another difference between him and Marty. Martin Lockham was all about letting her do what she wanted, rarely challenging her requests or putting his foot down on anything. Malik was different.

Natasha finished tidying her bedroom and headed to the kitchen. She wasn't surprised to see Marty sitting at the breakfast bar drinking a cup of coffee, probably his second cup.

"How do you feel this morning?" he asked, studying her over the top of his reading glasses. She could only imagine what he was thinking and hoped he wouldn't say anything about what he might have witnessed earlier.

"Better." Her migraine had leveled off to a mild headache. "Have you eaten?"

"Yeah, I ate a few minutes ago." He stood and went to the refrigerator, pulling out butter, jelly, and cream cheese, as well as some orange juice. "So, what will it be?" he asked, holding up three different bags of bagels.

Natasha sipped from the orange juice she had just poured. Again, she was reminded of the morning after the night she'd spent with Malik. Not only had he cooked for her, but he'd prepared the best vegetable omelet that she'd ever had in her life. As for Marty's cooking skills, purchasing bagels or pastries was pretty much the extent of his ability.

"I'll take a blueberry bagel with a little cream cheese." She pulled out the bar stool next to the one he had vacated. "Thanks for picking up breakfast. I've been putting in some long days and grocery shopping keeps getting pushed back."

He set a small plate with the bagel in front of her and reclaimed his seat.

"When is work not going to be your first priority? I'm sure the migraine last night had a lot to do with you not eating properly and not getting enough rest. Have you thought any more about my proposal?"

Natasha could feel Marty's gaze on her, but she didn't look up from spreading a small amount of cream cheese on her bagel. A couple of weeks ago he had suggested they start dating again. According to him, now that they were older and more established in their careers, they both were ready for something a little more serious than the occasional dating they'd been doing.

"So," Marty said, turning fully on the bar stool to face her, "have you?"

She bit into her bagel and nodded. "Yeah, I have thought about it." She chewed, trying to find the right words to tell him that she wasn't interested.

"And?"

"And I don't think it's a good idea." She finished chewing and held up a finger when he started to speak. "I'll always love you, Marty, but I like what we have."

"I thought you said you were ready to settle down and have a family."

"I am," she stated, not wanting to hurt him, but decided to be honest. "I am ready to settle down, but not with you."

"Oh ... okay." He released a long breath, fiddling with the coffee mug sitting in front of him.

"Listen, let me explain."

"No, you listen." He pushed the coffee mug away and folded his hands on top of the counter. Staring down at his clasped fingers, he said, "I know I hurt you when I cheated. I'll never be able to express just how sorry I am for my indiscretion, but I thought you forgave me."

"I have. My decision has nothing to do with that, Marty. We were kids when we married. Yes, you hurt me deeply, but I understood. I put my career before our marriage and for that, I will forever be sorry. Looking back, there are so many things that I wish I had done differently regarding our marriage." She shrugged. "But it is what it is. I see you as a friend and I appreciate your friendship, but that's all that we can be. Friends."

He turned to her. "Despite how our marriage ended, I thought we still had something special. For the past ten years I have been here for you, loving you. Now you're telling me that you don't feel the same. You don't want to give our love for each other another chance?"

He stood and took his empty coffee cup to the sink. Natasha knew he was disappointed, but she couldn't continue on the path that they were going. She should have put more space between them sooner.

"We have been divorced for years. It's time we started

behaving like a divorced couple. You can't continue to just show up at my job or house whenever you want."

He turned from the sink and stared at her. "Does this have anything to do with the guy from last night, Malik?"

Natasha fingered the condensation rolling down the side of her glass of orange juice. She wanted to tell Martin that her decision didn't have anything to do with Malik, but in a way it did. He had introduced her to feelings she had never experienced, and she now realized what she missed in her marriage to Martin. Passion. Sure, they cared for each other, but they were friends so long that marrying him seemed like the natural thing to do. What she experienced during her time with Malik is what she wanted in her life all the time.

"Tasha?"

Hearing Martin call her name brought her back to the present.

"No. Malik is just a friend." She stood with her plate and glass. Martin stepped aside when she approached the sink.

"Where'd you meet him?"

Martin knew her family, but she'd never shared with him that her sister, Alandra, had been a CIA spy and that she was married to Quinn, a special operative, which is how Natasha met Malik. All Martin knew is that while Alandra lived in Chicago, she'd been a nurse. He knew about her leaving town, but he thought that she moved back to Los Angeles.

"I met him a few months ago through a mutual friend."

"Why haven't I seen him around? Are you two dating? Is it serious?"

She placed the dishes in the dishwasher and dried her hands before giving her full attention to her ex-husband—operative word: ex.

"Marty, I mean no offense when I say this, but none of that

41

is any of your business. All the more reason why you and I can't continue on like this. I've moved on. You need to also."

He snatched his keys and newspaper from the counter. "Well, when you finish screwing Malik and come to your senses, you know where to find me."

Natasha jumped at the sound of her front door slamming. *Well, that went well.*

Chapter Four

"Layla, I appreciate you coming in so early this morning," Natasha said, and placed a cup of black coffee in front of her friend. "I'm sure I don't have to mention again how sensitive in nature this information is."

"Of course not. I'm hoping you and risk management can prove my suspicions are wrong." Layla added sugar and cream to the steaming liquid. "Dr. Halsey is such a nice guy. Even when I first became concerned, I couldn't imagine him being involved in anything like this."

"I know," Natasha mumbled. She skimmed the files before her, trying to see if there were any patterns. It had been two days since Layla had brought her concern to Natasha, and she had spent much of the weekend thinking about Dr. Halsey. "I hope we don't find anything, but if something shady is going on in my hospital, I want to know."

They worked in comfortable silence, reviewing the last few of Dr. Halsey's deliveries. Natasha didn't see anything out of order, but she also wasn't sure what exactly she was looking for.

"Okay, so there were three women who died within twenty-four hours of giving birth and this one," Natasha set the file between her and Layla, "had to have an emergency C-section."

"Yeah, she was nineteen years old, eight months pregnant and had a stroke. When she was brought in, she was complaining of a headache. They gave her something for the headache and shortly after, she complained of numbness in her left arm."

Natasha read the report. The medication given to her wasn't listed, which was a red flag. She then looked for any pre-existing issues. "Her blood pressure was normal, no history of headaches, and no problems during her pregnancy." Natasha laid the file down and sat back in her seat. Each woman's death was listed as pregnancy related complications. "Out of the blue, she comes to the hospital complaining of a headache," Natasha said, trying to get her mind to catch something that she might have been missing by speaking aloud. "Then when they give her something for the pain, she experiences numbness."

"And she has a stroke," Layla said, tapping her pencil on top of the pile of files. "They delivered the baby by emergency C-section."

"God, that poor family. I can't even imagine what her parents must have thought. Your pregnant child comes in for a routine visit, ends up having a stroke shortly before giving them a grandchild, and then dies."

Layla scanned the file. "Well, actually, Tasha," she skimmed the page, her finger sliding across the paper as she read, "this woman didn't have any family. The baby was picked up by social services."

Natasha's heart lurched at the thought of another child ending up in foster care. *That poor baby.*

She sat up straighter and grabbed two files that she'd read earlier. If her memory was correct, there were some similarities.

Quickly skimming the first one, she found what she was looking for.

"All of these women were single with no extended family and their babies went into foster care."

Layla shrugged. "That might not be that uncommon. I'm sure if we went through more files, we'd probably see that with other doctors as well."

Natasha shook her head. "No. Dr. Halsey has had five deaths in two months, with a pattern. Something is going on and I intend to find out what it is."

Layla stood, running her hand down the ponytail dangling at the back of her head. "I have to tell you ... this whole situation is scaring me. I haven't actually witnessed Dr. Halsey doing anything illegal. What if I'm wrong? I don't want to be responsible for him losing his license, or worse, sending an innocent man to jail." The anxiousness in her tone was evident by the concern in her eyes.

"Technically, he hasn't been accused of wrong-doing. However, if there are suspicions regarding any one of us doing something that will jeopardize our patients, it's all of our responsibility to bring concerns of this nature to light." Natasha watched Layla pace near the seat she'd vacated, sensing that she was holding back information. "Layla, is there something else you haven't told me?"

She stopped and released a long breath, her shoulders sagging. "Remember when I mentioned that I thought a baby was missing? Well, although one of the state's social workers signed for him, nobody seems to remember the baby leaving the hospital. So while I was here Saturday, I checked to see if that social worker had signed for any other babies."

"And had they?" Natasha sat on the edge of her seat, afraid of what she might hear next.

45

"Yes, twice this month, but no one knows who the person is or if they are male or female. The signature is illegible."

Natasha scribbled on her note pad, reminding herself to look into the matter, just in case there was a connection.

"Um, I don't know if this is anything, but there's a labor and delivery nurse that has been acting a little strange."

Natasha glanced up from her notes and her brows drew together. "Strange how?"

"About a month ago, some of my nurses had been complaining about one of the labor and delivery nurses. Her name is Tessa and she's been with the hospital for a little more than a year."

"What type of complaints?"

"That she's been late, missing shifts, and disappearing for long periods of time, to name a few." Layla returned to her seat and removed her ponytail holder, fluffing out her auburn hair. "I've noticed things about her, too. Coming to work looking as if she hasn't slept in weeks, missing some of her shifts, or getting the days mixed up. Anyway, I talked with her during her annual review and asked if something was going on at home. Was she burnt out? Did she need to cut her hours? I asked everything I could think of that would explain her behavior."

"And what was her response?"

"She has two small kids, a husband who works two jobs, and they only have one car. The juggling of schedules, kids, and the one car, I believe is taking its toll. Anyway, for the past few weeks I've been observing this nurse. I have monitored her during some deliveries as well as when she's been in the nursery. The thing that has stuck out more than anything is her behavior around Dr. Halsey."

This really got Natasha's attention.

"She's jumpy, very nervous around him. Don't get me wrong, it's not that she's incapable of doing the work. She's a very competent nurse and does fine with the other doctors. Dr. Halsey has even gotten to the point of requesting her assistance for certain deliveries."

Natasha could understand him requesting a specific nurse to work with if their schedules aligned and they worked well together. She felt the same way during her career as a surgeon.

"A few days ago, I walked by the nursery and saw the nurse and Dr. Halsey standing over a baby, arguing. The moment I stepped into the room, they stopped. Dr. Halsey nodded a greeting to me, and then he asked Tessa if she could take things from there. When she nodded yes, he left. Tessa was really upset."

"What do you mean?"

"She wasn't crying, but there were tears in her eyes and she was visibly shaking. I helped her to a chair and asked what was wrong, but she said 'nothing'. So then I went and checked on the baby, thinking that maybe the baby had issues, but he was in perfect health."

"Hmm, I can see why you're suspicious." Natasha drummed her fingers against the tabletop. "It might be nothing, but right now, I'm going to look into anything that involves Dr. Halsey."

A knock at the door halted their conversation. Natasha closed the files before leaving the table. Her assistant wasn't expected until eleven due to a meeting at her daughter's school, so Natasha wasn't sure who would be at the door.

"Hi," she said, surprised to see Ray. Now that her eyes were clearer and she didn't have a migraine, she realized he was more handsome than she first thought. Nut-brown, blemish free skin except for the faded scar down his right cheek, confident dark-brown eyes, and a smile that Natasha knew got him plenty of dates. She didn't realize how young he looked the other day, but now, if she ventured a guess, she'd say he was probably in his mid to late twenties.

She moved back and opened the door wider for him.

"Sorry to bother you." He stepped across the threshold, his back ramrod straight, confidence in his gait. "It looks like you recovered well." His gaze traveled the length of her. He flashed a smile that lit up his whole face and Natasha couldn't help but smile back.

"I did, and thank you so much for your help Friday night. I probably would have ended up face down in the middle of the hallway had it not been for your quick reflexes."

His smile deepened. "No problem at all. I'm glad I was there to help." He briefly glanced down at his shoes—the shiniest Natasha had ever seen on someone in their twenties. "I was wondering if you were free for lun ..." He trailed off when Natasha turned to her right where she'd left Layla sitting at the round table in the corner of the office. "Oh, I'm sorry. I didn't realize you were in a meeting," he stammered, clearly surprised to see Layla.

Natasha was stumped by the invite, and though she was flattered, she didn't think it was a good idea to go out with Ray. The hospital gossip would run rampant like an out of control freight train.

"Hey Ray," Layla said with a wicked grin. "I can leave if you two need some privacy."

Natasha ignored Layla. "Regarding lunch, unfortunately I have other plans," she lied, not wanting to hurt his feelings.

"No problem." Ray backed out of the office quicker than he had walked in. "Maybe some other time. I'll let you get back to your meeting. Take care."

"Okay. Well, thanks for the invite."

"Bye Ray," Layla said in a sing-song voice.

Natasha closed the door. She didn't have to look at Layla to know that she was still grinning. She could feel the rays of her smile bouncing off the walls.

"Well, I see someone's been holding out on me," Layla said when Natasha reclaimed her seat. "First he rescues you from hitting the floor, and now lunch."

"Don't go jumping to conclusions. There is nothing between us. Actually, this is the second time I've ever seen him. The first was the other night, and you can't really count almost passing out as seeing him."

"So I guess you made an impression. I noticed him just now checking you out."

"He seems like a nice guy. Young, but nice."

Natasha didn't tell her friend that he'd made an impression, too. However, she had a strict rule: no dating anyone she worked with. Besides that, he was too young. At thirty-five, there was no way she was going out with a twenty-something year old.

"Speaking of impressions," Layla's words cut into Natasha's thoughts, "can I just say that Malik is *way* hotter than you described. When he came to the information desk and asked for you, I practically tripped over my tongue trying to get my words together."

"So that's why you personally escorted him toward my office. I'm surprised you remembered his name. I haven't mentioned him in months, and when I did, it was one time."

"I can't ever remember you talking about a man, any man, the way you talked about Malik Lewis. And now that I've put a face with your story, I must say, I can't believe you haven't seen him since your trip out west." Layla narrowed her eyes. "Or have you seen him and you're just holding out on me?"

Natasha laughed and shook her head. "No. Friday night was the first time since my trip." Layla knew that she'd gone to L.A. for a few days, but she didn't know the reason.

"Okay, sooooo ..."

Natasha shrugged. "Okay, sooo what?"

"Are you and Malik seeing each other? He seemed a little

intense. No, actually, he was downright possessive when he showed up here. And I promise you, I thought he was going to pummel poor Ray."

"Ha! Poor Ray looks like he can take care of himself." Natasha grabbed her travel mug from her desk and brought it over to the table. Her herbal tea was now almost cold, but it wouldn't be the first time she'd drank lukewarm tea. "The guy doesn't have an ounce of fat anywhere. Have you seen his arms?"

Layla twisted her mouth and bit down on her bottom lip. "Yeah, but he doesn't look as dangerous, or fearless, as Malik. Your man might've been dressed like he just left a boardroom, but there is definitely some thug in him."

"He's not my man," Natasha corrected, though weakly. Since their time in California, she had entertained the thought of hooking up with him again. She discreetly shook her head. No. She and Malik lived in two very different worlds. Her life was centered around saving lives, and as a former SEAL, Malik probably took more lives than she saved.

"Yeah, you say he's not your man," Layla grabbed her purse and her lunch bag from on top of the table, "but I saw you two together. There was more heat bouncing between you guys than steam from a radiator. I would be willing to bet that before the month's end, you two will be a couple." She looped the strap of her purse over her shoulder. "Well, my shift starts in twenty. Let me know if you have any more questions." She nodded toward the files. "Hopefully you and risk management will get to the bottom of things and soon."

"Layla, remember—" Natasha started, but stopped when her cell phone rang. She lifted a finger for Layla to hold up a minute. "Natasha Lockham."

"Hey Tasha, this is Malik. Is this a bad time?"

"Uh, Malik." His deep, confident voice sent a sweet shiver

through her body. She felt like a school-girl who just caught the attention of the varsity football captain. She didn't miss the huge grin on Layla's face. "Well, I'm just finishing up a meeting, can I call you back?"

"Actually, I was just calling to see if you were free for dinner tomorrow night. Say, around sevenish?"

Her first thought was to scream yes, but then common sense settled in. She was definitely attracted to him in a way that she'd never been attracted to any man, but he was asking her on a date. That was different than admiring him from a distance. He was a retired SEAL and special ops. She wasn't afraid of Malik, but Alandra's world had been turned inside out because of Quinn's past life in the military. Natasha didn't want to end up like her sister by associating with someone like Malik. Then again, there was something so intriguing about him that Natasha couldn't deny.

"Tasha?" his voice intruded on her thoughts.

"Uh, yeah, yeah, I'm here. About tomorrow night ... I'm not sure us hooking up is a good idea." *There, I said it.*

Silence filled the space before he spoke. "What if I told you it wasn't a date?"

"Uh ..." The question caught her off guard and she felt like such a dork. "Then if it's not a date, what would you call it?"

"A fact-finding mission," he said, a tinge of humor in his voice.

She couldn't help laughing. "Well ... as long as it's not date, then I guess it would be okay."

"Good. I'll be at your place at seven."

"I'll see you then." Natasha disconnected the call, and kept a death grip on her cell phone as she held it to her chest.

"Like I said, I'll give it a month."

Layla's voice snapped Natasha back to the present. She blew off her comment and put her cell back into her bag.

"As I was saying, it's imperative that what we discussed earlier stays in this room." She leveled her friend with a firm look. "Dr. Halsey is a well-respected doctor and I don't want this information to get out, especially not without us knowing all of the facts."

"Don't worry. As far as I'm concerned, *nothing* that we discussed this morning will leave this room." She wiggled her eyebrows and laughed as she left the office.

Natasha smiled and dropped down in her seat, wondering what she would wear to this fact-finding mission.

Malik shoved his cell phone back into the holster clipped on his waist and laid back against the headrest of his truck. Thoughts of Natasha had occupied space in his mind all weekend and he knew he had to do something about it. Calling her was a spur of the moment decision as he sat outside Wiz's house.

Malik sucked in a breath and released it slowly, not realizing how anxious he felt in doing the simple task of calling her. Definitely another first. He didn't have a problem asking women out, but his feelings for Natasha were confusing. On one hand, he wanted to get to know her, see if their chemistry from months ago was a fluke. On the other hand, the thought of getting too close to her freaked him out. She didn't seem like the type of woman that would settle for an affair, and he wasn't the type of man who wanted forever.

Malik finally exited his truck and glanced around the quiet street before walking up to Wiz's door.

"What's up, man?" Wiz asked when he opened the door, looking at his watch. "Kinda early for a visit, isn't it?"

Wiz had been out of town over the weekend, otherwise Malik would have showed up the moment he left Natasha's house. Not only to vent, but to also to tell him about the visit from Rosalyn. He needed Wiz's expertise in looking into her claims.

"Who's at the door, babe?"

Malik heard Olivia from somewhere in the back of the house. He wouldn't have stopped by had he known she was in town. Last he heard, she was doing an art show in New York. As a world-renowned artist of oil and acrylic paintings, she had recently started doing photography.

"It's Malik," Wiz called over his shoulder.

Seconds later, Olivia came around the corner, drying her hands on a dishtowel. "Hey Malik."

"What's up, Ollie?"

She swatted his arm before kissing him on the cheek. "What did I tell you about calling me that? You know I don't do nicknames." She stepped back. "We just finished breakfast, but I can whip something up for you if you're hungry."

"Nah, I'm good. I just need to talk to your hus— I mean Wiz for a minute."

Wiz and Olivia had married straight out of high school, but when Wiz became a SEAL, she divorced him. She couldn't handle the middle of the night calls telling him that his team was going wheels up. Worse than that, she didn't like not knowing where he was going or when he'd return. Despite their divorce, they had remained close, and since Wiz had retired from the Navy, even closer. Malik wasn't sure why they were waiting to officially reunite. Seeing them together made it clear they were both still very much in love with each other.

"Come on back," Wiz said. "We can talk in the office."

Malik followed Wiz into the room he called an office, but it looked more like a military command center. The huge space had tons of computer equipment and a large monitor mounted on the wall. As a private investigator, Wiz now did contract work for the government and occasionally took on assignments that were more personal.

"What happened to you Friday night? You were supposed to stop by and pick up this file before I left for the airport."

"I stopped by the hospital to see Natasha."

Wiz turned from his computer screen, his lips easing into a grin. "Whaaat? You quit trippin' and finally went to see her, huh?"

Malik sat in the chair across from him. "Yeah, and it's a good thing I did." He told Wiz about finding her in the hallway and getting her home that evening.

"Damn, I would have loved to see the look on your face when she told you to get out." He laughed, amused and unmoved by Malik's glare.

"Laugh all you want. I talked to her a few minutes ago and she agreed to have dinner with me tomorrow evening." Considering how she'd dismissed him the other night, he was a little surprised she agreed.

"All right, dog." They bumped fists across the desk. "Sounds like there might be hope for you yet. So what made you suddenly stop by the hospital? Surely it wasn't something I said," he joked.

"Actually, I received some interesting ... no, make that disturbing news after you left my office Friday." Malik rubbed his eyes, still a bit tired from working the whole weekend. "Rosalyn, the lady that stopped by my office right before you left, was the sister of Susan Lee, a woman I dated off and on."

"And?"

"And Susan is dead." Malik stood and walked to one of the windows in the room. He didn't have any emotional ties to Susan, but he was still in shock and sorry to hear about what happened. "Supposedly she died during child birth a few months back. Rosalyn found out that though her sister died, the baby lived," he said over his shoulder. "She was able to get a death certificate for her sister, but there's no birth or death certificate for the baby."

Wiz typed something on his keyboard. "So why'd she come to you? Doesn't she know you provide personal security, not missing person's services?"

Malik turned from the window. "She thinks the baby is ... was mine."

Wiz stopped typing and lifted an eyebrow. "Say what?"

"You heard me. She thinks I'm the father. She found one of her sister's journals and one of the entries claimed that I was the father of her unborn child."

Wiz sat back in his seat and let his hands fall into his lap. "Well I'll be damned. All of your hopping from one bed to another has finally caught up with you."

Malik shook his head. "No. No way I have a kid out there. I have *always* wrapped it up. No exceptions. I don't care what her journal said, that kid is not mine."

Wiz shook his head. "So what do you need me for?"

"I want you to find the kid."

"Okay, let me get this straight. You don't believe you're the father, but yet you want me to find him or her."

Malik sat back down. "Yeah."

"Why?"

"Because."

"Because there's a chance the kid is yours."

"No! Man, quit sayin' that. I'm telling you that I'm not the father! Susan was cool and all, but I'm a hundred percent sure I wasn't the only man she was with. We were both out to have a good time."

"There is a chance, Tree." It had been a long time since anyone called him that. During their SEAL days, they all had nicknames. Quinn was Ghost, and because Malik had often been compared to being as big and solid as an oak tree, they called him Tree.

Malik refused to believe that he had fathered a child. He'd been too careful. Plenty of women had tried to trap him, wanting him to use condoms they provided, telling him that they were late and could be pregnant. He'd heard it all and made extra sure there were no slip ups.

"I want you to look into this because Rosalyn thinks there might have been foul play involved in her sister's death. As for the kid, I want him or her found in order to prove the kid is not mine."

Wiz threw up his hands. "All right, fine. I'll look into it. Did this Rosalyn lady happen to show you the journal?"

"No. I told her I'd be in touch. I want us to go over to Susan's place and look through everything."

"Yeah, there might be more journals. If she wrote about you, she probably wrote about other men." Wiz twirled a pen between his fingers. "Why does the sister think there was foul play?"

Malik shrugged. "Something about them not contacting next of kin, which would've been her and she claims Susan was perfectly healthy. She says she has access to her medical records and there's nothing that can explain why her sister suddenly died."

"Okay, well I'm going to need to ask Rosalyn a few questions. Did she happen to mention the name of her sister's doctor?"

Malik pulled a small slip of paper from his pocket and glanced at it. "Yeah, his name is ... Robert Halsey."

Chapter Five

Once the server took their food order, Natasha glanced around the Italian restaurant. The smell of garlic, basil, and fresh bread made her mouth water. She hadn't been there before, but loved the atmosphere of the quaint eatery. The gold and taupe mural of Italy spread across the walls, accented with black and gold wall sconces, and dim lighting gave the room a romantic feel.

Natasha returned her attention to the handsome man sitting in front of her. Being there with him seemed so surreal. The night they shared, the memories of their lovemaking, all of it came rushing back to her the moment she found him standing on her doorstep. Prior to the day he had shown up at the hospital, she had no idea if she would ever see him again. They made no promises to each other during their time in L.A. At least she hadn't made any promises, but he had. He promised to be only a phone call away if ever she needed him. Based on her erotic dream the other night, she definitely needed him.

"How long has this restaurant been here?" Natasha asked.

"I'm not sure," Malik looked around before returning his dark intense eyes to her, "but I've known about it for years. It's one of my favorite restaurants to get authentic Italian cuisine." "I love Italian food. Actually, I love food period." They both laughed and Natasha liked the way his face lit up whenever he smiled. "That's why I decided to join a gym. My poor diet is starting to catch up with me."

His gaze swept over her seductively and it took everything she had not to squirm in her seat. She couldn't remember the last time she was on the receiving end of a man's unabashed appraisal, but she kind of liked it.

"Well, it appears that it caught up with you in all of the right places." Malik brought his glass of beer up to his tempting lips, a small smile playing near the corners of his mouth. "Does that mean that you're no longer going to put in long hours? I remember you telling me that you often work as many as sixteen hours a day."

Natasha nodded, toying with the diamond hanging around her neck. In all actuality, working crazy long hours wasn't something to brag about. Sure, she got a lot done and prided herself on staying on top of her work, but she had no social life.

"You have a good memory. I probably average more like twelve to fourteen hour days, but that's still too much. It's not healthy." She sipped her white wine.

"I'm glad you realize that. Seeing you in the condition I found you the other night had me concerned."

"Me too. It was a definite sign for me to slow down and start taking better care of myself." Considering she had left work earlier than usual and was having dinner with an intriguing man, most would say that she was off to a good start.

"Okay, we have the Tortelloni ai funghi porcini, Tortelloni with porcini mushrooms for you." The server placed a huge oval plate of piping hot food in front of Natasha. "And for you," she said to Malik, "we have the Stinco di agnello con patate arrosto ed aparagi, the lamb shank with roasted potatoes and sautéed asparagus."

Natasha studied both plates. She was used to large portion sizes whenever she visited an Italian restaurant, but this place had taken it to a different level. Her mouth watered, eager to take her first bite.

"Is there anything else I can get for either of you?" The server glanced at Natasha and then at Malik, her gaze staying on him a little longer than Natasha thought necessary. She couldn't blame the woman, though. Everything about Malik warranted a second glance, from his size to those amazing eyes that didn't seem to miss anything. If you added his great sense of humor and sexy smile, you had a man any woman would love to get to know better.

"Tasha," Malik prompted, "is everything to your liking?"

"Uh, yeah. This looks amazing."

"Good, I'm glad to hear that." The server nodded her head, sending her long, reddish curls bobbing up and down. She turned back to Malik. "And you, is there anything else I can get you?"

Malik looked over his plate and shook his head, oblivious to the server's rapt attention. "Nah, I'm good. Thanks." He gave her a quick glance before diving into his food.

"So tell me more about your company. How did you get started in the bodyguard business?" Natasha asked, cutting into the bread and then dipping it into the small plate of olive oil in the center of the table. She loved Italian food, but bread was definitely her weakness.

"Well, actually Supreme Security is a personal security company. We offer more than just *bodyguard* service." He winked. Natasha had no doubt that the enticing smile gracing his full lips probably made him very popular with the women. The man was just too damn sexy.

"I guess I don't really have to ask how or why you got into the business." She imagined most retired military would do something along the same line or become a cop. "What type of services do you provide?"

Malik's eyebrows rose in amusement. "For you? Anything you want, baby."

Natasha choked on her pasta when she realized how her words must've sounded. Having a hard time catching her breath, she patted her chest and scooted her chair back.

Malik's mischievous grin slid from his lips. "You okay?" He rose from his seat.

She waved him off, tears filling her eyes. "I'm fine," she croaked, dabbing at the corners of her eyes with the edge of her napkin. "My food just went down wrong."

He didn't look too convinced, but reclaimed his seat.

"What I meant was, what else do you and your team do besides provide personal security for people."

"That's a big bulk of what we do." He continued staring at her warily while she settled back down, totally embarrassed. "We also have a division that installs and monitors state-of-the-art home alarm systems. But for the most part, we provide personal security to individuals and organizations."

"I guess that means you probably get to meet some pretty famous people."

He shrugged. "Yeah, a few."

She knew he was being modest. Alandra had told her some of his clients included well-known singers, talk show hosts, and professional sports figures.

"So when you take women out, do they know that you once worked in Special Forces?"

"No, most don't." He cut a slice of bread and dipped it in the small dish of olive oil. "It's not something I advertise. People have different reactions." He wiped his mouth, leaned forward, and lowered his voice. "Take you for instance. When we first met, Quinn, Wiz and I were in the middle of trying to find out who was threatening your sister. I remember the suspicion in your eyes when you found out we were taking her to D.C. to track down the person responsible for trying to kill her."

Natasha laid her fork down and hunched forward. She remembered being scared to death for Alandra. Even understanding that the three SEALs in her sister's life were going to keep her safe didn't help the despair that had invaded her body knowing that things could go terribly wrong.

"Who wouldn't be worried? First of all, the thought of knowing someone is trying to kill your sister, after failing once, would freak out anyone. You guys talked as if it were normal to hunt someone down and make them ... disappear." She looked around, hoping that no one overheard them.

When Alandra was being hunted by members of *Los Hermanos* drug cartel, it was like a scene out of a horror movie for Natasha. Someone had already put a bullet in Alandra's chest. When word got out that Alandra had survived, the cartel hunted her with a vengeance.

"Hey," Malik grabbed hold of Natasha's hand and squeezed, "I didn't mean to upset you. I only wanted to show you that most people don't see us as everyday guys who breathe the same way they do; who feel pain the way they feel pain, and who put their pants on one leg at a time, just like they do."

Natasha sighed and focused on calming her rapid heartbeat. He was right. At the end of the day, he and his friends were just men ... men who happened to be trained killers.

"Okay, enough about me." Malik sat back in his seat. "Let's talk about you. I'm a little surprised you agreed to come out with me."

Natasha crinkled her eyebrows. "You are? Why?"

"I figured that ex-husband of yours wouldn't let you."

"Martin doesn't dictate who I go out with."

"No?" Malik cocked his head. "I find that hard to believe, especially considering how possessive he was when I dropped you off the other night."

"Possessive?" She narrowed her eyes. "What about when you stopped by the hospital and Ray was there helping me. You practically bit the poor guy's head off."

Some men would say they were sorry or at least show some remorse, but not Malik. If anything, his gaze grew harder and the tightness in his strong jaw made him look even more dangerous.

"So who is that guy to you?"

Natasha shrugged. "Just someone who works at the hospital. Someone who was only trying to help."

"It looked to me that he had other interests than just trying to *help*. There was something about him that didn't sit right with me, and it wasn't because he had his hands all over you," Malik said, his voice dropping an octave.

Someone is jealous. Natasha held back a smile. "Before that night, I had never even seen Ray before," she stated. "He's only been with the hospital for a month or two. And I'm sure his intentions were pure."

"Yeah, if you say so," Malik said, sounding unconvinced.

They talked throughout their meal, discussing everything from favorite foods to world news. Their vast range of conversation surprised Natasha. She thought that with their different backgrounds, they wouldn't have much to talk about. Instead, the connection she felt months ago was just as strong.

"I have a question for you." Malik pushed his empty plate to the side and folded his large forearms on top of the table. "What happens to orphaned babies at your hospital?"

Natasha lifted her wine glass to her lips. "What do you mean?"

"Maybe nothing," Malik said, pushing back from the table. "I recently found out a friend of mine died a few months ago, after giving birth. Her sister has been in touch with people at your hospital. Supposedly, the baby was taken into the state's custody. The thing is, when my friend's sister contacted them, they had no record of the child. Do you ..."

Unease crawled up Natasha's spine. She could see Malik's mouth moving, but didn't hear anything else after he said the state has no records of the child. Panic like she'd never known before welled in her throat and an icy fear wrapped around her heart.

Oh my God, Layla might be right. Something is going on.

"Tasha? Tasha?"

Natasha finally glanced up to see Malik standing near her. He held one of her hands, and his other one rested on her back. The server was cleaning up broken glass from the once white tablecloth. Natasha didn't know what scared her the most, Malik's questions, or the fact that she didn't remember dropping her wine glass.

"I would ask if you're okay, but apparently you're not." Malik removed the napkin from her lap, which held slivers of glass. After helping her to her feet, he turned to the server. "Can you bring the check?"

Malik kept part of his attention on Natasha while he paid for their meal. Sitting near the entrance, where patrons waited for a table, she toyed with the diamond pendant around her neck. Malik hadn't missed the shock on her face when he mentioned talking to Rosalyn, and when he asked Natasha about orphaned babies. He couldn't figure out if she knew and was just holding back, or if she was shocked that there might be something terribly wrong going on at her hospital.

"Come on, baby, let's head out." With his hand gently on her elbow, he walked with her out of the restaurant.

"Malik, I ... I'm not sure what happened." She looked up at him with her gorgeous brown eyes. He'd been in a constant state of arousal from the moment he picked her up from home. Wearing a fitted, fuchsia wrapped blouse and a straight black skirt that stopped above her knees showing off amazing legs, she was easily the sexiest woman he'd ever taken out.

He draped his arm around her shoulders. "It's like you blacked out, but with your eyes wide open. Was it something I said?"

"I ... I ..." Her eyes blinked several times and she avoided looking at him. "I don't think so. I'm not sure." She stepped away from him, and brushed invisible lint from her clothes. Malik knew she was lying. "To answer your original question, if a mother dies giving birth, the state gets involved. If a child can't be placed with a family member, they place the child in foster care. I can look into it if you give me the name of the mother."

"All right," he said as they waited for the valet to bring his truck. "But first—" His cell phone vibrated for the third time within minutes. He pulled the iPhone out of his pocket and read the text from Wiz.

Is Natasha with you? Explosion at the hospital. Call me ASAP.

Shit. Malik stepped back with Natasha when the valet, who looked barely old enough to drive, pulled up with his truck. After helping her climb in, Malik slapped a few bills into the valet's hand.

"Thanks, young-blood."

"Thank you!" The kid grinned after glancing at the amount of his tip. "Have a good evening."

Malik's phone vibrated again.

Five minutes to call me. Otherwise, sending the troops.

Malik knew why Wiz was anxious. With not knowing how deep the threat went regarding Quinn and Alandra's life, they all knew that their families could easily be targets.

He looked at Natasha, preparing to tell her about the situation at the hospital, when his phone rang. He answered.

"She's safe. She's with me." Natasha studied him expectantly and he switched the call to the Bluetooth feature built into his truck. "Something happened at the hospital," Malik said to Tasha. "You're on speaker, Wiz."

"Hey Natasha," Wiz's voice boomed through the truck and Malik turned the volume down, "there was some type of explosion at the hospital. Just checking to make sure you're safe."

"What? What happened?" Natasha frantically reached for her bag, which was on the floor, and pulled out her cell. After pushing a couple of buttons, she glanced at Malik. "I didn't get a call."

"Wiz, do you have any details?" Malik asked, merging into traffic.

"Right now, the only thing the media is saying is that a car blew up in the employee parking lot. Not sure if anyone was hurt."

"I have to get there," Natasha said. Malik heard the concern in her voice. Before she could say more, her cell phone rang.

"Hello," Natasha answered and listened for a moment, her forehead crinkled with worry. "Layla," she had to repeat herself several times, "Layla, I need you to calm down. I can't understand a word you're saying."

"Wiz, thanks for the heads up," Malik said, trying not to speak too loud so that Natasha could hear Layla. "I'll give you a call back."

Malik made a U-turn and headed in the direction of the

hospital. He wasn't ready for the date to end, but as the chief of staff, he figured Natasha should probably be there.

"Okay. Okay, I'm on my way. I'll get there as fast as I can." Natasha drew her phone to her chest and laid her head against the headrest. "I'm sorry to cut our date short," she said to Malik, apparently noticing that he was going in the direction of the hospital.

"No problem."

"That was Layla, the nurse you met the other night. She's pretty messed up, I couldn't make out anything she was saying."

"Well, we'll see what's going on. You can do what you need to do, and then I'll take you home."

Natasha turned to him, her mouth slightly ajar. "Malik, I don't expect you to sit around and wait for me. There's no telling how long I'll need to be there."

"I'll wait."

"Malik," he heard the exasperation in her tone, "you don't have to—"

Malik shot her a quick glance. "I know I don't have to, but I am. So you might as well save your breath."

He didn't have to look at her to know that she was staring at him, but he did like that she squashed the debate. He hated repeating himself, and he definitely had no intention of arguing with her.

With her guiding him, he drove around to the employee parking lot. He heard her gasp when she saw all of the fire trucks, police cars, and people standing around.

"Oh my God." Her hand shook against her mouth. "There's no way there would be this many emergency vehicles and cops here if there wasn't some injuries, or worse, fatalities."

Malik didn't respond. He hurried around to the passenger's side and helped her out of the truck.

"Come on. Let's see what we can find out." With her hand securely in his, he guided her through the mass of onlookers.

"I'm sorry, you can't get through here." A police officer stopped them. They could see what was left of the smoldering car.

"I'm the chief of staff of this hospital." Natasha showed him her ID. "I need to talk to whoever is in charge."

The officer scanned her credentials and handed them back. When he looked at Malik, Natasha was quick to tell him that he was with her.

"I see someone I know who can give us answers," Malik stated, spotting Detective Sheldon Baker. Whenever a situation arose with Malik, Wiz, or Quinn and they needed some help from someone inside of the police force, Sheldon was the person they called.

They walked toward him and he looked up. "What's up, Malik? What brings you out here?" Sheldon shook his hand and gave him a one-arm hug, and turned his attention to Natasha.

"Hey, man, this is Natasha Lockham, chief of staff here." He put his hand at the small of Natasha's back, encouraging her forward. "Can you give her any information?"

Sheldon shook Natasha's hand. "How you doin'?"

"I'm okay, but I'd be better if I knew what was going on." A shiver skittered down her back when she saw the charred vehicle, praying no one was inside. "Do you know what happened? Was anyone hurt?" Malik kept his hand at the small of her back, not missing the worry he saw on her face.

"The fire department just put out the fire, so we're just getting started." Sheldon glanced at the notepad in his hand. "Unfortunately, there was one person in the car and one of your nurses suffered some minor injuries. According to Layla Sanders, the person in the car was Tessa—"

"Oh my God." Natasha's hands hovered over her mouth.

"Tessa was a nurse who worked in L&D, labor and delivery. Oh no ... h–how did this happen? Cars don't just blow up ... do they?" Her frantic eyes shifted from Sheldon to Malik.

Malik shook his head slightly. He understood Natasha being upset, but he sensed there was something else. He couldn't put his finger on it, but he'd bet all of the money in his wallet that Natasha knew something about this incident.

"Tasha!" Layla came barreling toward her and might've knocked her over had Malik not been standing behind her.

She held Natasha tight, her sobs growing louder by the minute.

"Layla." Natasha gently pushed her back, her hands on Layla's shoulders as she looked at the bandage around her wrist and the large Band-Aid on the side of her temple. "What happened?"

"It was terrible." Layla swiped at her tears. "Tessa forgot one of her bags at the desk. So I grabbed it and ran after her, hoping she hadn't left the parking lot yet." Layla took a breath, her hand covering her heart. "I saw her walking toward the car and I called out to her, but ... but she didn't hear me. So I hurried toward her, figuring that she'd see me when she backed out of her parking space. I was about twenty feet from her when," Layla said on a sob, "she started the car. Suddenly, there was this loud boom. Before I knew it, I was thrown through the air and landed over there."

Malik's gaze followed to where she pointed.

"Do you know if she was having any trouble with anyone?" Sheldon asked.

A knowing look passed between Natasha and Layla. Malik knew they were hiding something.

Sheldon met Malik's gaze, apparently thinking the same thing.

Malik placed his hand against Natasha's waist and pulled

her close, her butt bumping against the front of his body. *Damn she feels good.* This wasn't the time for his body to spring to attention, but everything about the woman threw him off his game. Using all of his restraint, he reined in his self-control. His lips brushed up against her ear and he whispered, "If you know something, now would be a good time to speak up. You can trust him."

She turned and her gaze landed on his lips. He desperately wanted to kiss her at that moment, but then she looked up. His heart slammed into his chest. Her beautiful brown eyes held something: fear, concern, he wasn't sure what, but he planned to find out.

Seconds passed with them staring into each other's eyes, and despite the seriousness of the situation, he wanted to bend down and kiss her tempting lips. This woman did things to him that no other woman had ever done. Sure she was sexy as hell and he was attracted to her physically, but he had a burning desire to protect her.

She finally shook her head. "I didn't know Tessa personally," she said softly. "I'm ... I just can't believe that something like this has happened again."

"Again?" Malik and Sheldon said at the same time. Malik had temporarily forgotten Sheldon and Layla were standing close enough to hear his and Natasha's conversation.

"What do you mean again?" Malik asked, turning her so that she was fully facing him. "When did something like this happen before?"

She looked at Malik expectantly, as if he should know what she was talking about. When he didn't speak, she turned to Sheldon.

"Isabella. She was a nurse here. A few months ago, her house blew up and she died inside."

Malik gave himself a mental slap. No wonder Natasha

looked at him as if he should understand. When Alandra had reemerged from the dead, the former CIA agent, Isabella, provided information about the person who tried to kill her. Alandra and Quinn sought her out for answers, and they barely escaped with their life when the woman's house exploded, killing her in the process. Natasha didn't know that Alandra and Quinn had been in the house or were connected to Isabella in any way. Only a handful of people knew she was former CIA.

Terror crept up his back as he did a mental catalog of what had taken place before and after the house explosion. There was no way the two situations were connected ... or were they?

Malik glanced around the parking lot, the crowd slowly thinning. His gut told him that the bombings weren't connected, but right now he wasn't ruling anything out. He continued to scan the lot until his gaze fell upon a small group of hospital staff and a familiar face came into view. *Ray Newton.* Their gazes held and the same foreboding Malik felt during their first encounter swirled around in the pit of his stomach, slowly making its way up his throat. He didn't care what title the hospital gave the guy, he had a feeling he was more than a health records technician.

Chapter Six

Natasha swiveled back and forth in her office chair, twirling her pen between her fingers, trying to decide her next move. Between assisting with grief counseling for the staff, to attending meeting after meeting regarding the car explosion, the last three days had been the busiest since she stepped into her new position. There was a time when she thought she could make a difference at the hospital as chief of staff, but now she wasn't so sure.

A stab of pain pierced her heart each time she thought about Tessa and the family she left behind. In addition, finding out the car explosion was caused by a bomb attached to the fuel tank of Tessa's car brought on a level of fear for her and her staff, thinking that they might be next.

Natasha leaned forward in her chair, and according to the time, she had fifteen minutes to get to a meeting with the administrative team. Since her telephone call to them regarding Dr. Halsey, it seemed as though she was meeting with them daily; answering their questions, reviewing information and patient's records. It made her even more concerned that Dr. Halsey might have been at fault for at least three of the deaths in the last two months.

A shudder crawled up Natasha's spine and she shivered at the thought. She gathered her notepad and pen, as well as the file she had put together. The whole situation didn't seem real. How could someone who took an oath to never do harm to his patients intentionally take their life? A nauseating, sinking feeling of despair settled in her gut. She still hadn't told risk management of her suspicions that Dr. Halsey and Tessa might have been working together. But what could she say? She didn't have concrete evidence that there was anything illegal going on between him and Tessa. What Natasha needed was proof.

She grabbed her keys and hurried out of her office, opting to take the stairs instead of the elevator, since she only had to go up one floor.

"Good afternoon, Dr. Lockham," a familiar deep voice called out from behind her.

Natasha turned to find Ray strolling toward her. Funny how she'd seen him practically every day this week, when she had never seen him prior to their run-in last week. His grin and cool demeanor always brought a smile to her face.

"Hi Ray. It's good to see you."

"You too." He glanced around. "Do you have a moment to talk?"

"Unfortunately, I'm on my way to a meeting. Can it—"

"Actually, it'll only take a moment." He gestured with his hand for them to step off to the side. "I wanted to see if you were free for lunch tomorrow. I know this real nice Mexican restaurant not too far from here that I'd love to take you to."

What is going on today?

Earlier, Martin had called to invite her to breakfast, despite her telling him that she needed to put some space between them. *Now Ray.* In his defense, Natasha hadn't come out and told him she wasn't interested. She liked him and didn't want to hurt his feelings.

"Ray, I appreciate your invitation, but I have to be honest with you. I don't date people I work with."

"Who said anything about dating?" he asked, his tone combative and his eyes narrowed. "I just thought it would be nice to take you out to lunch."

Natasha took a step back, surprised by his tone. Malik's words popped into her mind. *There's something about him that doesn't sit right with me.* Natasha had waved his words off, but at Ray's tone and the lethal aura bouncing off him, she was starting to wonder if Malik might've been right.

Ray ran his hands over his low-cut hair and then dropped his arms to his side, his eyes brimming with defeat. "Listen, I'm sorry. It's just that ... it has been an exhausting day. Between taking care of my sick mother, moving, and dealing with the stress of the bomb, life is a bit much these days. The energy around here is a little depressing. That's still no excuse for my tone. I shouldn't be taking my frustration out on you."

For the first time since he'd stopped her, Natasha took in his appearance. The tail of his shirt was hanging out, his nametag was on crooked, and most noticeably his shoes weren't as shiny as usual. Each time she'd seen him, he'd been impeccably groomed, but not today.

She relaxed her stance. "Believe me, I understand. It has been a tough few days for everyone. If you need to talk to some-one," she tried to choose her words carefully so as not to make him go into defense mode, "there are grief counselors on site. They are not only for those who are having trouble dealing with what happened a few days ago. If you need to, please don't hesi-tate to speak to one of them."

"Dr. Lockham?" Natasha looked back at the door of the conference room. "We're ready to start."

"I'll be right there." Natasha turned back to Ray. "I'm sorry I have to cut this short," she said backing away, "but don't forget what I said. Talk to someone if you need to."

Ray nodded, but Natasha had a feeling he didn't intend on speaking to a counselor. She wasn't surprised. Most of her male staff members hadn't taken advantage of having the counselors on site. She just hoped Ray got help before the stress of his life became too much for him.

Two hours later, Natasha sat at her desk, her head in her hands. Tides of weariness flowing through her body. The meeting with risk management had gone as expected. Dr. Halsey was suspended until a thorough investigation could be done on his most recent cases. She hated convicting anyone before knowing the whole truth, yet she understood why the hospital was taking such measures. They took threats to the well-being of their patients very seriously, and now there was enough evidence to prove the doctor's methods of late were a hindrance. If word got out that they had a doctor on staff who might be intentionally killing new mothers, all hell would break loose. Regardless, the question that burned in Natasha's mind was why. Why would he risk his career like this? And had Tessa been involved? If so, had he killed her?

Natasha's heart broke for him and his family. Three years ago, he and his wife had lost their youngest son to leukemia. As a couple, they had struggled to get over the loss. There was even rumor of divorce. It wasn't until Dr. Halsey started the *Rescue a Child* foundation did he and his wife start to heal from their loss. *Now this.* Risk management had tried reaching Dr. Halsey by phone, but as of yet, he hadn't returned the call. Natasha wondered if he knew this was coming. The fact that he suddenly took vacation didn't help his case, only prolonged the inevitable.

The ringing of Natasha's cell phone broke the silence surrounding her. She dug through her purse and pulled it out.

"Hello."

"Natasha? This is Malik."

"Hi," she said, her voice flat, matching the lack of enthusiasm she felt. She honestly didn't feel like talking to anyone and had answered the telephone on automatic pilot.

"Everything okay?" Malik's baritone voice held a tinge of concern. "You don't sound like yourself."

Natasha sighed loudly. "Yeah. Just another day at the job. I need a damn vacation," she muttered.

"Wow, it must have been a helluva day if it has you cursing and thinking about vacation. Anything I can do to make it better?"

Normally his suggestive questions or comments made her smile, taking her back to the last time he made her feel better. Today was different. She didn't want to feel better. She just wanted to wallow in misery, unsure of how the news of Dr. Halsey's suspension would affect the rest of her staff.

"Thanks, but I'm good." She planned to go home, slip into some pajamas, and curl up with a good gallon of butter pecan ice cream.

"Well, how about dinner tonight? I can—"

"Malik, thanks, but I want to be alone tonight." Most women would be happy to receive invites for breakfast, lunch, and dinner from three good-looking men, but not Natasha. Not today. "I appreciate the offer, but now is not a good time. I have some major things going on here at the hospital, and I need for all of my focus to be on work and my career, but thanks. You've been a good friend." He had called to check on her every day since the car bomb. If she weren't careful, she could get used to his thoughtfulness.

"Okay," Malik finally said. "Well, you know how to reach me if you need me. I'm only a phone call away."

Malik sat at his desk, his hands folded on top of his head, thinking about his brief conversation with Natasha. She'd been brushing him off since the day after the car bombing incident. Normally, he was the one brushing women off, so this was a new experience.

"Hey Malik." Victoria strutted into his office on her brown four-inch stilts that she referred to as shoes. "Bowker decided to extend his contract for another six months. I told him that I wasn't sure whether or not we could keep the same team with him, but I wanted to check with you first." She laid the file down on his desk in front him and sat in one of the guest chairs, crossing her jean-clad legs. "What do you want me to tell him?"

Malik rubbed his forehead before he opened the file. Scanning the content, he closed it and pushed it toward Victoria. "Keep it the same except for Travis. Stan has been giving me some good reports about the kid. I want to try him on a couple of other teams to see how he handles himself."

He released a breath and slouched in his seat, tapping his fingers against the desk. He had to do something about Natasha. He didn't take rejection well. It wasn't like he was looking for anything serious, but he did want to see if their electrifying connection months ago was a fluke. He enjoyed the chase as much as the next guy, but he still hadn't fully decided if he wanted to chase her, remembering that she wasn't the type of woman who would agree to an affair. Besides that, he liked her. He liked everything about her from her intelligence to her independent nature. Throw in her killer body and the way she screamed his name when she tumbled over the edge of an orgasm and he had the perfect woman.

Damn. I gotta get laid.

That had to be why his mind had latched on to his time with Natasha. He couldn't remember the last time he had gone three months without getting some. It wasn't like he hadn't had the opportunity. He had a few "go to" women who weren't looking for a forever type of love, and were quick to spread their legs for him.

"You want to talk about it?"

Malik lifted his gaze to find Victoria studying him. He was so caught up in his thoughts, he had temporarily forgotten she was sitting across from him.

He shook his head. "I'm sorry, what?"

"What is going on with you? I have never seen you this distracted." She folded her arms across her chest, her leg swinging back and forth. "Let me guess ... woman troubles. Is this about the doctor you took out a few days ago?"

Malik brows drew together. "How do you know who—"

"The night of the car bombing, Wiz called looking for you. He might have mentioned you had a date." She smirked.

"I'm going to have to talk to that brotha about sharing my business with just anyone," he murmured, knowing that Victoria had a way of getting any information she wanted. "Dr. Natasha Lockham is the woman, and we're friends."

"But you want to be more than friends, right?"

Good question. Too bad he didn't have an easy answer. If he were honest ... "I wouldn't mind getting to know her better, and I think the feelings are mutual. Only I don't think we want the same thing. Besides, right now she has a lot going on at work and doesn't have time for much else."

"You're not getting any younger, boss man. There comes a time when you have to start thinking about the future. At some point, dating different women is going to get old." She stood and leaned against the back of her chair. "Oh, and if you're really interested, don't let her excuse of too much work get in the way. Just put on the old Malik Lewis charm and let her have it. I guarantee she'll make time for you." Victoria had always been more than an employee. She was more like his sister, always butting into his business, but always having his back.

A slow smile lifted the corner of his lips. "Is that right? So you got all the damn answers, huh?"

"You know it. Now I'm outta here. Good luck."

Malik sat back in his seat and thought about what Victoria had said. He always went after what he wanted. His problem was deciding if he wanted to pursue Natasha. Considering he hadn't been with another woman, or even interested in another since meeting Natasha, said it all.

Standing suddenly, he shoved a few files into his briefcase and grabbed his keys. It was time he turned on the Malik Lewis charm. *She's not going to know what hit her.*

"I can't believe I let you talk me into this," Natasha said when she climbed onto the bar stool next to Layla. "I had planned to go home and curl up with some ice cream and a chick flick. Not sit around a bar fighting off unwanted advances from men who have had a little too much to drink." She glanced around the small establishment, not surprised to see so many people taking advantage of happy hour. At least ten people were sitting at the semi-circle bar and all of the tables were occupied.

"If you hadn't declined all of the offers you received today, you probably could be home curled up with one of three men. But no, you had to turn them all down. What's that all about anyway? Are you determined to live the rest of your life alone, hanging out in places like this?" She waved her hands at their surroundings.

Natasha smiled and looped her arm through Layla's. "Hanging out with you is not all bad. I get to spend quality time with my best friend. At least being here with you I'm guaranteed some good laughs, and now that I have legitimate plans for the evening, I don't feel bad about turning down Malik's invite."

"Yeah right." Layla signaled for the bartender. "I can understand why you might not want to spend time with Martin or Ray, but are you telling me you would rather be hanging out with me instead of that tall, dark knight that I met the other day?"

"Ah, Layla, don't start. I shouldn't have mentioned him." Natasha dropped her arm and placed her elbows on top of the bar. She knew why she'd mentioned Malik; she hadn't stopped thinking about him since he'd called that afternoon. "Let's just finish our drink and then head out."

Layla once again signaled for the bartender and asked for another glass of wine. "The best time to discuss men is over a second drink." She turned and crossed her long legs. She had changed out of her scrubs before leaving the hospital and replaced them with a fitted yellow blouse that accentuated her light brown eyes, and a short brown skirt that showed off her legs.

"Okay, so you say that you and Martin are over ... for real this time, and there won't be any more lunch dates, dinners, or anniversary celebrations with him. Which, by the way, I think was weird, but that's beside the point."

"So what is your point?" Natasha didn't bother telling her

friend that she didn't want to talk about the state of her social life, knowing it wouldn't do any good.

"My point is, if you say you're moving on, why don't you? I don't think you should go out with Ray since he works with you, sort of, but I do think you should give Malik a chance. Hanging out with him might be fun and you deserve to have a little fun."

Natasha shook her head. "I don't do affairs." She felt like a hypocrite considering she'd spent a night with him. "Malik has a reputation of being a player and that's not what I'm looking for. I want a relationship that will lead to marriage and children."

"Do you know if he has any children?"

"No. He doesn't."

"Well, that's good. At least you don't have to deal with any baby-mama-drama." Layla sipped from her glass of white wine and set it back down on the bar. "You said that you and Malik had a connection. I have never heard you say that about any man, not even your ex. There might really be something to build on there. Besides, how do you know Malik doesn't want the same things you want?"

She didn't know. All she had to go by was what she knew of him. He traveled a lot, he'd do anything for his friends, and he didn't do relationships—according to her sister. Natasha knew his type even if Alandra hadn't told her about his playboy ways. He was about enjoying himself. She couldn't be mad at him if that's the life he wanted to live. She knew spending time with him could be fun, but the last thing she needed was to fall for a man who wasn't looking for anything serious.

Natasha continued playing with the straw in her strawberry mojito. She wasn't much of a drinker, but whenever she did have alcohol, mojitos were her drink of choice.

"My indiscretion with Malik was something that just happened." Natasha shook her head, still surprised that she had gone all the way with him. "It won't happen again," she mumbled, sadness in her tone. Deep down, she would love many more nights with Malik and she couldn't help wondering 'what if'. What if they could be more than friends?

"Don't look now, but one of your admirers just walked in," Layla murmured and nodded her head to Natasha's left.

Natasha turned and her gaze met Ray's. *Oh great. There's definitely a disadvantage to stopping by a bar that's only a few blocks from the hospital.* She wasn't sure how to greet him. If she waved, he might see the gesture as an invitation to come over to where they were. If she didn't do or say something, he might feel slighted. She wasn't interested in him, but she wasn't looking to make any enemies either. Instead of waving, she smiled and nodded, then returned her attention back to Layla.

"As I said before. I should have gone home after work."

"It must be rough being you," Layla cracked. She pinched her lips together, her cheeks puffing out as if trying to stifle a laugh. "I'm surprised he isn't coming over. You must have really scared him off."

"I wasn't trying to scare him off, but maybe he understands that I'm not interested."

"Excuse me. Is anyone sitting here?" a nice looking man standing next to the bar stool on Layla's right asked.

"Nope. It's all yours," Layla said, moving her small handbag that was sitting on the bar to her lap. She returned her attention back to Natasha and leaned in. "Okay, let's get back to Malik. You know what I think?"

"No, but I'm sure you're going to tell me." She fingered the condensation sliding down the side of her glass.

"I think you're afraid to give Malik some attention because he might turn out to be everything you want and need in a man. What if you continue avoiding him and it turns out he is the one, and that he does want what you want?"

"Then fate will step in. For now, I plan to protect my heart."

"Yeah, that sounds good and all, but you're never going to get married and have those children you want if you don't take a chance on love." Layla placed her hand on Natasha's arm. "Promise me that you won't succumb to fear and possibly miss out on the love of your life."

Natasha glanced at her friend, a smile tugging on her lips. "I promise."

Chapter Seven

"**D**r. Lockham?" Natasha's administrative assistant called over the intercom.

"Yes."

"You have a call on line one, a Malik Lewis. Are you available?"

I think you're afraid to give Malik some attention because he might turn out to be everything you want and need in a man. Layla's words from the night before popped into Natasha's head.

Malik had left a message on her voicemail the night before, but by the time Natasha listened to the message, it was too late to call. Actually, it probably wasn't too late to call him, but after the conversation she'd had with Layla, Natasha wasn't ready to talk to him.

"Yes. I'll take it," Natasha responded. "Thank you."

She pushed the button for line one. "Hello."

"Dr. Lockham, this is Mr. Malik Lewis," he said, humor in his deep voice. "Is this a bad time?"

Natasha smiled and glanced at the files on her desk, which she had ignored most of the morning. "No, this is a good time.

Sorry about not returning your call last night, but it was too late. So how's your day going?"

"My day is going all right, but it would be better if I had a lunch date. Are you interested and available?"

Natasha drew her bottom lip between her teeth. *What if you continue avoiding him and it turns out that he is the one?* Layla's words continued to rattle around in her head. Natasha lifted her appointment calendar. She would love to have lunch with Malik, but by the time she met him somewhere it would take at least a half an hour. She would only have thirty minutes to get back before her first afternoon meeting.

"Malik, I would love to have lunch with you, but I have a meeting in an hour. If—" A knock sounded at the door before she could continue. "Hold on a second." She placed him on hold and hurried to the door.

She swung the door open and a wave of excitement washed over her. There before her stood the man she couldn't get out of her mind.

Malik disconnected his cell phone and shoved it into the holster on his hip. That was when Natasha noticed the picnic basket in his hand. He lifted it up.

"So, you were saying?"

She shook her head and opened the door wider. A quick glance at her assistant and the grin on her face proved that Malik must have charmed her into letting him knock on her door. She shrugged and lifted her hands. "Sorry," she mouthed. Natasha smiled at her, closed the door, and leaned against it. She watched as he unloaded the items from the picnic basket. Like the other night, he wore a suit that emphasized his wide shoulders and narrow waist. The dark blue pinstripe garment draped over his muscular body as if specifically made for him. He definitely didn't look like a man who had spent twenty years running through jungles or swimming in shark infested waters to protect this country. Malik was meticulously dressed from head to toe and could have easily passed for a CEO of a Fortune 500 company.

"If you're done checking me out, maybe we can eat before you have to leave for your meeting," Malik said facing her, a dark eyebrow raised and his devastating smile chipping away at the shield around her heart.

Natasha brought her hand to her mouth to stifle her laugh. Besides the way he looked in a suit, the other thing she liked about him was his sense of humor.

"I wasn't checking you out. I ... I'm just surprised you're here." She pushed away from the door and accepted the chair he'd pulled out for her. *And he's a gentleman.* She took in all of the food on her round conference table. The fried chicken appeared homemade, and she wondered if he had made the potato salad and baked beans himself. "Wow, this looks amazing. Did you prepare all of this?"

"I did, except the cheese and crackers, strawberries, cheesecake, and iced tea are from the store up the street."

Natasha's hand rested over her heart. "I can't believe you went to all of this trouble." She couldn't remember anyone ever doing anything this thoughtful for her.

"No trouble. I just didn't want to eat alone."

Fond memories of the morning, actually, the afternoon of that amazing night they'd spent together flashed in her mind.

"So you cooked, prepared a picnic basket, and brought it to my job all because you didn't want to eat alone?"

He shrugged. "Also because I figured you would probably work through lunch." He sat in the seat next to her. "Dig in. You don't want to be late for your meeting."

They ate and talked. If Natasha bothered to take a lunch break every day, she could easily get used to spending her lunch hour with him. Coming from two different worlds it was amazing they had anything to talk about.

"This chicken is so good." Her eyes rolled and she moaned. "It's almost as good as the omelet you made for me the morning after we ... uh ... you know." *Crap!* She hadn't planned to talk about that night with him unless he brought it up.

He wiped his mouth and laid down his fork. "I was wondering if what happened between us would ever come up."

"I hadn't planned to mention that night," she leaned in and lowered her voice, "but I want you to know that I don't usually have casual sex with a stranger."

"I know you don't."

She leaned back and narrowed her eyes. "How do you know?" She didn't appreciate the smugness in his voice. "I might've just been saying that so you wouldn't think I was easy. For all you know, I just might indulge in ... in ... you know."

A cocky grin lifted the corner of his lips. "What? Sex?"

"No! One night stands," she countered, not caring that she was raising her voice and giving him a neck roll. "I'm not some goody two-shoes who doesn't know how to have a good time. I can let loose and drop my panties with the best of them."

Malik threw back his head and let out a peal of laughter that bounced off the walls and shook the room.

"It's not that funny," she grumbled after watching him hold his stomach and wipe tears from his eyes. "Okay, maybe it was funny. I can't believe I said that." Natasha shook her head and joined in laughing, realizing how childish she probably sounded. Several minutes passed before they both composed themselves.

"I know you're not a woman who jumps into bed with just anyone, and I respect that." Malik picked up his fork and moved potato salad around on his plate without taking a bite. He glanced at her, his eyes solemn. "I hope you know I didn't intend for that night to happen. I'll admit, I was attracted to you from the moment I came by your house to pick you up that day, but," he shrugged, "I had no intentions of seducing you. And for the record, I'm not sorry it happened."

Natasha lowered her head and smiled. Contentment edged with excitement wrapped around her like a silken cocoon knowing that he enjoyed their time together as much as she had. She picked up her fork and resumed eating. They ate in silence until Malik spoke.

"I remember your sister saying that you were the youngest chief of staff in the hospital's history. What did you do, start medical school right out of grade school?"

Natasha laughed. "Not quite, but close. I skipped a couple of grades and then started my undergrad when I was sixteen, finishing in three years instead of the usual four." She hoped her words didn't come across as if she were bragging, but she was very proud of her accomplishments. "I completed medical school at twenty-three and then did my residency in Connecticut at Stamford Hospital." She had sacrificed so much, including her marriage, to reach her goal of becoming a surgeon. Landing the chief of staff position was a bonus.

Malik studied her with that intense gaze she was growing used to. "I was impressed with you before, but now I'm just scared of you."

Natasha threw her head back and laughed. "Oh please, if anyone should be afraid, it should be me of you. I don't know many SEALs or people who have expertise in weapons of mass destruction and can take out an enemy without breaking a sweat." The moment Natasha noticed the change in him, she regretted her words. "I didn't mean—"

He wrapped his large hand around hers. "You never have to be afraid of me. I would never do anything to hurt you."

"Oh Malik," she turned her hand within his and held on, "I

know that. I definitely didn't mean to suggest otherwise. I feel very safe with you." What was her problem today? Everything she said came out wrong or shouldn't have come out at all. She'd never been attracted to the bad-boy types, at least not in her adult life, but there was something about Malik that made her feel all warm and cozy inside.

A knock sounded against the door. Natasha squinted down at her watch, glad to see that she still had a half an hour before she had to head to her meeting. She wiped her mouth and went to answer the door.

"Sorry to bother you," her assistant said in a rush. "I'm heading to lunch, but these came for you a few minutes ago."

Natasha gasped at the beautiful bouquet of Peruvian lilies mixed with red, yellow, and pink roses. She mouthed thank you and closed the door. She couldn't remember the last time she had received flowers.

"These are breathtaking," she mumbled. Malik was definitely pouring on the charm. First lunch and now flowers.

She set the bouquet on the table near her plate and pulled out the envelope stuck between the stems. "You know you didn't have ..." Her voice trailed off as she read the card.

Sorry about yesterday. I was a total jerk. I hope you can forgive me. Ray

Who the hell is sending her flowers? Malik wondered.

Natasha looked at Malik. "Sorry, I thought—"

"That the flowers came from me." He wiped his mouth and dropped his napkin on the table. Leaning back in his chair, he folded his arms across his chest. His gaze roamed over her womanly curves. Instead of the sexy vixen he'd taken to dinner the other night, today she looked like the epitome of professionalism. Her light blue button down blouse, tucked neatly inside her dark slacks, might have hid some of her sexiness, but he knew what lay beneath the conservative attire.

"So, who are they from?" He didn't really have a right to ask her questions about gifts she received from other men, but if she didn't want him to know, she could tell him none of his business.

She tapped the card against the palm of her other hand, her gaze trained on the bouquet. For a moment, Malik thought she wouldn't respond, but then she glanced at him.

"Ray."

"Ray? The kid who works here?" he asked, not only surprised that she'd told him, but shocked that the kid, who barely looked twenty-five, was sending someone like Natasha flowers.

She nodded. "Yes."

"So why is he sending you flowers? You two have something going on?" He knew older women dating younger men was popular these days, but he didn't take Natasha as the type to date someone ten years her junior. Especially one of her subordinates.

She dropped the card on the desk and returned to her seat. "That's none of your business."

"It is if he's stepping to a woman who I'm interested in." *Damn.* The words slipped out of his mouth before he had a chance to rein them in, but what the hell, they were true. He had decided last night that he would see where this attraction to her led. He still didn't want forever, but until he got her out of his system, he wouldn't be able to move on. "Nothing to say?"

She regarded him with an eyebrow raised, and seconds passed before she spoke. "I ... I'm surprised." She placed a couple of strawberries on her plate next to the slice of cheesecake.

"So tell me. Is it a problem if I'm interested in getting to know you better, Dr. Lockham?"

She stuffed a fork-full of cheesecake into her mouth and chewed, her eyes trained on him. The longer it took her to answer, the more interested he became. A smile spread across his mouth. He always did like a good challenge.

She wiped her mouth. "Why the cocky grin when I haven't answered you yet?"

"Because the interest is mutual." He grabbed a chicken leg and bit into it, finishing it off before speaking again. "And your attraction to me is written all over your face. So, I'll tell you what. You can ask me anything you want if it will help make up your mind." He wiped his mouth and hands on a napkin and dropped it in his empty plate.

Natasha rolled her eyes and returned her attention to her cheesecake. *"No aguanto hombres arrogantes,"* she mumbled.

"No aguanto mujeres tercas," he said in perfect Spanish, countering her comment about disliking arrogant men.

Her head jerked up and she stared at him, a smile inching across her beautiful lips. "Can't stand stubborn women, huh?" Natasha bit into a strawberry, turning him on with every move of her luscious mouth. He had never witnessed a woman make eating a piece of fruit look so sexy. "I have a feeling, Mr. Lewis, that getting to know you better is going to be very interesting."

"I guarantee it." Most people didn't know he spoke three languages. He liked that instead of her questioning his multi-lingual abilities, she was willing to allow the process of getting to know him better unfold naturally.

"Okay, I have a question for you. Considering how tall you are, did you ever consider playing basketball professionally?"

Of all the questions she could have asked, Malik wasn't expecting that one. "Yeah. I was headed in that direction. A NBA recruiter noticed me during my junior year of high school." He slouched a bit in his seat, remembering one of the most devastating times in his life. "Our school went up state that year—we were that good—and in the last game I tore my ACL."

"Oh no."

"Yeah. I worked like hell during that summer to recover and get back on my game before senior year, but I wasn't as good."

"You must have been crushed."

"You have no idea. Basketball was everything to me. So when I realized that I wasn't going into the NBA and had no desire to go to college, the day after I graduated high school I joined the Navy."

Sitting there with her, sharing a meal, felt right. Felt good. For the last few days, he had settled for talking with her on the telephone, but being there in her presence was so much better.

"When did you become a Navy SEAL?" Natasha asked.

"A few years into my Navy career. As a kid I had always been a strong swimmer, athletic and thrived on danger." He shrugged. "My commanding officer thought I'd be the perfect candidate."

"And that's when you met Cameron and Quinn?"

Malik didn't know what it was about her, Alandra, and Olivia, but rarely did any of them refer to Cameron as Wiz.

"Yep. We went through Hell Week together and have been best friends ever since."

"I could tell how close you three were while we were in Los Angeles."

The mention of L.A. brought with it memories of the brief time he'd spent with her. A time that would be forever engrained in his mind. The memory also included saying goodbye to a man who was more than his SEAL teammate, but also his brother.

Natasha toyed with the diamond around her neck, the one she wore every time he'd seen her.

"So what do you do for fun?" She finished off her cheesecake. He loved a woman who wasn't afraid to eat in front of him. They had practically wiped out the whole meal. Some of the model-type women he'd dated in the past would barely eat a salad for fear of gaining weight.

"When it's nice outside, I usually try to get in a couple of rounds of golf," he finally answered.

"Are you any good?"

He grinned. "I'd like to think so. I'm no Tiger Woods, but I know for a fact that I can beat Charles Barkley."

She laughed. "That's not saying much. Rumor has it he's not that good."

"The rumors are true." Malik chuckled. "I've played with him. He may not be that good at golf, but he's a helluva nice guy."

Her mouth dropped opened. "You've played golf with Charles Barkley?"

He shrugged. "Yeah, Michael Jordan, too."

"What? You know Michael Jordan? Oh my goodness. Next to Hunter Graham, he's like my all-time favorite basketball player."

"You like Hunter Graham, huh?"

"Who doesn't like him? Not only is he the best NBA center in the league, but he's real easy on the eyes."

"Is that right?" Malik teased, amused that she had a crush.

She dropped her head in her hands. "I can't believe I actually told you that." She lifted her head. "What did you do, put truth serum in this food? I've been running off at the mouth from the moment you walked in."

"Don't worry," he covered her hand with his, loving how soft it felt, "your secret crush on him is safe with me. I won't tell him the next time I see him."

She narrowed her eyes at him. "Don't tell me you know Hunter Graham."

"Okay, I won't tell you."

"I know he doesn't golf, so how do you know him?"

"He's my brother."

She gripped his arm, her eyes as round as saucers. "Hunter Graham is your brother?" she asked in a lower, huskier tone. When he nodded, her hands flew to her chest. "Oh my God! I can't believe you're related to Hunter Graham!"

Malik fell out laughing, finding it hard to believe that a gorgeous, straight-laced doctor and the new chief of staff was going crazy over his kid brother.

"I happen to have two tickets to his playoff game Friday night. Are you interested?"

"Are you kidding? Yes I'm interested!"

Chapter Eight

Malik and Natasha pulled up to the United Center, ending Malik's stories about how he, Wiz, and Quinn used to attend almost every Chicago home game. Natasha could tell he missed hanging out with his friends. According to Malik, he and Wiz didn't spend as much time together now that Wiz had reunited with his ex-wife.

Malik opened the passenger side door and extended his hand to help Natasha out of his truck. As they approached the arena, she wasn't surprised that a few people knew Malik by name. Her sister had once told her that Quinn and his friends seemed to have their finger on the pulse of the city, knowing everyone from government heads to common criminals.

They entered through the back of the building with other VIPs, and Natasha felt like a kid visiting Disney World for the first time, taking in her surroundings. This was so different from the world she lived in. Sure, she received some special treatment tossing the word doctor around, especially when she traveled for the hospital, but she couldn't remember ever rubbing shoulders with the rich and famous. Basketball was her favorite sport, but with her work schedule, she rarely attended games or did much socializing outside of the hospital.

"Here, come this way." Malik guided her, his large hand at the small of her back, heat from his powerful touch radiating up her spine. "There's someone I want you to meet."

They entered a tunnel-like hallway where the media camped out, as well as the player's agents talking on their cell phones. When they finally came to a stop outside a set of double doors, Malik greeted the two burly guards by name. He had told her on the ride over that the United Center was one of his clients.

"Is he here?" Malik asked the guard to the right of the door.

"I'll get him." Minutes later, Hunter Graham walked out.

"What's up, bro." Hunter greeted Malik with a one-arm hug, pounding him on his back. "I thought you were going to be here earlier so we could talk about a few things."

"We'll talk before you leave town, assuming you guys are going to win tonight and there will be a game five," Malik smirked. They had grown up in Chicago, but Hunter lived and played for the Los Angeles Rivers. Right now, L.A was behind in the series—one to Chicago's three—and needed this win.

"Don't you worry, big brother. There will be a game five." Hunter pulled a ponytail holder from around his wrist and his gaze met Natasha's. Heat rose to her cheeks when that same gaze traveled the length of her body as she stood silently, partially blocked by Malik. Standing with them, Natasha felt like an ant in a forest of tall oak trees. An inch or two shorter than Malik, Hunter was even better looking in person. Besides his long hair—which he pulled back into a ponytail at the nape of his neck—and skin a slight shade lighter than Malik's, there was no doubt that they were brothers.

"There's someone I want you to meet," Malik told his brother, wrapping his arm around Natasha's waist protectively.

"This is Dr. Natasha Lockham. Natasha, this is my little brother, Hunter Graham."

"Dr. Lockham," Hunter said, humor in his voice and a smirk on his lips as he glanced from her to his brother and back again.

"Natasha, please." Natasha extended her hand, but Hunter didn't accept it.

"Nah, Doc. If my brother has brought you here to meet me, we are way past handshakes." He pulled her out of Malik's grasp and wrapped his long arms around her, placing a kiss on her cheek before setting her back, his hands on her shoulders. "We're practically family."

"Man, let her go." Malik pulled her against him, the hard planes of his body behind hers making her insides turn to mush. "And keep your damn lips to yourself," he added with humor in his tone.

Hunter threw his head back and laughed. "Do I sense a bit of jealousy, my brother?" Malik punched him playfully in the chest and they passed a few punches back and forth. "Okay, all jokes aside." Hunter turned to Natasha. "It's a pleasure to meet you. I'm glad you were able to make it to the game tonight."

"It's my pleasure," she stated, her hand against her chest, still unable to believe that she was meeting *the* Hunter Graham. "This will be my first playoff game. The only thing is, I don't know whether to root for the home team or you, my favorite player."

Hunter grinned. "I like her. She's definitely a keeper."

Malik didn't agree or disagree. His eyes bore into her like a laser. Natasha had no idea what he was thinking, but the intensity deeply seated in his gaze had her looking away.

They talked a few minutes longer, Natasha asking Hunter questions about being in the league, while he and Malik lobbed jokes back and forth, the love for each other evident. Seeing the camaraderie between them made her miss her sisters even more.

"Well, we better go so you can get ready," Malik said to Hunter. The brothers exchanged a hug before Hunter pulled Natasha back into his arms. He hugged and kissed her on the cheek, not caring that Malik was glaring at him.

"I look forward to seeing you again, Doc." He pointed at Malik, but kept his attention on her. "If you get tired of the big guy, feel free to give me a call," he joked, his eyebrows dancing up and down.

Natasha laughed. "I'll keep that in mind."

Minutes later, they were in their VIP seats.

"Are you hungry or thirsty?" Malik asked close to her ear, the bass in his voice sending a delicious shiver up and down her arms. The undeniable chemistry between them was growing stronger by the moment, and Natasha knew that it wouldn't take much for her to fall for Malik.

She shook her head. "No. I'm still full from dinner, but maybe a bottled water."

"You got it. I'll be right back."

She watched his tall frame weave through the crowd before turning her attention to the court. She couldn't believe they were at center court. They weren't on the floor, but were close enough for her to see all of the action first hand. This night was turning into one of the best nights she'd had in a long time, and she owed it all to Malik.

"All right, here you go."

"Wow, that was quick," Natasha said when he returned with a bottle of water and a beer. "I thought you would get stuck out there."

"Nah, one of the vendors happened to be walking around with water and beer."

His body brushed hers when he reclaimed his seat. A warm, cozy feeling engulfed her as she sat next to him. The row they were in had individual seats that weren't connected like the ones higher up, and had more walking space between the rows. Yet, Malik still took up a lot of space, his knees touching the seat in front of them.

"Thank you again for bringing me," she said, leaning in close so that he could hear her over the noise growing in the auditorium. "I still can't believe that I'm actually at a playoff game. Tickets sold out within hours, and I know I couldn't get seats this good even if I wanted to."

"I'm glad you were able to come. With this possibly being the last game of the season, I can't think of anyone else I'd rather be here with."

Natasha's eyebrows rose. "I never pegged you for being a sweet talker."

His wholehearted laugh caught the attention of others around them. "I'm not going to lie. I'm not all that sweet, baby, but I can be sweet at times."

"Is that right?" Every time his penetrating gaze met hers, her heart did somersaults within her chest. She had witnessed his laid back, joking side, and lately this sweet side that she doubted many people saw. "So tell me about your family. Do you have any other siblings?"

Malik shook his head. "Nope, only Hunter. We have the same mother, but different fathers. My mother and Hunter moved to L.A. shortly after I left for the service."

"How many years between you two?"

"Ten."

When someone passed in front of them, Malik placed his arm on the back of Natasha's seat and turned his body so that they could get by, bringing him closer to her. The scent of his cologne, sandalwood with a trace of citrus, flowed past her nostrils, making her want to lean in to get a better whiff. *God, he always smells so good.*

"So why haven't you remarried?" Malik asked her out of

nowhere. "You seem like the marrying type who would have two-point-five kids and a white picket fence by now."

Natasha grunted. "Yeah right. Well, I tried the marriage thing once, and as you know that didn't turn out too well for me."

"Have you ever thought about trying it again?"

Natasha was surprised by the question, especially coming from a confirmed bachelor who, from what she'd heard, had never been in a relationship for more than two months.

"I've thought about it," she answered honestly. "Even more so the last couple of months. I have been so focused on my career that I rarely do stuff like this." She waved her hand around, indicating their surroundings. "Now that I feel a little more comfortable in my career, I'd like to try marriage again and maybe have one or two children." She turned slightly in her seat toward him. "What about you? Is marriage and kids in your future?"

Damn. He had walked right into that, not thinking that she might turn the question on him. Discussing marriage and kids with a single woman was risky considering most of them were trying to snag a man. Yet, with Natasha it was different. She didn't come across as a woman whose sole purpose of going out with a guy was to make him fall in love or lust after her, and then expect a marriage proposal within a few weeks.

"Had you asked me six months ago I would have said *no,* and probably would've said a few more things that your delicate ears wouldn't have been able to handle." They both laughed.

"But now?" she prompted.

He stretched his other arm along the back of the empty seat next to him, finding it impossible to get comfortable. A few seconds passed as he debated on how to respond to her question, but decided to be honest with her.

"Now ... maybe." He glanced at her. "And if you ever tell Wiz or Quinn I said that, I will throw you over my shoulder and carry you out to the woods never to be seen again."

"Well, dang, you act like someone is asking you to give up a kidney or something. Marriage is not that bad."

"No?" He looked at her pointedly. "Then why aren't you still married?"

Seeing her deep in thought made him wonder if he shouldn't have saved the question for another day. The last thing Malik wanted to do was ruin the good time they were having. The game wouldn't start for another twenty minutes and he was enjoying their small talk.

"He cheated on me."

Malik sat up straight. He knew he didn't like her ex before, but now he was tempted to hunt the bastard down and beat his ass.

"It wasn't his fault, though."

"How the hell wasn't it his fault? Nobody accidently cheats," Malik said before thinking.

"Okay, it wasn't *totally* his fault. I wasn't there. I wasn't present in our marriage." She shrugged. "He got tired of sleeping alone, eating alone, and point blank being alone. Unfortunately, I put my career first."

"You were young, ambitious, and working to become a surgeon. He should've understood."

"Would you have understood?" She looked at him expectantly.

Silence fell between them as he searched her face, finally zoning in on her tempting lips. "For you, yeah. I would have understood." He pushed a lock of hair out of her face and the back of his finger glided down her cheek. "I would have understood, but I probably would have been at the hospital every damn day. Either bringing you a meal, pulling you into a broom closet for a quickie, or I might have done something real stupid like cut off a finger so that I could get you to sew it back on for me."

"That is the sweetest ... and the most disturbing thing anyone has ever said to me."

Her undiluted laughter was a sweet sound to his ears, a sound he wanted to hear long after their night together was over. Attending the game with her was turning out to be better than he expected. Normally the seats they were in were reserved for his boys, but she was a good fill in. She looked amazing in an orange one-shoulder top that stretched lovingly across her ample bosom. And Malik loved seeing a woman in jeans. Hers didn't disappoint. The skinny jeans, with a belt that matched the color of her shirt, fit like a second skin. The woman was hot, and tonight she was his, but right now, he wanted to know more about the stupid Dr. Martin Lockham.

"Being divorced definitely looks different than I would expect. First Wiz and Olivia, now you and your ex. What's that all about? When you get married these days, do you have to sign something that says you're going to remain friends if you decide later to split up?"

Smiling, Natasha shook her head. "I don't know about all of that. But seeing Cameron and Olivia together in California, no one would ever believe that they were divorced." Natasha took a swig from her water. "As for Marty and I, we were friends long before we married. Although he gets on my nerves at times, he's actually a nice guy."

"If you say so." Malik took a swig from his beer, noticing how quickly the auditorium had filled. Something else about Natasha's relationship with her husband had been rattling around in his mind. He leaned in and asked, "So ... do all of your friends have a key to your house?"

She briefly stared at him before shaking her head. "No, and I'm done answering questions."

Malik studied her, a glazed look of disappointment in her eyes and a slight slump in her shoulders. "All righty then. No more questions. Let's sit back and enjoy the game."

Chapter Nine

Malik and Natasha walked hand in hand to his truck. She wasn't a petite woman, but next to Malik she felt tiny, feminine, and safe. She was also happy. The worries of the week were placed securely in the back of her mind, giving her an opportunity to enjoy being Natasha Lockham, the woman.

They approached Malik's Chevy Tahoe and he disarmed the vehicle. Instead of opening the passenger door, he wrapped his strong arm around her waist and backed her against the truck, the hard wall of his body against hers. He stared down at her and she didn't miss the sensual look in his eyes.

"There is something I've wanted to do from the moment I picked you up from your house this evening."

He pressed his mouth over hers, smothering her lips with demanding mastery. She didn't fight the boldness of his gesture or the desire strumming through her veins. Like him, she wanted this too, giving herself freely to the passion of his kiss.

Malik cradled the back of her head with his hand, increasing the intensity of his mouth against hers. As far as Natasha was concerned, they could stay that way forever. Her arm wrapped around his waist, and her fingers caressed the hard planes of his back turning her on even more. What was it about this man that made her want to throw caution out the window and let the desires of her body take control?

Malik moaned against her mouth and his other hand slid up the side of her body, crawling along her waist and fiddling with the edge of her shirt. Natasha's senses reeled from the feel of his fingers against her heated skin and the way his tongue dipped and explored the inner recesses of her mouth.

What was he doing to her? His expert lips had her heart thumping loudly inside her chest, pleasure radiating through her body. She clung to Malik, not trusting her legs to keep her upright.

A phone chirped and Natasha pretended not to hear it. She didn't want the sweet torture of his mouth on hers to stop. The phone chirped again. The moment was broken.

Malik lifted his head and Natasha's hand went to her mouth, her lips still warm from his kiss. The fervent passion brewing in the depths of his eyes showed she wasn't the only one affected. Had it not been for the cell phone, there was no telling how long she would have stayed pinned against his truck.

The phone chirped again and Natasha realized it was hers.

"I'm sorry, I have to get that." She pulled away from him and dug her cell from the side of her Coach bag. "Hello." Malik opened the passenger door and she climbed into the truck.

"Dr. Lockham," the voice on the other end of the phone line rasped, "I need to see you as soon as possible."

"Who is this?" she asked, her fingers gripping her cell tighter. She chewed on her bottom lip as Malik climbed in on the other side, his gaze meeting hers.

"Dr. Halsey."

"What is it?" Malik asked, his voice low and throaty.

"Dr. Halsey?" Natasha whispered, and swallowed audibly.

All types of thoughts were running through her mind. Should she contact the hospital? Risk management had been trying to reach him for days. "Bob, we've been trying to rea—"

"I need to see you immediately. It's ... it's important."

Thirty minutes later, Malik pulled up to a small building with a crooked, wooden sign hanging over the roof that simply read, Coffee House.

"So why did he want to meet here?" Malik shut off the ignition, turning his head left and right as if looking for something.

"I'm not sure. Maybe he was in the area," Natasha said, even though she doubted Bob hung out on this side of town, especially at this time of the night. Near the corner of the building, a drunk stumbled down the street, swaying back and forth. Cans and bottles littered the sidewalk near the building. Turning in her seat, Natasha saw a small group of men sitting on a stoop, loud music pumping out of the speakers in the window above them.

Returning her attention to the front of the truck, she had to admit that she was happy Malik was with her. Had Bob called and she not been with anyone, she might've made the trip alone, which wouldn't have been a good idea.

Malik stepped out of the truck and walked around to her side. She slipped her arm through the strap of her purse and accepted the hand that he offered. Natasha wasn't sure what Bob had to say and she didn't know what she'd say to him.

With his hand at the small of her back, Malik glanced around discretely as if memorizing the area. He guided her toward the entrance.

"I don't like this, Tasha."

She looked up at him, her eyebrows knitted together. "You don't like what?"

"All of this. I say you tell the doctor that you'll listen to anything he has to say, but not here."

"Oh, Malik, you're being ridiculous," she said in a low voice. She grabbed hold of his arm and leaned into him. "I think your training has you paranoid. I'm just going to see what he has to say and then we can go."

Malik looked down at her, his serious expression unreadable. He grabbed hold of her hand and opened the door. They stood near the entrance and several beats passed before he spoke. "Is he here?"

"Yeah, he's in the back booth next to the window with the black baseball cap." She gestured with her head. There were only five or six people in the whole establishment, and again Natasha had to admit it was a little weird that Bob had chosen such an out of the way place. She also couldn't ever remember seeing him in a baseball cap.

"You're telling me that the old white guy, who's trying too hard to fit in by wearing urban gear, is the doctor you're here to meet?" Natasha nodded, her discomfort rising by the moment.

"I really don't like this, but make it quick." He kissed the top of her head and released her hand. "I'm giving you ten minutes, and then we're out of here. I need to make a call, but I'll be at the table over there." He pointed to a table a few feet from where the doctor sat.

"Hi Bob, aren't you supposed to be on vacation in Mexico or someplace?" She searched his face. His weathered skin held more wrinkles around his gray eyes, and he looked tired, as if he hadn't slept in days.

"Change of plans." He pulled the bib of his cap down lower over his eyes. "Who's the guy you came in with?" he asked, his tone rough and disapproving.

"My date." She hadn't had a real date in so long, it felt weird attaching the title to Malik.

Her gaze moved to Bob's freckled hands; they shook uncontrollably when he lifted the glass of water to his lips. *Something is definitely wrong.* Whatever was bothering him was bad and Natasha was beginning to think that Malik might have been correct in his initial assessment of Bob and their meeting location.

She glanced over at Malik; he was staring at Bob, his eyes narrowed and his jaw clenched. Natasha didn't know what he was thinking, but his intense gaze sent goose bumps up and down her arms. She looked around nervously before returning her attention to Bob. The sooner they got out of there, the better.

"Bob, why'd you ask to meet with me, especially here?"

He toyed with the bib of his cap again, still not making eye contact. Natasha reached over and touched his hand, to keep it from shaking.

"I'm not sure what's going on, but whatever you're involved in, I'll do whatever I can to help." She pulled her hand away, folding them on top of the table. "So talk to me."

"Over twenty-five years ago, I dedicated my life to medicine, wanting to save lives and help people who couldn't help themselves." He toyed with the paper that once held his straw, folding it into a small square and then unfolding it. "I never thought I'd be in this position, questioning poor decisions and fearing for my life ... and my family's life."

"What are you talking about? Is someone after you?" An intense silence settled between them. When it didn't look as if he would answer her questions, she spoke. "If you don't start talking soon, the man I came in with will carry me out of here and you'll never have this opportunity again."

"I lost my medical license prior to moving to Chicago."

Natasha gripped the edge of the table, slowly releasing the breath that had lodged in her throat. "Wha—" The weight of what he'd just revealed hit her like a steel beam to the stomach.

"Please let me finish," he interrupted.

A wave of fear and anger gripped her gut. Her muscles tightened into a ball with each second that passed. There was no way a doctor was working under her leadership without the proper credentials. Was there? *No. That's impossible.*

"All I've ever wanted to do was save lives and help people. I thought I would die when I lived in Texas and the medical board unfairly stripped me of something I treasured more than anything ... my medical license." He rubbed his forehead and swiped at his eyes. Natasha sat stunned, the meaning of his words tearing at her insides. For the first time since she had arrived, he looked into her eyes. "I didn't care what I had to do, I wasn't about to let anyone tell me that I couldn't help people, that I couldn't do what I had dreamt about doing since I was eight years old."

"I don't understand. There's no way you could've gotten this job without having a medical license!" she said angrily, her voice rising with each word. She felt Malik's movement more so than saw him, so she lowered her voice. She leaned in and whispered, "If what you say is true, how did you get hired?"

"I hired a lawyer. A damn good ruthless lawyer. He helped me get a new identity and presented me with a new medical license." Bob ran his hands down his face. It was as if he was aging before Natasha's eyes. "I'm glad I finally have someone I can talk to. I've been living a lie for over nine years and the secret is slowly killing me."

Natasha collapsed against her seat, trying to maintain her fragile control. If any of this ever got out, the hospital would be ruined. The lawsuits would no doubt come rolling in. Part of her wanted to scream and shake some sense into the doctor, but there was nothing she could do about what he'd already done.

Malik, who was now looking at her, squinted. She wasn't sure what he saw on her face, but he started to stand. She quickly shook her head and raised her hand, praying that he would stay put. Although she didn't think she was ready for Bob's complete story, she had to listen. If what he said was true, it was way past time to put an end to his deception.

"A few years ago," Bob continued, "the lawyer who helped me change my identity, approached me about joining an organization that he was a part of. My Child Adoption Agency." Natasha made a mental note to do research on the agency. "I told him I wasn't interested. Actually, after all that he'd done for me, I didn't trust him."

Natasha was getting madder by the moment, not believing what she was hearing as she slowly started piecing things together. It was like a horrible nightmare that she couldn't wake from.

"I assume your call this evening has something to do with the women who have mysteriously died in your care."

"When I told the lawyer I wanted nothing to do with whatever he was involved in," Bob continued as if she hadn't spoken, "he told me that he would destroy me. I would never be able to practice medicine anywhere, and even worse, he would destroy the foundation. Destroy my efforts to support families who have children with leukemia. I couldn't let that happen." He wrapped his hands around his water glass. "Besides, that foundation is my wife's whole life. She would be devastated."

¡Dios mío!

Natasha maintained her death grip of the edge of the table in order to keep from slapping him. He said the words as if killing innocent women and putting the whole hospital in jeopardy was no big deal.

This man had to be sick. There had to be something wrong with a person who would intentionally take the lives of others for any reason.

She reined in her anger in order to get as much information from him as possible. "So let me make sure that I'm clear,"

Natasha said, her voice shaking with every word. "You're telling me that you killed innocent women and stole their babies because some lawyer told you that if you didn't, he would ruin your foundation and tell the world that you were a fake?"

"Do not judge me!" he growled. Natasha leaned back, putting some distance between them. Malik stood, but again she gave the slightest shake of her head to halt his approach. "You don't know the hell that I've been through. You don't know what it's like to work day and night, sacrificing time with my family. You're only in your early thirties and don't have a clue what it is like for someone to rip everything away from you that you've worked so hard to create. So don't you sit there and judge me," he said through gritted teeth.

Natasha swallowed hard and glanced at Malik again, not surprised at how intently he was watching. He looked as if he would pounce at any moment, and it gave Natasha a semblance of comfort knowing that he had her back. He lifted his hand and mouthed five minutes.

Natasha turned back to Bob, disgust rolling around in her gut. "You're not the only one who has been through hell all in the name of being the best doctor you can be. I, too, have a story. The difference between you and I, is that I didn't sell my soul to the devil and take the lives of innocent people just to protect my good name."

He dropped back in his seat as if the fight had gone out of him. Numerous emotions swept across his face, and Natasha knew she had to get as much information as possible before he shut down.

"Bob, I can't help you unless you fill in some of the missing pieces. Tell me the person or the organization that is behind this. And most importantly, where are the babies?"

. . .

There was only one reason why someone would want to meet and talk at a little hole in the wall such as the Coffee House, Malik thought. Either they had something to hide or they were hiding from someone. Malik suspected in the case of Dr. Robert Halsey, it was a little of both.

Recognizing the doctor's name as being the same as the attending physician for his friend Susan, he had taken a picture of Halsey with his cell phone and texted it to Wiz. He knew his friend would find everything he could on the doctor.

Malik didn't know what Natasha and Dr. Halsey were discussing, but he didn't like how heated their conversation was getting. He inched to the edge of his seat, prepared to step in if necessary. He didn't sit back and relax until the doctor sat back in his seat and Natasha appeared to have the conversation under control.

However, something was still off; he could feel it in his gut. It was the same nagging at the nape of his neck he had felt when he was in Tybekystan. His and Quinn's last mission together before retiring. The mission that almost cost Quinn's life. The mission from hell.

"Can I get you anything else, doll?" the waitress, old enough to be his mother, asked. Her raspy voice, stained teeth, and weathered skin were a sure sign that she had probably lived a rough life with cigarettes, coffee, and booze.

"Nah, I'm good. Thanks." He pulled his money clip from his front pocket and slipped her enough bills to cover his cup of coffee.

Besides Natasha, there were only a few people occupying two of the six booths, and no one was sitting at the tables that made up the middle of the room. Malik remembered when the café was rebuilt after burning down five years ago. No one was as surprised as he was when the owners rebuilt in the same location, despite the gang activity in the neighborhood.

The gnawing in his gut grew more intense, surrounding him. No one looked suspicious, but it was as if the air in the small space had shifted.

His cell phone rang and he debated on answering. After the second ring, he pulled it from his pocket and glimpsed at the screen.

"What's up, Wiz?"

"It's going to take me at least a day to pull up information on the doc, but my initial finding is that he is an obstetrician and has been with the hospital for five years. He and his family, a wife and two sons, moved to Chicago from Texas. He and his wife lost another son a few years back."

"I know you're just getting started with the research, but are there any red flags that you can see? Anything look out of order?"

"Mm, not really. Wait, actually, there is something. Two years prior to the doctor moving to Chicago, it's like ..."

Malik tuned in and out, his attention on Natasha and the doctor. He didn't care what she said, something was up with this guy. His body language said it all. The disguise, the fidgeting, and trepidation bouncing off him in waves. *Something doesn't feel right here.*

"Malik? Are you still there?" Wiz asked. "You know, this could—"

"I'm sorry, man. I'm still at the Coffee House waiting for Natasha and ... something feels off." His gaze went to the window when he thought he saw a flash of light. He wasn't sure what it was or if it was anything. "I'm ... uh...Wiz, let me call you back in a few."

He disconnected before Wiz had a chance to respond. A sense of foreboding grabbed hold of Malik and all he could think was that they needed to get the hell out of there.

Time's up, baby. We're out of here.

Malik stood, but before he could take a step forward, the front window shattered. Shards of glass sprinkled every flat surface like rain hitting hot pavement. He dropped to the floor. Screams bounced off the walls as another gunshot splintered through the air.

Oh shit! "Get down!" Malik yelled at Natasha, pulling her on to the floor.

His heart pounded in his ear as he wrapped his arm around her waist. Shielding her body with his, he pulled her toward the back of the building. She had a choke-hold around his neck, her deafening screams piercing his ear drums. Glass from framed pictures shattered around them, but he didn't stop until they were in the kitchen.

"Ohmygod, ohmygod!" Natasha cried, her body shaking against his.

"Shh, shh you're okay," he whispered, quickly scanning her body for injury. Natasha, still shivering but surprisingly calm, lifted her head from the crook of his neck. Then, as if suddenly remembering something, her hands flew to her mouth and her eyes grew wide.

"Bob, we have to check on Bob." She struggled to free herself from Malik's grasp, but he didn't loosen his grip.

"I don't give a damn about Bob," he growled. "Right now my only concern is you. Are you okay?" he asked, pulling his 9mm from his ankle holster with one hand. His other hand cupping her cheek. "Are ... you ... okay?" Natasha's jerky nod was all he received, her eyes focused on his weapon. "All right, I need you to stay right here."

"No!" She grabbed hold of his arm, her nails digging into his skin. "Don't leave me here."

He pulled out of her grasp and squeezed her hand. "I promise you, I'll be back."

Chapter Ten

Forty-five minutes later, Natasha sat in the chair Malik had dragged into the kitchen. She was giving her statement to the police, reliving the most horrific experience she had ever undergone in her life.

"Tom? Got a minute?" someone called for the officer who was taking her statement.

"Excuse me, Dr. Lockham. I'll be right back."

Rocking back and forth, her arms securely wrapped around her midsection, flashbacks of the evening dominated every space inside her head. *I could have been killed.* A shiver stormed through her body and she slammed her eyes shut. Memories of Malik tackling her to the floor played over and over in her mind. Had it not been for him, she'd be the one lying on the floor across the room with a tarp over her body.

Dr. Halsey is dead. Malik's words had slammed into her like a car involved in a high speed chase, ramming into her. *Bob is dead.*

Natasha blinked back tears, refusing to fall apart while sitting in a kitchen surrounded by tons of emergency personnel. If she could just hang on until she got home. Hang on until she was alone. Then she could cry. She could scream until she was hoarse and had nothing left. But for now, she would remain strong.

Holding her raw emotions in check, Natasha pulled the blanket someone had wrapped around her shoulders tighter. Closing her eyes again, she prayed the night would soon end.

"Dr. Lockham?" Natasha's eyes snapped open to find that the officer had returned. "I know this has to be hard for you, but any information you can give us will be very helpful in catching the person who did this."

"I told you everything I know." She swallowed the despair in her heart. "He called and said he wanted to talk. When I arrived, he wasn't himself. Paranoid. Jumpy. Something was bothering him and he was rambling." She struggled with how much information to share. Bob had answered the important questions, but what he had shared could easily ruin the hospital. Protecting the hospital's reputation was Natasha's number one concern at the moment. Once she had a chance to talk to the hospital's lawyers, she'd share more if instructed to. "I'm sorry. I don't know what else to tell you."

The officer studied her as if he didn't believe she was telling the truth. "I know it's been a tough night," he said, "but if you think of anything else, please give me a call." He handed her his business card. "We'll also be in contact if we have any further questions." She nodded with a rigid jerk of her head.

God, please let this night hurry up and be over.

"What the hell? First Quinn, and now you?" Detective Sheldon Baker said to Malik. "You care to tell me what's going on? And you sure as hell better not say that this has anything to do with Mexican drug cartels or terrorists."

Malik scrubbed his hands down his face and let them settle

on his waist as he paced in front of his long-time friend. Sheldon's reservations weren't unwarranted considering the drama that periodically followed Malik and his boys upon returning from missions over the years.

"I'm not sure what's going on," Malik said, "but I don't think it's anything like that."

"All right. Tell me what happened."

"Natasha got a call from Dr. Halsey." Malik nodded toward the body that was covered with a white tarp. "The guy with a bullet in his head is one of the doctors at the hospital where she works. Anyway, they were sitting over there." He pointed at the booth and told Sheldon everything that happened from the moment Natasha received the call, including the doctor's weird behavior.

Malik continued to pace. If only he had listened to his gut and insisted they not enter the café, Natasha wouldn't have had to witness the doctor's murder.

"He was incognito and everything about this meeting didn't feel right. The sudden call, the meeting place, and the way he was behaving seemed off." Malik stopped moving and faced his friend. "Before I knew it, the front window blew out, screams erupted, and then I saw the single shot to the doctor's head."

"Did you see anyone when you went outside?"

"I didn't see anyone, but I did see a black Ford utility van speeding away. And before you ask, there were no plates. The only distinguishable features were on the right side of the vehicle. It looked as if there was some wording on the side panel that had been painted over, or maybe taped over. It also had a roof rack, but nothing on top."

"All right, that's good." He jotted something down on his notepad. "Going back to the doctor's conversation. Do you know what they were discussing?"

"I have no idea. All I know is that Halsey was agitated and

occasionally raised his voice while they were talking." Malik leaned against one of the kitchen counters, rubbing his eyes. "Whoever took out that doctor was a professional."

"Yeah, I noticed," Sheldon said.

"A solid shot in the forehead. That type of precision ..." Malik balled his fists, tension gripping his body. "Shell, man, that damn shot was on point, clean. Considering where Natasha was sitting, a half-an-inch to the left and she would've been dead." He cleared his throat. Emotion gnawed away at the unbendable shield around his heart. Now he understood the fear that Wiz and Quinn carried around with them when it came to their women's safety. Malik and Natasha were only friends, yet the unexplainable need to keep her safe chipped away at him. He didn't know if he could ever let her out of his sight again.

"Do you think the car bombing at the hospital and this shooting are related?" Malik asked.

"Maybe, but right now I don't have enough information to connect the two, unless there's something you're not telling me." He narrowed his eyes at Malik. "Is there? Do you know something that I should know?"

Malik had his suspicions, but there were answers he needed from Natasha before he shared them with anyone.

"I'm not sure what this is about yet, but you better believe I plan to find out," Malik said, the conviction in his tone matching the determination lodged in the depth of his soul.

"Oh no you don't!" Sheldon shoved the notepad into his inside jacket pocket, and pointed his ink pen at Malik. "You're going to let me and my guys do our job. Do I make myself clear? I can't have you and your people going all vigilante out there and getting in the way of this investigation."

Malik sighed. Folding his hands on top of his head, he stared up at the food-speckled ceiling. He'd let them do their job, but that wasn't going to stop him from pulling his team together to find their own answers.

"I already warned Wiz and Stan when I spotted them lurking around outside the building across the street." Malik dropped his arms and returned his attention to Sheldon when he sensed him moving closer. His friend lowered his voice. "If you guys find anything, I expect you to share the information with me."

Moments passed as they stared each other down before Malik gave a slight nod, the message between them clear. "I'll stay out of your way if you agree to keep me informed of what you find."

When Sheldon silently agreed, Malik glanced at Natasha, surprised at how well she was holding up. There were only a few moments that he thought she would break down, but she hadn't, impressing him even more. His past life was comprised of scenes like the one that had just played out in the dining area, but for her, this had to be like something out of a bad dream.

Sheldon cleared his throat. "Oh how the mighty have fallen." He chuckled. "Wiz was already a goner with Olivia, but then Quinn and now you. *Damn.* I never thought I'd see the day. Although I have to admit, you guys sure know how to pick them. Tough and cute. Nice combination.

"We're just friends," Malik said, still looking at Natasha. He had to agree, she was a tough woman. Watching her now, no one would ever believe that she'd just witnessed a murder, and had barely walked away with her life considering the gunman had only missed her by a fraction of an inch. That alone let Malik know whoever had taken out the doctor was skilled. Someone that precise didn't miss Natasha by chance. She wasn't the target, but now she might be.

Malik realized Sheldon was still staring at him. "What, man? I told you. We're just friends."

"Mm hmm, you keep telling yourself that, buddy. Looks like I'll be holding up the bachelorhood all by myself." Sheldon slapped him on the back, shaking his head. "But getting back to business. I might have more questions after we sort some of this out. Where's she going to be?" Sheldon nodded his head toward Natasha.

Malik returned his attention to her. "She'll be with me."

He approached Natasha after the police officer who was questioning her walked away. Their gazes met. Now that he was close to her, exhaustion showed in her eyes. Usually she had a ready smile for him, but now her features were withdrawn and wary. He hated seeing her like this.

"Come here," he said when he reached her, wanting ... no, needing to hold her close.

Natasha stood slowly, letting the blanket fall from her narrow shoulders, and walked into his embrace. He held her tight, loving the feel of her soft curves molded against his body. If anything had happened to her, he wasn't sure what he would've done. Despite what he had told Sheldon, he had to admit that somehow the woman in his arms had penetrated the shield around his heart.

He kissed the top of her head. "I'm so sorry you had to experience this." As soon as he whispered the last word, the floodgates opened and she broke down.

"Ah, baby ..." He whispered comforting words close to her ear, hoping to say something that would make her feel better. Peering over Natasha's head, he noticed Wiz across the room trying to get his attention. Instead of approaching, Wiz gave the hand signal for Malik to give him a call. With a small nod, he agreed.

Natasha's sobs eventually quieted, and Malik snatched a few napkins from the counter and handed them to her. She stepped back and peeked at him, tears lacing her lashes. The inside of his chest felt as if someone had reached in and had a strong grasp on his heart. Normally she always looked as if she were in control and in charge, but now she seemed small and fragile. Everything in him wanted to just hold her and never let her go, keeping all harm away from her.

"That could have been me," she said quietly as she wiped her face. "I've seen my share of injuries, blood, and even death, but this ... this was too much. He was killed right in front of me. Every time I close my eyes, I'm taken back to that moment ..." Their gazes met and tears filled her eyes again.

"Baby, I can't handle the tears." He pulled her close, catching the tears streaming down her cheeks with the pads of his thumb. "I promise you, the memories will slowly fade. Just give it time. I'll do whatever I can to shield you from ever having to go through anything like this again."

Her tears fell faster. Apparently, his words were having the opposite affect that he was going for.

"You saved my life." She reached up and cupped his cheek, her thumb rubbing against the light stubble on his jaw. "I will forever be grateful for what you did for me. Thank you."

At that moment, he felt that he would walk on water for her if he had to. *Shit. This is not good.* Every second he spent with her another layer of resistance fell from around his heart.

"I hope you're going to be okay with this." He wrapped his arm around her waist, and guided her toward the door. "Tonight, you're going home with me."

Chapter Eleven

Malik pulled his truck into the three-car garage. Natasha vaguely remembered the long ride. All she could think about was the nightmare of an evening she'd just experienced. Each time she closed her eyes, she heard the glass shattering, the screams in the café, including her own. And then there was the hole in Dr. Halsey's forehead; the memory forever engrained in her mind.

Natasha wrapped her arms around herself. On top of reliving the nightmare from two hours ago, thoughts of going home with a man she barely knew made her just as uncomfortable. *What was I thinking?* Truth be told, she hadn't been thinking. All she knew is that she didn't want to go home, nor did she want to be alone.

Malik ran his hand up and down her arm. "Are you sure you're okay and don't need me to take you to the hospital?"

She appreciated his concern, wondering if he'd forgotten she was a doctor. Except for the ache in her right side from when Malik yanked her to the floor, physically she was fine. Her mental state was another story. "Thanks, but I'll be all right."

Sharon C. Cooper

"Okay, but just say the word if you change your mind."

The moment Malik climbed out of the truck and walked around to the passenger side Natasha heard loud barking.

"I didn't know you had a dog," she said.

"Yeah, a Rottweiler. His name is Tank. How do you feel about dogs?"

"I like dogs. I didn't picture you as having one, though."

Natasha followed behind Malik as he climbed the two concrete steps inside the garage that led into the house.

"Hey boy," Malik greeted an excited Tank, who was more interested in sniffing Natasha.

"Good evening, Malik," his alarm system's sultry voice chimed when he deactivated the code.

"Hi Darla. Code one."

"Roger that," the alarm system responded.

"Your alarm system talks to you. Impressive. So instead of coming home to a wife, you come home to Darla."

A grin slid across his full lips as he ushered her into the mudroom. "I usually try out some of the security systems before we offer them to clients. Darla here is our most recent unit, ideal for people who live alone and who might want someone to welcome them home when they arrive."

"I see." She rubbed Tank's short fur and the dog leaned into her, enjoying the attention. "It's nice to meet you, Tank." He barked, as if understanding her words.

"Come on in." Malik moved around the kitchen and then the family room, turning on more lights. "Tank. Go." He snapped his finger and pointed to a designated spot in the family room. "He likes you. At the rate you were going, showing him all that love, he'd be following you around like a shadow."

"Do you live here alone?"

Malik frowned. "Yeah, why?"

She took in all of the maple wood, custom kitchen cabinets, granite countertops, and the state of the art stainless steel appliances. The whole first floor of her house could fit inside the kitchen. It was a cook's paradise. "This place is huge. Why so much space?" she asked, strolling into the family room. She loved the arched openings, and the impressive crown molding throughout the room captured her attention.

"I'm a large man," he said from the kitchen. "I like everything big." She turned back and watched as he rinsed his hands in the sink and dried them before opening the refrigerator. "Are you hungry? Thirsty?"

"Do you have tea?" she asked, her energy starting to wane. She sat at the breakfast bar, her elbow on the counter and her chin in her hand.

"Yeah, actually I do." He reached into the pantry. "What kind do you like?" he asked, displaying a container, housing a variety of tea packets.

Natasha arched an eyebrow, deciding on the one she wanted. "You don't seem like a tea drinker. Why the big selection?"

"My mother visits often. She's a big tea drinker." He stood on the other side of the breakfast bar, staring down at her. "You look exhausted. Why don't I show you to the guest room and you can shower and try to relax."

She shook her head. "Not yet. I'm not ready to close my eyes again. The images ..." She stopped, not wanting to think about the last couple of hours. She had pulled plenty of all-nighters during her residency, staying awake for a couple of days straight. She could do it again. However, the yawn that had her eyes watering said otherwise.

"This is what we're going to do." Malik reached for her hand and pulled her off the barstool. "I'm going to show you to your room. While you shower, I'll find something for you to sleep in. By the time you're refreshed, I'll have a drink prepared for you that will be a tad bit stronger than tea and will help you relax."

Natasha leaned into him when he wrapped his arm around her waist. "I guess you have all the answers." It had been a long time since anyone took care of her. She realized she liked it.

Before they made it to the stairs, Malik's cell phone rang. Considering it was well after one in the morning, she hoped it wasn't any bad news or some woman making a booty call.

A half an hour later, they lounged in Malik's family room, with Tank, the traitor, who now sat at Natasha's feet. Malik had never invited a woman to spend the night. Normally he'd take her to a hotel or spend time at her place. Yet, bringing Natasha home seemed like the most natural thing to do.

He sat facing her on the other end of the sofa. Bringing his beer bottle to his lips, he allowed his gaze to travel down her body. Malik couldn't ever remember being so turned on by a woman in a man's T-shirt. The shirt he'd given her to sleep in skimmed over her curvaceous figure, tempting him so much that he had to put some distance between them to ensure he kept his hands to himself.

Her smooth shapely legs, which he longed to run his hands over, were curled beneath her and her hands wrapped securely around a coffee mug. Instead of a simple hot cup of tea, Malik prepared her a hot toddy; a whiskey, cinnamon, and honey concoction. She yawned for the second time in five minutes and he knew he only had a small window of opportunity to get some answers from her.

"You and Dr. Halsey were in a pretty heated conversation tonight. Care to share what you two were discussing?"

Narrowed eyes zoned in on him. "You don't think I had anything to do with his death, do you?"

Malik frowned. "Of course not. Why would you even asked that?"

Some of the worry lines slowly left her face and she stared down into her cup. "The cops questioned me as if I were a suspect, like I could set anyone up like that."

Anger stirred inside Malik. The police might have been doing their job, but he didn't like it.

Malik slid closer to her. Compassion wasn't one of his strengths, but she looked as though she was going to fall apart. He knew he wouldn't be able to handle more tears, especially hers.

"You having anything to do with the doctor's death never crossed my mind."

She glanced down at Tank, who was looking back and forth between her and Malik, as if waiting to see what would happened next. Malik had no idea what she was thinking, but the tension radiating off her spoke volumes.

"Tasha, I hope you know that you can trust me. Whatever you two were discussing might have something to do with why Halsey's dead now. Why don't we talk about it? Besides, it'll make you feel better to get whatever's bothering you off your chest." Natasha turned to him, tears filling her eyes.

Oh damn. He sat his beer down on an end table and went to the half bath for the box of Kleenex.

"I don't know who killed him," she said when he handed her a few sheets of tissue, her voice barely a whisper, "but I know why he's dead."

Natasha felt Malik stiffen next to her, his intense dark eyes growing darker. He sat studying her for the longest time. She wished he would say something. Anything. Every nerve ending in her body was slowly starting to fray. She couldn't handle the silence. She needed to talk to someone. Someone outside of the hospital. Someone she could trust. Since Alandra, her confidant, wasn't there, she'd have to take a chance on Malik.

"If you know anything," Malik's voice dropped an octave, "and I mean *anything* about why he might be dead, you need to tell me. Your life could be in danger."

Her hand clenched around the mug and Malik eased it from her grasp. "No. I ... I have no association with him. All I know is that he is ... well, he was a respected doctor at the hospital."

"I have a feeling you know more than what you're saying. Why don't you start from the beginning?"

The warmth flowing through her body from the drink Malik had given her—along with the cozy room they were sitting in, with its dark woods and overstuffed furniture—no longer provided her with peace. She swallowed hard trying to decide what to tell him. She had known Malik would question her about her conversation with Bob. She was surprised he hadn't asked earlier.

"I could lose my job," she fidgeted with her hands, "but I have to tell someone. Please, you have to promise me that you won't say anything."

He grasped her hand. "If you're in trouble or in danger, you have to tell me. As for not telling anyone, I think you know me well enough to know that if I have to say anything to anybody, it won't be anyone but Wiz. And the only reason I would confide in him is if we needed his help."

Natasha studied him. His strong jaw and the serious look on his face reminded her of when they all sat around Quinn's kitchen, before he and Alandra prepared to leave the country. If Quinn and Alandra trusted him, then she would, too.

She sucked in a long breath and released it slowly. "Dr.

Halsey is ... or was under investigation for killing new mothers." Natasha glanced at Malik, whose expression didn't change. "Tonight he pretty much admitted to it, claiming that he didn't have a choice because he was being blackmailed."

"By who? Did he say who was blackmailing him?"

Natasha shook her head. "No, not exactly. He said a few years ago some lawyer helped him get a fake medical license."

"He was practicing medicine without a legitimate license?" Malik asked, his tone remaining neutral. Natasha had no idea how he could sit there so calm, no reaction, just questions.

She nodded. "And from what Dr. Halsey said, this lawyer contacted him later about doing some work for him. At first Dr. Halsey was totally against the idea."

"What type of work?"

"I assume taking the lives of these new mothers."

Malik shrugged. "Why? I don't understand. Why would this lawyer want these mothers dead? It doesn't make sense."

"To steal their babies."

Malik looked confused. She saw a flash in his eyes. Understanding. Anger. A lethalness he'd never shown before.

"Dr. Halsey said that this lawyer is connected to an adoption agency."

"Which one?" he asked.

She uncoiled her legs, placed her feet on the floor, and leaned forward, her elbows on her knees. "With everything that's happened ... I can't remember the name of the agency." Misery floundered in the pit of her stomach like granite rocks, crashing against the inside of her body. One of the most important pieces of the puzzle and she couldn't remember.

He squeezed her hand. "Don't be too hard on yourself," he said, the shell-shocked look in his eyes growing deeper. "You'll remember."

She took a deep breath and sat back against the sofa, willing herself to be strong. "What I do know is the agency he mentioned isn't familiar to me. Tomorrow I'll check our list of the agencies the hospital is affiliated with to see if any trigger my memory."

Malik stood and ran his hand over his baldhead, his back toward her. "I can't believe that someone is fucking stealing babies," he said, incredulous. A few other choice words rolled off his tongue. Suddenly, he turned to face her. "Does the hospital know how long this shit's been going on?"

Natasha cringed each time he cursed. It wasn't so much the words he chose, it was the way he said them with enough venom to strike a person down. He had told her he'd been working on cleaning up his language, but apparently he still had work to do.

"We're not sure. The hospital has been investigating. The administrators and the legal department have been reviewing all of his files, patient's charts, everything, for the past couple of weeks. Dr. Halsey was on vacation. No one could reach him. That is ... until tonight."

Malik paced in front of her like a Tyrannosaurus Rex lumbering the earth, moving powerfully from one side of the family room to the other and back. "This explains your reaction to my question at dinner that one night, when I told you about my friend who died giving birth ... and I asked about how things are handled with orphans." He continued to pace, talking under his breath; his colorful vocabulary getting raunchier with each word out of his mouth. He stopped abruptly, turning to her with his jaw clenched and a dangerous glint in his eyes. "We have to find out what happened to those babies."

Malik carried a sleeping Natasha up the stairs to the guest room. Normally it was just him and Tank in the four bedroom, three bathroom colonial, but he had to admit, despite the circumstances it was nice having her there.

She snuggled closer, her head against his chest, her body molded against his. The fresh smell of soap mixed with her natural scent wafted around him, sending his libido into overdrive. He was tempted to carry her to his bed, but had promised himself that he would keep his hands to himself. The next time they shared a bed, he wanted it to be intentional, and not a one-nighter.He kissed her forehead and stared down into her angelic face, recalling their conversation from earlier. He hoped like hell that she had told him everything. There was nothing worse than going into a situation with only half the intel.

His cell phone vibrated in his pants pocket and he reluctantly laid her in the bed, waiting to answer the call until he was in the hallway.

"Yeah?"

"Is she okay?" Wiz asked.

Malik stood in the doorway to Natasha's room, watching her. "She's a little shaken, but she's holding up good. So what did you find out?"

"The area across the street from the café was clean. No brass or anything else was left behind, but that was no surprise considering we're dealing with a professional. I did find a witness, though."

"Oh yeah? Please tell me he was able to give a description of the person."

"Not exactly. He said a black man practically knocked him down when he was leaving the apartment building across from the café. Said the guy had a long duffle bag and was about my size. No real description of the perp, except that he wore all black, including a wool hat pulled low, almost hiding his eyes."

Malik cursed under his breath.

"He did get a look at the getaway vehicle. He said there was some white lettering on the side of the black van that the guy sped away in."

This got Malik's attention.

"He said the same thing as you. Something was covering the lettering, but he said that he was able to see a few letters ... d, y, man. He said the van was a dark color, but he didn't know if it were black or blue."

"Well, at least that's something. My first guess would be that the word spelled handyman, but it doesn't help much."

"Did Natasha tell you what she and the doc discussed?" Wiz asked.

Malik shared the information that Natasha had given him. He wasn't sure where to start searching for answers, but he knew Wiz would know. "I have a feeling that Susan might have been one of the doctor's victims."

Wiz blew out a long whistle. "That's some crazy shit."

"I'm sure I don't have to tell you that we need to handle this with as much discretion and under the radar as possible."

"Definitely. At least this gives me something to work with. Let's hook up later tomorrow. I'll give you all of the information I have on Dr. Halsey. And based on what Natasha told you, I'm sure we both agree that there's a huge possibility the car bombing is related to this incident."

"Yeah, I was thinking the same thing."

"I have a contact at the hospital. I'll see if I can get a copy of the video of the employee parking lot from that night. Maybe it'll give us some clues. We're also going to need to go and see Rosalyn. Maybe there's something in Susan's journal that can help us piece more of the situation together."

"Yeah, that's a good idea. Let's see if we can meet up with her tomorrow."

"One more thing," Wiz said. "How do you feel knowing that

this doctor might've killed Susan, and whoever he's working with might have sold her baby? Possibly your child."

"Dammit, Wiz!" Malik growled. Turning away from Natasha's doorway, he went into his bedroom. "How many fuckin' times I gotta tell you? The kid is not mine!"

Chapter Twelve

Natasha sluggishly opened her eyes, blackness surrounding her. In the distance, the hum of an air conditioner pierced the silence of the room and a surge of anxiety leapt within her body. *Wha ... Where am I?* Her hands fisted the sheet as her gaze darted back and forth in the dark trying to figure out where she was.

Okay. Okay. Calm down and relax. Calm down and relax, she told herself, using the same chant she had used plenty of times when doing a surgery. *Just calm down.* She breathed, inhaling a deep breath and releasing it slowly as her eyes began to adjust to the darkness. Memories of the evening slowly penetrated her mind.

Malik. I'm at Malik's house.

She sighed in relief and turned onto her side, snuggling into the pillow and hoping that sleep would once again claim her. Time passed and like earlier, when she closed her eyes, the scene at the café infiltrated her mind. She didn't want to think. She didn't want to remember. All she wanted was to be lulled back into the mindless, dreamless state she'd just come out of.

When she realized that wasn't going to happen, she sat up

in bed, only to sway to the left and then to the right. *Whoa.* She grabbed her head. Once the room stopped spinning, she planted her feet on the floor and felt her way to the adjoining bathroom. She wasn't much of a drinker and the queasiness flowing through her body reminded her why. She hated the after effects of alcohol.

Happy to see a new toothbrush and toothpaste near the sink, she brushed her teeth and splashed cold water on her face. The small gesture had her feeling somewhat alive. Returning to the bedroom, she sat on the edge of the bed. It was too quiet. She could turn on the television mounted on the wall, but that's not what she wanted. What she really wanted was to be wherever Malik was.

That's not a good idea.

Ignoring her inner voice, she went in search of him. When she stepped into the hallway, it was just as quiet and dark. A light from the lower level illuminated part of the staircase, whereas the other end of the hallway was pitch-black. She didn't hear Tank, so she assumed Malik had put him in the basement since he had mentioned it earlier.

She glanced across the hall at Malik's bedroom, his door slightly opened.

Natasha brought her hand up to her mouth, her bottom lip folded between her teeth. She knew she was asking for trouble if she went to him in the middle of the night, but the need to be held was overriding all common sense.

With one foot in front of the other, she approached his door and slowly pushed it open. He had showed her around upstairs, but with the darkness, she could barely see her hand in front of her face. A sliver of moonlight shone through the slats of the blinds, guiding her to the massive bed in the middle of the room.

There wasn't enough light for her to see him clearly, but it didn't matter. She remembered every inch of his strong, enticing body. She licked her lips recalling how she dug her fingernails into his unbelievably broad shoulders the night he rocked her world. And she would never forget his wide chest, sprinkled with soft, dark hair perfect for running her fingers through.

Natasha swallowed hard. Why was she torturing herself? Torturing herself with memories of making love with a man who didn't want the same things she wanted? Marriage. Children. She asked herself the question, but she knew the answer. Malik had brought her more pleasure in one night than her own husband had brought her in all the years they were together. She shook her head knowing she should go back to her room, but she couldn't. She wanted him. Right now, she needed him.

Natasha stepped closer to the bed. Her heart lurched when her gaze landed on the spot where he'd been shot just below his ribcage during a mission in Afghanistan years earlier. She stretched out her hand, her fingers grazing the wound that had almost cost him his life.

Malik bolted upright with his gun drawn.

Natasha screamed when he grabbed her by the front of her T-shirt, the barrel of his gun between her eyes. Her heart slammed against her chest. Fear kept her from breathing. "Ma–Malik!" she cried, tears clouding her vision. "Please ..."

Malik released her and slapped his hand against the side table. Light illuminated the room.

"What the hell?" he roared, his gun still drawn. "Are you crazy? You could have been killed!"

Natasha stumbled back. Tripping over his shoes, she landed hard on her tailbone. Fear kept her moving. She shuffled her feet and scooted away from him until she hit a wall, unable to go any further, unable to breathe.

Shit!

Malik shoved his pistol into the side table drawer and leapt off the bed, not caring that he was only in his boxer briefs. The fog in his head barely lifted as he hurried toward Natasha, her eyes wild with panic, her arms flailing around.

He dropped onto the floor and wrapped his arms around her, pulling her onto his lap. "Okay, baby, I've got you. I've got you," he said calmly near her ear, barely able to contain her as she fought against him, her chest heaving uncontrollably in full panic attack mode. "I need you to breathe for me." Tears streamed down her cheeks as she struggled to catch her breath. "Come on, baby. Just breathe," he repeated over and over again, showing her by going through the motions himself. "That's it. In ... and out."

Malik didn't know how long he sat there with her, his back literally against the wall. She had finally calmed down, but still hadn't spoken. He'd had enough heart-stopping moments in the last few hours to last him a lifetime. First the café shit and now this. His heart thumped wildly, remembering the look on her face. He wasn't used to having anyone in the house, especially in his bedroom. He hated to be the cause of her panic attack.

Natasha shifted in his arms, her head on his chest, her body molded against him. His body reacted to every move she made on his lap. The skimpy T-shirt covered her, but her soft curves were driving him crazy. Even considering her mental state, he wanted her more than he had ever wanted a woman before.

"Have you ever had a panic attack before?" he asked, and placed a kiss on top of her head, willing his body to settle down.

"Once." She snuggled closer, her small hands gripping his upper arm. "During my residency. I hadn't slept in three days and on one particular day there had been a ten-car pileup. The emergency room was like nothing I had ever experienced and we were literally running around trying to keep up." She rubbed her forehead and Malik could feel the tension radiating from her body. "We had a code blue and um ... a little boy went into cardiac arrest and I had ... I had a panic attack."

Malik tightened his arms around her.

"Thank God someone else was able to help him." She sighed. "That day I almost gave up on my dream of being a doctor."

"What changed your mind?"

"More like *who* changed my mind." She was silent for a moment. "I called home and told Marty what happened and he pretty much talked me down off the ledge so to speak."

Malik was glad Martin had been there for her, but the last thing he wanted was to hear anything about her ex-husband. Besides that, his legs were getting stiff.

Instead of asking her to get up, he stood with her in his arms and set her on the bed. Sitting next her, he leaned forward, his elbows on his thighs.

"Sorry about the gun. I didn't mean to scare you."

She shook her head. "No, I'm sorry. I shouldn't have snuck up on you like that."

He studied her solemn expression, the color slowly coming back into her cheeks. With all the activity over the past half hour, he hadn't asked why she was in his room, not that he minded. The only thing was, it brought back memories of their night together, memories he wanted to repeat.

"Sleeping with my gun is a force of habit," he said, interlocking his fingers together and staring down at the floor. He needed to stop looking at her, stop thinking about all that he wanted to do to her and all of the positions he wanted them to try. Sitting in only his boxer briefs did nothing to hide his desire for her, and if she hadn't already noticed his state of arousal, she would eventually.

She cleared her throat and fidgeted beside him. Trying to

maintain some semblance of modesty, he kept his arms in front of him, but turned slightly to look at her.

"You okay?"

"Yeah, just thinking about you sleeping with your gun."

He shrugged. "It's what I do."

"But wouldn't you prefer to sleep with a woman tonight?"

Malik froze. It wasn't often he was left speechless, but damn if she hadn't caught him off guard. He turned fully, suddenly not caring if she noticed his erection. His gaze traveled from her disheveled hair hanging loosely around her shoulders to her gorgeous face, free of makeup. The T-shirt he'd given her to wear did nothing to hide her perky breasts, her nipples standing at attention, begging to be tweaked. Since the moment they stepped into his home, he'd been struggling to keep his hands to himself.

He continued his inspection, zoning in on those smooth legs that he'd wanted to run his hands down all night. The thought of them wrapped around his waist took his erection to new lengths. And she had pretty feet. The hot red toenail polish coupled with the rest of her sexy ass body had his libido fully awake now.

He leaned back on the bed, staring up at her. "In answer to your question ... it would depend on the woman." When he didn't get a response or a reaction he asked, "So, why are you in my bedroom?"

She fiddled with the tail of her T-shirt before meeting his gaze.

"I couldn't sleep."

This day for Natasha had been like no other day in her life. Now, here she was, sitting in a man's room, who she barely knew, trying to figure out how to tell him that she wanted him.

She wanted him in all the ways a woman could want a man and she wasn't sure how to proceed. And the way he was studying her, it didn't appear that he would make this easy.

"I thought ... I thought if I came in here, then maybe ... I'd be able to fall back to sleep."

He still didn't say anything. Instead, he laid on his back and stretched, his long arms extending over the side of the bed. His sculpted body was displayed in a way where all she had to do was reach out and slide her hands down his dark skin. Unlike some women, her favorite body part of a man were his thighs, and Malik didn't disappoint. Nice, solid, tree-trunk like thighs, with a light dusting of dark hair were calling out for her. If only she could run the tip of her fingers up the inside of his powerful thigh and ... An involuntary tremor surged through her body as her gaze went higher, his thick shaft straining against his underwear. Apparently, she wasn't the only one in need of sexual release.

"There you go, checking me out again," Malik said, jarring her from her inspection of his man parts. He climbed fully onto the bed, his back against the fabric-covered headboard, his legs spread apart. "C'mere." He extended his hand and she accepted it, allowing him to pull her to him. Positioned between his legs, she was on her knees and they were face to face. Her pulse pounded loudly in her ears at their nearness. "Tell me what you want." He cupped her cheek and she closed her eyes, leaning into his touch.

This man made her feel things that she couldn't put a name to. Every nerve came alive when he was near, when he touched her. She couldn't explain the sensation sparked by the tenderness of his fingers against her heated skin.

His hand glided down the side of her face and he lifted her chin, forcing her to look at him. "Tell me what you want," he repeated. The velvet edge in his voice was as sexually stimulating as his touch.

"You ... I want you."

With his hands cradling her face, he drew her closer, their lips only a breath apart.

"And I want you." His deep voice dripped like warm honey tantalizing her with unadulterated desire. He lowered his head and his mouth covered hers. His kiss was slow, thoughtful, and almost torturous.

For months, Natasha wondered if she'd ever see him. Wondered if she would ever get to experience what it felt like to be in his strong, muscular arms again. And wondered if she'd ever feel him inside her, stroking her, stirring everything within her, making love to her.

Malik pulled his mouth away from her lips and kissed the slender column of her throat, his heated breath caressing the sensitive area behind her ear. Her body tingled from the contact, goose bumps popping up on her arms. This is what she'd been missing the last three months. No actually, all of her adult life. When she was with him, he brought her senses to life like jumper cables to a dead battery, surging power to every cell in her body.

"You have on way too many clothes," he said, yanking on her T-shirt. His large hands slipped beneath it and he lifted the oversized garment over her head, allowing her bare breasts to burst free. His eyes brimmed with tenderness and passion, sending a flood of delight rising within her. "You're absolutely breathtaking." The huskiness of his voice was as much of a turn on as his hands and lips on her skin.

He gently laid her on her back and hovered above her. She almost looked away as he boldly skimmed her body, but she couldn't. His unwavering gaze met hers and had her rooted in place. Despite her desire for him to hurry and be inside of her. He would not be rushed.

Malik cupped her breasts, gently kneading them, the pads of his thumbs caressing her sensitive buds. When he lowered his head and took her nipple into his mouth, Natasha swallowed hard. His tongue twirled around the harden peaks, sending wicked jolts of pleasure throughout every sensitive inch of her body. She moaned and her eyes drifted shut. Her nails dug into his shoulders at the pleasure he elicited, especially when he paid the other breast the same attention. Just when she thought she couldn't handle any more, he pulled her harden peak gently between his teeth, the euphoria pure and explosive. She wouldn't have ever guessed that a man Malik's size could display such tenderness, but she couldn't take much more of the sweet torture. The ache between her thighs growing more intense.

"Malik," she whimpered.

"I know, baby," he murmured as if reading her mind, "but tonight I want to take my time and reacquaint myself with your body."

He stripped her of her lacy red panties, tossing them to the floor. Her pulse raced as his gaze roamed over her once again, as if cataloguing every curve and dip of her body. He made her feel things she had never felt with any other man and at that moment there was no one she'd rather be with.

He moved to kiss her again. She placed her hands on his face, forcing him to look into her eyes. "You asked me what I wanted and I told you – I want you. I want you inside me... now." Her throbbing sex had waited long enough. If he didn't make a move soon, she was going to burst.

· · ·

Malik chuckled. "I like it when you tell me what you want." He discarded his briefs, tossing them to the floor with her clothes. He leaned over her to grab a few condoms from his nightstand, keeping one and placing the rest on top. He sat back on his haunches, glanced at Natasha and caught her sizing up his rigid shaft. "There you go checking me out again," he taunted, enjoying her appreciative gaze. "Do you like what you see?"

A wanton smile slid across her lips. "As a matter of fact I do." Her words dripped with seduction as she wrapped her soft hand around his erection, sliding up and down his length.

Ahh shit.

His eyes slammed shut and a surge of heat swept through his body like a roaring fire. He swallowed hard, crumbling the silver packet in his hand as her grip tightened around him. Natasha fondled and squeezed him with a mastery of a baker kneading dough, his length growing longer and harder with every stroke. When her thumb slid over the tip of his penis, he almost lost it.

"Okay, okay, okay." He grabbed her hand, trying to catch his breath. "Damn girl," he said between shallow breaths. "I like that you're not afraid to take matters into your own hands, but ...." His voice trailed off and he ripped the condom packet open with his teeth. *To hell with taking it slow.*

He nudged her thighs apart. His hand slid over her flat stomach and didn't stop until he reached the V between her thighs. He dipped a finger inside her womanly folds. *Wet and hot.* "Oh yeah, you're ready for me." His mouth covered hers hungrily as he added yet another finger, sliding in and out of her. Deeper. Faster. Harder.

She lurched against his hand and tore her lips from his. "Malik!" she cried and lifted her lower body off the bed, clawing at his back.

The sexy sounds she made sent adrenaline rushing through

his veins. His pulse pounded and his erection throbbed with need, needing to be inside her.

Malik removed his finger and gripped her butt, pulling her toward him. He eased into her sweet heat. Inch ... by inch, by excruciating inch, giving her body a chance to adjust to his size. He'd swear he heard angels singing when he entered her. Her tightness wrapped around him like a snug-fitting glove. She moved beneath him, her muscles contracting around his shaft as he buried himself deeper inside of her.

Balanced above her, his weight supported by his hands and arms on either side of her body, Malik pressed his mouth to hers. Natasha draped her arms around his neck and kissed him with a hunger that matched his own. This is what he missed. Three long months since he'd last had her, and not a day had gone by that he didn't think about how sexually combustible they were together.

She felt so damn good. He knew he wouldn't be able to hang on much longer. Especially with the way her tongue tangled with his, spurring him to thrust faster, harder. Their bodies moved in perfect sync with each other

When an acute surge of adrenaline hit him, Malik pulled his mouth from hers. "Natasha," he growled, his movements more jerky, his grip on her hips tighter.

A whimper slipped through her lips with every thrust and Malik could feel her nearing her release. Like her, he was barely hanging on.

"Malik!" She screamed and jerked against him violently, her nails digging into his arms as his explosive release followed right behind her.

Malik collapsed on top of her, but quickly rolled to his side, taking her with him. It was a while before either of them could speak.

"All I can say is ... damn, girl!"

Chapter Thirteen

Natasha awoke to birds chirping outside of the window and the smell of bacon permeating the air. She snuggled further under the covers, burying her face into the feather down pillow, Malik's masculine scent surrounding her. Since he was a morning person, she wasn't surprised to wake up and he not be in bed. He had once told her that he could live on as little as three or four hours of sleep.

Natasha eased over onto her back and yawned. When she stretched, the welcomed ache between her thighs quickly reminded her of the activities hours ago. Malik had more stamina than anyone she'd ever met, and for the first time in her life, she'd spent the night in the arms of a man who made her feel desired, cherished.

She climbed out of the bed and practically glided to the bathroom feeling lighter on her feet than she'd felt in years. *That's what good lovin' does to you.*

Natasha used the bathroom, admiring the beautiful color scheme of shades of blue and brown. The room was the size of her living room. Dual vanities, a humongous jetted tub, and a shower that looked as if it could hold a basketball team. The space could easily be featured in a bathroom design magazine.

She washed her hands then splashed cold water on her face, before running her fingers through her disheveled hair. Hearing noise in the bedroom, she opened the door to find Tank standing on the other side of it, knowing Malik wouldn't be far behind.

"Hey there." She bent down and held Tank's large head between her hands, ruffling his dark fur. "How are you?" He barked and tried to lick her face, but caught her neck when she turned her head. She had always loved dogs and would have one of her own if it weren't for the long hours she worked. Tank was a beautiful, well-trained dog, but bigger than she'd want. Malik had told her that he was a rescue dog. Tank had showed up on his doorstep a few months after Malik retired from the military, and when no one claimed him, Malik kept him as his own. They'd been together ever since.

Natasha found Malik standing near the door observing her. The man was a walking billboard for all things powerful and strong. Sexy in his sleeveless tank, his biceps were as big and round as her thighs. Her gaze moved down to the jeans that hung low on his hips, the button unfastened and his belt undone. She swallowed hard. Images of their three rounds of lovemaking came to the forefront. She didn't think she would ever get tired of being with him.

"Hi," she said shyly, suddenly feeling nervous under his penetrating gaze.

"What? Tank gets a hug and a whole lot of love, and all I get is 'hi'?"

Natasha laughed and moved toward him, kissing him on the lips.

"That's better," he said, and held up the tray of food he was carrying. "I thought you might be hungry. How about breakfast in bed?"

"Wow. No one has ever made me breakfast in bed."

Malik's eyebrows drew up in surprise. "You're kidding."

"Nope. I'm serious."

"You know, I like that ex-husband of yours less and less every day. I can't believe that chump never made you breakfast in bed."

Natasha didn't bother telling Malik that Martin had fallen short in a number of areas in their marriage.

"Come over here and let me show you how breakfast in bed works." She followed behind him. "Climb back in," he gestured with his head toward the bed, "and lean against the headboard. Use some of those pillows to put behind you."

She did as he instructed and watched as he set the tray over her lap, the tray legs straddling her thighs.

"Now relax and dig in."

Natasha examined the tray, loaded with pancakes, bacon, hash browns, fruit, and a mug filled with hot water. He even had a small bottle of hand sanitizer and a variety of tea bags sitting next to the plate of pancakes.

"I hope you're planning to help me. I can't eat all of this."

"Eat what you can. Tank and I will take care of the rest."

He climbed on the other side of the bed and stretched out next to her. They talked and laughed while she ate, periodically sharing bacon with Tank and feeding Malik from her fork. She could definitely get used to the attention Malik showered on her so effortlessly.

"What time is your meeting at the hospital?"

"One thirty. I guess I should get ready, considering I need to go home and get changed." She had received a number of calls last night, letting them all go to voicemail. She didn't check the voicemail until after she had a chance to shower and relax the night before. Martin had called at least ten times and her boss, Dave, had called, insisting that she call him back. When she did, he told her that there was a meeting set up for this afternoon for her, a couple of administrators, and the legal department. A meeting she wasn't looking forward to.

When they finished breakfast, Malik moved the tray to the floor and kicked Tank out of the room.

"Alone at last," he said, and pulled her into his arms, placing soft, feathery kisses along her neck. "Allow me to show you what happens after breakfast in bed."

Oh yeah, I can definitely get used to this.

Hours later, Natasha strolled up to her front door all set to stick the key in the lock, but the door swung open.

"Where have you been?" Martin snatched off his reading glasses and glared at her. "I have been worried sick about you. Why haven't you returned any of my calls?"

Natasha glanced behind her outside. Malik was walking around the perimeter of the house, looking for what she didn't know, but he insisted that she needed an alarm system. After last night's event, she didn't argue with him. She'd been thinking about getting a house alarm for months and just hadn't gotten around to it.

"Martin, you shouldn't be here." She dropped her handbag on the sofa, noticing the folded blanket and pillow. A talk with him about not inviting himself over and making himself comfortable in her home was long overdue.

"You were involved in a shootout, stayed out all night, and that's all you have to say to me? Do you know how many people I called looking for you?"

"Ah, damn. Not this shit again."

Natasha turned to find Malik standing inside the doorway, glaring at Martin. "I thought you said you two were divorced," Malik said to Natasha. "If that's the case, why is he always here?"

"You!" Martin raised his voice and stupidly got in Malik's

face. "You need to learn how to keep your mouth shut. You're probably the reason she almost got killed last night. And now you bring her home in the middle of the morning as if it's the most natural thing to do."

"Martin!" Natasha didn't know what had gotten in to him.

"Are you fucking kidding me?" Malik grabbed the front of Martin's shirt, pinning him against the wall. "Your ass is the *ex*-husband and you're up in her house, uninvited, talking shit to me? Do you have a death wish or something?"

The scene was so high school that Natasha was tempted to leave the two idiots standing there and let them battle it out. Unfortunately, she knew how it would end. Martin wasn't a fighter, and she had no doubt Malik would pummel him without blinking an eye.

She closed her eyes and rubbed her temples as their voices grew louder. What was her life coming to? For the past few years, every day was much of the same. Yet in the last couple of weeks, there had been more drama around her than she had ever experienced in her life.

"Get your hands off of me!" Martin jerked out of Malik's grasp, knocking several family pictures to the floor.

"Stop it, both of you!" Natasha screamed. She was tired and frustrated. Therefore, the last thing she wanted to do was break up a fight between two grown men.

She wasn't sure what they saw on her face, but they stared at her. Malik stepped back and slowly approached her.

"Don't." She threw up her hands to halt him midstride. "Don't say anything, just go."

Malik lifted a questionable eyebrow. "Let me get this right. You're asking *me* to leave?" He pointed at himself. "Your *ex*-asshole here is the one who is out of place, but you want *me* to leave?"

"Malik, please, let's not do this right now. Let me talk to Martin alone. Please, just go and I'll talk to you later."

She narrowed her eyes at Martin when he grunted, looking pretty proud of himself. She'd never known him to be so childish, but lately she'd seen a side of him she didn't like.

Malik's eyes bore into her, as if glaring would make her change her mind. "Please just leave," she said again. "I'll call you later."

He stepped back and cursed under his breath, shaking his head. When he did return his gaze to her, the disappointment she saw in his eyes nearly broke her heart and she knew things had changed between them.

"Someone will be here in an hour to install your alarm system," he said, still glaring at her as if it were taking every ounce of control within him to not explode. "His name is Reuben and—"

"She doesn't need an alarm system." Martin moved forward, a couple of feet from her, and joined the conversation. "She has never had a problem until you came along."

"Enough! Martin, what is wrong with you?" Natasha yelled. "This has nothing to do with you. So shut up and back off!"

"His name is Reuben," Malik continued as if she and Martin hadn't spoken. "It should only take him a couple of hours to install it. Then he'll make sure everything is working properly. Call the office and talk with Victoria if there's a problem."

Malik turned and headed for the door. A sense of foreboding came upon Natasha and it felt as if this was good-bye. That's not what she wanted, but ...

"I'm also going to assign a bodyguard to you," Malik said, his back to her as he stood at the door. "Victoria will give you the details. I'd prefer they shadow you wherever you go." He finally turned to face her. "But if you don't want them in the house, interrupting anything the two of you," he said, and jerked his head toward Martin who was finally quiet, "might have going on, then they can stay outside."

"Malik, I appreciate the precautions you're trying to take, but I really don't think I need a bodyguard. The alarm system should be enough."

"Victoria will let you know who'll be assigned to you," he said, ignoring her plea.

He turned to leave and Natasha grabbed hold of his thick arm. "Malik, please don't leave like this."

His dark gaze held her in place, and a deafening silence lay between them.

"This is the second time you've asked me to leave because of him. There won't be a third time." He eased out of her grasp, slipped on his dark shades, and left.

Natasha stood at the door long after Malik drove away from the house. She liked Malik. Heck, she more than liked him. She just wasn't sure about them. He was made up of everything mothers warned their daughters about. He had no fear of danger, which made him just as dangerous as some of the hoodlums lurking around outside. She thought about how she'd stared down the barrel of his gun in the middle of the night, scaring her half to death. If that was his norm, there was no way the two of them could have anything more. He was a shoot first and ask questions later kind of guy. Even with all of that, he was everything a woman could ask or hope for. He was thoughtful, caring, and she had no doubt that he would give his life in order to protect hers. And when it came to making love ...

"So what happened last night?" Martin asked from behind her. She had temporarily forgotten he was in the room, witnessing Malik walk out on her. "Were you hurt?" He spun her around to face him. "What exactly happened? The media said there was a shooting, and that there was a doctor dead and you were injured. Are you okay? Did you go to the hospital to get checked out?"

She pulled away from him. "I'm fine."

"You don't look fine, and I'm wondering what you were even doing with that guy. You seem to be hanging out with him more and more. He's not your type."

Natasha swung around, and within two steps stood before her ex-husband. "Martin, we've already had this conversation. You and I are *not* married anymore. You don't have the right to interfere in my life and you sure as hell don't have a say in who I date." She backed away and shook her head. "I can't believe that I let our strange relationship go on for this long. I consider you a friend, but we will never be anything more."

"Sweetheart, you don't mean that." Martin touched her arm, but dropped his hand when she stiffened at his touch. "You and I have been through a lot together. Of course I'm going to worry about you and be concerned about the people you hang out with. And Malik is bad news."

Frustration coiled through her body at how she'd treated Malik. After all that he'd done for her in the past couple of weeks, he didn't deserve her coldness. Flashbacks of their night together, the way he made her body hum and her toes curl, crowded her mind.

"He's like a thug playing dress-up in a business suit," Martin continued, and began picking up the pictures on the floor that had fallen when Malik shoved him. "I think you did right in kicking him out. He's nothing but trouble. Besides, he's not your type. A little rough around the edges, don't you think?"

Natasha balled her hands into a fist, her nails digging into her palms as she approached Martin. "How dare you come into my house and insult my guest. You might not realize this, but you don't live here anymore!"

She couldn't ever remember being so angry. The worst part:

she sent a wonderful man away. The same man who had saved her life less than twenty-four hours ago and took care of her without any expectations.

She dropped down in the chair next to the sofa. "God, I am so stupid," she mumbled. Malik didn't come across as the type of guy who would forgive and forget. *This is the second time you've asked me to leave because of him. There won't be a third time.* His words stomped around in her head.

"Listen, you're probably just tired." Martin's hands went to where her shoulders met her neck, kneading the tight muscles. "Why don't I go out and get you something to eat? That big lug you've been hanging out with probably hasn't even fed you."

Natasha gripped the arms of the chair, digging her fingernails into them to keep from digging her nails into Martin's pretty face.

"That *lug* that you're referring to has not only cooked for me on numerous occasions, but saved my life last night." She stood slowly, coming face to face with Martin. She didn't care what Malik said about the bullet being meant for Dr. Halsey, she knew if it weren't for Malik's quick thinking, Dr. Halsey wouldn't have been the only fatality.

Martin stood straighter, standing over her by three inches. "What's gotten into you? Are you sleeping with this guy? Is that what this is all about? You're screwing him?" He raised his voice. "He put it on you so good, and now you feel like you have to defend him."

The palm of Natasha's hand went up and across Martin's face before she could stop herself. His glasses flew off and landed on the carpeted floor near the sofa.

"You have truly lost your mind, woman!" Martin rubbed the side of his face where her handprint still showed and glared at her before moving. He went to the sofa without taking his gaze from her and picked up his glasses.

151

"Get out of my house," she seethed, her body shaking with the rage roaring through her veins. "And don't you ever come back."

"After all that we've been through, has it really come to this?" he asked, tucking his glasses into his shirt pocket. "You're pushing me out of your life to make room for some giant Neanderthal?"

"*Llevate tu mierda y salte de mi casa!*" She moved to the door and opened it. "Better yet, just get out. I'll FedEx anything you've left behind."

Malik stormed into Wiz's office and slammed the door closed. He didn't care that photos and the large screen monitor rattled against the walls.

Wiz stood at his desk, his green eyes shooting daggers at Malik.

"I don't know what the hell is wrong with you, but you better have a damn good reason for slamming my door."

Malik was too pissed to speak. After leaving Natasha's house, he drove to a boxing gym he frequented often to burn off some steam. Instead of helping, he was madder than he'd been before going to gym.

"What's your problem?" Wiz asked, returning to his seat, but still not looking too pleased about the way Malik entered his office.

"Women and their fucking ex-husbands." He dropped down in the chair closest to Wiz's desk.

"Ahh, I should've known." Wiz grinned before returning his attention to his computer monitor. "Natasha and her ex."

Malik filled him in on the scene at Natasha's house, his anger subsiding a bit. He didn't know who he was angrier at—himself or Natasha. Himself for falling for her when she clearly wasn't over her ex, or her for still being in love with her ex-husband.

"So does this mean that you're done obsessing over her?"

Malik narrowed his eyes at his friend. "I've never obsessed over a woman and you know that."

"Before Tasha came along, I might've agreed with you, but when it comes to her, you're different. And the most telling thing is that she spent the night at your place. I've known you a long time and I can't ever remember you taking a woman to your house, let alone her spending the night."

Malik closed his eyes and pinched the bridge of his nose. Who was he kidding? Natasha had gotten under his skin. He wasn't exactly sure when it happened. Yet, if he were honest with himself, he'd have to say it was the first time he met her ... the day he escorted her to L.A. to say good-bye to Quinn and Alandra.

He shook his head. "I'm done. I refuse to be second to her asshole ex." Malik stood and went to the small refrigerator in the corner of Wiz's office to grab a beer. "I'll keep one of my guys on her until I'm satisfied that she's not in danger, but after that, I'm done."

"Yeah right," Wiz said, his fingers flying across his computer keyboard. Malik didn't know how Wiz could have a conversation and focus on what he was typing. "You're not done with her. You can lie to yourself if you want to, but the truth is on your face and in your tone. Right now you're mad because she's the first woman who's ever slighted the almighty Malik Lewis."

Malik didn't respond. This whole, yet brief, experience with Natasha was new to him. Wiz was right about one thing: this was the first time in a long time that a woman had kicked his ass to the curb. If he wasn't still pissed, he'd laugh.

"Now, if you're done bitching and moaning, I'll tell you what I found so far." He handed Malik a file. "That's the dossier on the good Dr. Robert Halsey, or should I say Dr. Anthony Hailstock. The name he went by in New York and Texas."

Malik opened the file and sifted through some of the pages. He couldn't believe the type of information Wiz could dig up on a person. His friend's talent to find the impossible never ceased to amaze him.

"Check this out." He pointed a remote to the large monitor hanging over a short bookcase. On the screen were photos of two men. "Guess who that is."

Malik's eyebrows shot upward. "Don't tell me that's Dr. Halsey."

"Yep. Not only did his identity change on paper, but he had some work done on his face as well."

"Wow! He looks totally different." Malik sat on the corner of the desk. "My thing is, though, I still can't believe he was able to practice medicine with a fake license."

"Apparently you haven't looked at the license yet." Wiz nodded toward the file he'd given Malik. "It looks legit. Whoever this lawyer is that helped him pull this off was good. Damn good."

Malik continued perusing the file, which included photos of the doctor's family, information about the foundation that he and his wife created years ago, and financial statements.

"I expected to find huge sums of money in the doctor's bank account, but that wasn't the case. I'm still waiting for some information, but so far, it doesn't look as if the doctor was killing off his patients for money."

"The way Natasha made it sound he was killing them in order to keep his identity a secret."

"Surely he had to be smarter than that." Wiz stood and walked around his desk, leaning on the back of the chair that Malik had vacated. "He had to know that this lawyer guy was going to keep asking for more babies."

"Speaking of babies, did you find out anything about underground adoption agencies?"

"Well, it would help if Natasha could remember the name, but I have some feelers out there. Hopefully I'll hear something soon."

Malik closed the file. "Anything else?"

"I talked with the husband of the woman who died in the car bombing. Needless to say, he wasn't in a talkative mood considering the police had been questioning him."

"But I assume you were able to convince him to share info."

"Of course." Wiz grinned and walked over to the large window overlooking his huge backyard. He opened the blinds and turned back to Malik. "He's a retired Marine, so I played the military-brotherhood card."

"And?"

"After his wife was killed, he found a bank account. He knew nothing about it, but it had over sixty thousand dollars in it."

Malik smiled. He knew where this conversation was going. "I trust that you'll be able to trace back the deposits to find out where the money came from."

"I'm working on it." He opened his office door. "I'll keep you posted on anything else I find, but right now you got to go."

Malik laughed and stuck the file Wiz had given him under his arm. "I see how this day is going, and already I'm a little sick of people kicking me out of their homes. Y'all don't know who you're dealing with," he moved toward the door, "I'm Malik Goddamn Lewis! I don't have to leave until I'm good and ready. You're just lucky I'm ready."

Chapter Fourteen

"All set?" Stan, the bodyguard Malik had assigned to Natasha, asked when she exited the hospital's conference room.

She nodded and he fell in step with her. Natasha was so ready to leave. Meeting with hospital administrators to discuss Dr. Halsey was like reliving the night before all over again. And if one more person asked how she was doing she was going to scream. She knew they meant well, but since the moment Malik walked out of her house earlier, she'd been on edge.

Stan opened the door that led to the stairs. That was one good thing about having a bodyguard; he opened and held doors for her. She had first met Stan when he was assigned to guard her sister, Alandra. Natasha remembered teasing Alandra when Quinn insisted that Stan go wherever she went, and now here Natasha was in the same situation. She had to admit that she liked Stan and appreciated Malik's concern about her safety, but she didn't want a bodyguard. Whoever killed Bob was after him, not her. She might've been a little nervous about being alone the night before, but today she felt like her old self. Independent and in charge.

"Dr. Lockham," a male voice called out from behind her. Natasha slowed and glanced over her shoulder to see Ray heading in her direction.

"Hi Ray," she said, actually glad to see him. With her workload and meetings during the past week, she hadn't had a chance to thank him for the flowers. She turned to Stan. "Can you give us a minute?"

He hesitated, giving Ray a once over before saying, "Sure, I'll be right over there." He pointed to a spot about ten feet away.

"How's it going?" Ray asked. "I heard about last night. Were you hurt?" His gaze took a bold stroll down her body before returning to her face, appreciation brimming in his eyes. "You look amazing by the way."

Natasha—caught off guard—smiled at him, wondering about his boldness. A couple of weeks ago when he invited her out for lunch, he seemed somewhat shy. Yet, the other day in the hallway, there was almost a cockiness to his behavior. She didn't know what to make of him, but he seemed like a nice enough guy.

"Thank you, and no I wasn't hurt. It was just a case of being in the wrong place at the wrong time." She downplayed the situation. Many members of the staff were looking for details regarding the previous night and the death of Dr. Halsey, but she was asked not to share specifics.

"I'm sorry to hear about Dr. Halsey," Ray said. "I never met him, but I heard he was a good doctor and a nice guy."

Natasha nodded. She wasn't exactly sure how she felt about Bob at the moment. She would never wish death on anyone, but knowing what she knew, she struggled to come to terms with what he'd done. She also hated the vulnerable position he had put the hospital in.

"Yeah, it's a sad situation all the way around," she finally said. "By the way, I was hoping to run into you. I wanted to thank you for the flowers you sent the other day. They were absolutely beautiful."

His mouth spread into a wide grin and Natasha thought he was even more handsome when he smiled. "I'm glad you liked them. It was the least I could do considering my outburst the other day. I shouldn't have taken my shi– I'm sorry, my crappy mood out on you."

"Believe me, I understand." And she did. Today she would have preferred to stay at home behind closed doors and not talk to anyone. It seemed her tolerance level decreased the longer she stayed at the hospital.

Natasha shifted the strap of her handbag to her other shoulder. Since they'd been standing there, Ray had looked over at Stan at least three times during the conversation. Stan's expression never wavered and his gaze stayed on Ray. Malik insisted that something was off about Ray, but couldn't explain the feeling in his gut. Natasha wondered if Stan was picking up the same vibe.

"Well, I'll let you get going," Ray said, shoving his hands into his pants pocket, rocking back and forth on the balls of his feet. "I need to get a quick workout in at the gym before I head to my next job."

"Oh, what gym? I recently joined the one up the street."

Ray flashed his straight-teeth smile again. "That's the one I'm at. Maybe we'll run into each other there sometime."

"Yeah, maybe."

They said their good-byes, leaving Natasha thinking that he seemed like such a nice guy. If he was a little older and she weren't interested in Malik Lewis ... She stopped herself from completing the thought. Not only was Ray too young, they worked at the same place and she definitely wasn't trying to be a part of any hospital gossip.

Stan slipped on his dark shades and they proceeded to the exit.

"Dr. Lockham!"

Natasha was blinded by a camera flash, and then another. *What the...*

"Dr. Lockham!" a reporter shouted, charging toward her like moths to a light.

"Dr. Lockham, why were you and Dr. Halsey meeting at the Coffee House on the south side of Chicago last night?"

"Were you having an affair with Dr. Halsey?" another person asked.

"Did you see the killer?"

Questions bombarded her from every direction. Stan shielded her from the onslaught of microphones and pushy reporters, making her happy that he was there.

"No comment," he growled and pushed his way through the small crowd, guiding her through the parking lot. Trying to keep up with him in her heels, she took three steps to his every one. When he led her away from the direction of her car, she wondered why, until she spotted his Lincoln Town Car.

"Get in." He opened the back door and she practically dived into the car, shocked that reporters had followed them. Despite the dark tinted windows, she covered her face from the flashes bombarding her from outside of the vehicle.

Stan charged out of his parking spot, as if not caring that reporters were blocking his way. Natasha heard him curse a few times, but he managed to get them out without killing anyone.

"You okay?" he asked, glancing back at her through his rearview mirror while speeding down the street.

Natasha ran her hands up and down her arms. Despite the seventy-degree weather, chill bumps covered her arms. "Yes," she finally answered. She had often seen the same scene play out on television with celebrities, but never in a million years did she expect to be the subject of media attention.

"Vicky, I need to speak to the boss," Natasha heard Stan say. The car must've contained a hands free telephone system because she didn't see a cell phone and he didn't have an earpiece. "We have a situation."

"What's up, Stan?" a woman asked, her voice bouncing off the interior of the vehicle. "Everything okay?"

"It is now, but the media was outside of the hospital."

"Is Dr. Lockham all right?"

"Appears to be. Is the boss around?"

"No he's not, but I'll see if I can get a hold of him. In the meantime, bring her here."

Stan shot Natasha another look and she shook her head no.

"That's a negative, Vicky. I'll take her home and wait there until further instructions."

Natasha really wanted to see Malik, but right now, she just wanted to go home and climb into her own bed. She was still reeling from her conversation with Martin, the meeting at the hospital, and now the media.

She thought back on the incident at her house that morning. Malik might have been hurt that she asked him to leave instead of Martin, but he should have said something. Instead, he stalked away like a stubborn child. All she wanted to do was talk to Martin alone to make him understand that what they once had was over. Maybe she could have handled both situations differently, but after what she and Malik had shared only hours earlier, he should have known that she wasn't saying good-bye to him.

"Do you need to stop anywhere before you head home?" Stan asked from the front seat.

"No, but thanks for asking. Also ... thanks for what you did back there."

"No problem."

Natasha closed her eyes and settled in for the short ride home. Instead of flashbacks of the scene at the Café the night before, she recalled her night with Malik. A night with him and suddenly she couldn't imagine sleeping alone.

Two days later, Natasha stepped off the elevator and on to the floor where Malik's company was located, followed by Stan. She didn't know what type of money Stan made working for Malik, but whatever it was, he earned it. At first, she was leery about having him around, especially in her house, but if Malik trusted him, she trusted him.

Natasha glanced around, impressed by the sheer size and décor of the space, taking in the amazing artwork and statues. She didn't know what she expected, but the office looked as if it should belong to a Fortune 500 company more so than a personal security firm.

The words Supreme Security Agency stood out in big, bold silver lettering on the wall behind the customer service desk.

"Hey Stan," the cute, petite brunette behind the desk said. She nodded at Natasha and gave her a friendly smile.

"Hey, can you get the boss?" Stan asked. "Tell him Dr. Lockham is here."

"Okay." She eyed Natasha, as if unsure of whether something was wrong, and made a brief phone call. Finally, she spoke to Natasha. "His assistant will be with you shortly. You're welcome to have a seat over there if you'd like." She pointed to several cushioned chairs. "Stan, Vicky said she can take it from here."

He nodded. "All right." He turned to Natasha. "You take care," he said and returned to the elevator.

Instead of sitting, Natasha roamed around the space and

admired the paintings as well as the large black and white photos gracing the walls. A gorgeous photo of the sun peeking behind a few clouds over Lake Michigan caught her attention.

"Beautiful, isn't it?" a woman's cheerful voice asked from behind her.

Natasha swung around and came face to face with a woman who could have easily been a supermodel. "Yes it is." She glanced back at the photo. "Do you know who the photographer is?"

"As a matter of fact I do. It's Wiz's wife, Olivia Miller. She's responsible for all of the artwork and photos in the entire office." The woman stuck out her hand. "By the way, I'm Victoria Bracero, Malik's assistant. It's a pleasure to finally meet you, Dr. Lockham."

Natasha accepted her hand, surprised that Victoria knew of her. "Please, call me Natasha."

Victoria nodded. "All right, Natasha it is. If you'll follow me, I'll take you back to Malik's office."

Alandra had mentioned that Wiz's wife, Olivia, was an artist, but Natasha had no idea how talented she was. Natasha stopped periodically along the way to admire some of Olivia's pieces, impressed by the vast uniqueness of each item.

"These are amazing," Natasha mumbled as she got back in step with Victoria.

"They are, aren't they?" They continued their walk down the hallway, passing several closed doors along the way. "If you haven't attended any of her art shows, you'll have to check one out. They are always well attended. I've been to a few here in Chicago and one in New York, and her work just seems to get more impressive each time I see a new piece."

They approached an area enclosed with glass and stepped through the double doors. The space wasn't as big as the one they'd just left, but impressive nonetheless. Two large desks sat on each side of the room, with a small sitting area in the corner.

"Hey Tasha." Wiz stepped out of the office closest to Victoria's desk, closing the door behind him. "It's been a while. How are you?" They hugged.

Natasha liked Wiz from the moment she met him in L.A. He had a quiet spirit about him, but since he was a retired Navy SEAL, she'd bet there was a dangerous side to him, like Malik and Quinn. Built like a linebacker, Wiz wasn't as tall as Malik, but still towered over her. He had skin the color of café au lait, and the most unique hazel-greenish eyes she'd ever seen.

"So how've you been?"

"I'm all right." She wanted to tell him that Malik wasn't accepting her calls and ask Wiz how she should go about making things right, but she didn't.

"Malik's on the phone right now," Victoria said, standing at her desk. "Once he's off, you'll be able to go on in. I have to warn you, enter at your own risk. He's been a bear the last couple of days."

Natasha wasn't sure what Malik had told Victoria about her, but she was surprised that Victoria was comfortable talking about her boss in front of her.

Wiz's eyes sparkled and he chuckled. He rubbed the slight stubble growing on his jaws and chin. "Yeah, I noticed he's been wound pretty tight, but I think Natasha's just what he needs."

Natasha ducked her head, her cheeks burning as Wiz and Victoria gave her a knowing look. She and Malik hadn't put a name or a title to what was going on between them, but she had a feeling that what they felt was mutual. Or at least she hoped. If she could, she would take a do-over of the other day and not insist on him leaving without explaining why she wanted to speak with Martin alone. Looking back, she could see how he might have interpreted the situation differently.

"Well, I'm going to head out," Wiz announced. He touched Natasha's arm in passing, but moved closer and whispered, "He's as stubborn as a mule, but stand your ground and I think you'll be able to soften him up some." He squeezed her arm and smiled. "Good luck."

"Thank you," she said quietly. She appreciated any inside information she could get.

"Vicky, I'll catch you later."

"Okay, Wiz." She threw him a small wave. When he left, she sighed and covered her heart with her hand. "He is such a sweetheart."

"He seems like it," Natasha added.

"Okay, you're on. Malik's off the phone."

Natasha blew out a breath. "Wish me luck."

"Good luck, but I don't think you'll need it. His bark is worse than his bite. Uh, I take that back. When it comes to you, his bark is worse than his bite. But he gives everyone else hell."

They both laughed. Natasha drummed up her courage, unsure of what she was going to say when she came face to face with him.

After two quick knocks, she opened the door and walked in.

Chapter Fifteen

M alik glanced up from reviewing the documents Wiz had just dropped off, surprised to see Natasha. He hadn't been able to stop thinking about her. His anger had lingered, but seeing her curvy figure near the door began to slowly thaw the ice running through his veins.

"Hi," she said shyly, keeping her distance.

Malik, though still pissed, had never been happier to see anyone in all of his life. Stan told him about the reporters at the hospital and how shaken she was when more media people showed up at her house. Malik almost went to her. Almost.

He stood, but didn't move from behind his desk. His gaze traveled over her body from her hair loosely piled on top of her head, down to the short-sleeved wrap dress that hugged her hourglass shape. He didn't stop his perusal until he got to her slender feet, which were encased in high-heeled orange strappy sandals that matched her dress. Her favorite color was orange and it was quickly becoming his favorite, too.

Damn she looks good.

Seeing her now, dressed as she was, he couldn't help but

think about something he once heard someone say. The first step in getting what you want is looking like you mean business. And damn if she wasn't dressed to get whatever the hell she wanted from him.

"Hey," he finally said. He wasn't going to make this easy for her, yet it was taking everything in him not to bolt across the room and pull her into his arms. What helped him stay put was the fact that she'd kicked him out of her house. Never had a woman dismissed him, especially twice, and it was about time she understood exactly what he wouldn't accept.

"I'm surprised to see you here. What can I do for you?" he asked coldly.

She didn't move from where she stood and her nervousness showed with the death grip she had on the strap of her handbag.

"Thank you for having the house alarm installed. I just wanted to stop by and pay for the system and the services."

He studied her for a long time. He didn't want her money. He wanted her.

"The bill has been taken care of. Anything else?"

"Uh," she glanced around the room, still standing near the door, "I'd like for you to call off the bodyguard."

"That's not going to happen," he said. The media had backed off, but he still wasn't comfortable with her roaming around the city alone.

"Why not?"

"Because it's not."

He wasn't convinced that she wasn't in danger. Sheldon and his men still didn't have much on Halsey's death. Knowing that, not only was Malik going to keep eyes on Natasha, but he had also decided to start his own covert investigation.

"Malik, I'm sorry, all right?" Natasha said, taking a step toward him. He looked up just as she captured her lower lip between her teeth. "I know you're mad, and you have every right to be. I was wrong asking you to leave."

Malik said nothing. The only reason he could come up with of why she asked him to leave instead of Martin was because she was still in love with her ex. And there was no way in hell he was sharing her with anyone else.

"You scare me."

Malik drew his eyebrows together. "Excuse me?" Her voice was so low he wasn't sure he'd heard her correctly.

"You make me nervous. We come from two different worlds. You're like the star basketball player being pursued by a hundred colleges to play for their school, and I'm the geeky nerd who always gets looked over by the popular kids."

Malik frowned, not knowing what she was talking about, but he had to admit she was damn cute.

"I don't understand."

She sighed and narrowed her eyes at him as if he was the one who'd done something wrong.

"Why are you making this so hard?" She raised her voice and put her hands on her hips. "I like you, all right? I *really* like you and I can't stand the thought of you being angry with me."

The jerk in Malik wanted to let her stew, but Malik the man wanted to pull her into his arms and taste those sweet, pouty lips. There was something about this woman that stirred things within him that had never been touched, and he wasn't sure how he felt about that.

Her shoulders drooped. "Malik, don't look at me like that. Say something."

He laid down the file and walked around the desk, one hand stuffed into his pants pocket and the other rubbing his forehead. It was no wonder he didn't do relationships, because whatever was transpiring between him and Natasha was frustrating as hell. He couldn't imagine what it would be like to be seriously involved, or even married for that matter.

"Let's get something straight. I don't play games," he said, staring into her beautiful brown eyes. "I mean what I say and I say what I mean. So whatever the hell type of game you and your ex are playing, count me out. I like you," he eased up on her, "but I will not come second to some punk-ass professor, who doesn't know how to move on when it's over. Do we understand each other?"

Her jerky nod came without words so he continued, "I want *you*. Baby, I want you in every way a man wants a woman. If you're not ready for what you know I can offer, then you need to tell me now. Otherwise, I'm going to pursue you to no end."

Natasha visibly swallowed. "Okay."

So much for not wanting to be in a relationship. Malik didn't want to put a title on whatever he was feeling for Natasha, but he knew he wanted her in his life in some capacity.

"There's something I've wanted to do since the moment you walked in here."

He closed the distance between them and captured her mouth without hesitation. Feeling her lips against his was like returning home after an op. A sense of peace surrounded him like nothing he had ever experienced. They had kissed before, but this, this was different. This was a soul-stirring, heart throbbing, I'll never be able to let you go type of sensation. Right then and there he knew ... there was nothing he wouldn't do for this woman.

Natasha snaked her arms around his midsection. The feel of her soft hands caressing him through his dress shirt sent a jolt of pleasure straight to his groin. Lustful yearning coursed through his veins. One kiss would not be enough. He wanted all of her, every sweet, delectable inch of her, and he needed her to know. He needed her to know that she was special and desired. He needed her to know that no other man would ever be able to please her the way he could. And most importantly, he needed to make sure she knew that he had no intention of sharing her.

She sighed against his mouth and his palms circled her butt. Caressing. Squeezing. Pulling her closer. He deepened the kiss and held her softness against his throbbing shaft, wanting to be inside of her.

He eased back without removing his hand and blew out a breath. "You're something else." He touched his forehead to hers, both of them out of breath, and he stared into her eyes. Feeling better than he'd felt in the last few days, he grabbed her by the hand and led her over to the sofa. "I need to know for sure that there is nothing between you and the professor." He sat next to her.

Natasha squeezed his hand. "I already told you, we're done. We've been done for years, and after the other day, I doubt I'll ever see him again."

"What happened the other day?" Malik asked.

She told him about her conversation with Martin, but Malik had a feeling there was more to it than she was sharing.

"I also slapped him."

Malik leaned back and stared at her, surprised. "I never pictured you as the violent type."

She released his hand and stood abruptly. Malik loved all women, any nationality, shape, or size. Yet observing Natasha as she moved toward the window—her tiny waist, and the sexy sway of her hips—made him appreciate her on a whole different level. *Damn, this was going to be a long evening.* He had a meeting shortly, and then dinner plans with Wiz and Olivia. However, what he really wanted to do was take Natasha home, strip her out of that sexy outfit, and make sweet, passionate love to her.

"Normally I'm not violent, but he said some things ..."

Natasha's words regained Malik's attention, had him wondering if the professor had stepped out of line. He walked up behind her, his arm circling her waist, his lips kissing the side of her neck. "He said some things like what?" he asked against her heated skin.

"Some things that I didn't like. He caught me off guard and before I knew it," she shrugged, "I slapped him."

Malik straightened. "And what did he do?" His words came out harsher than he intended, but he wanted to make sure that fool hadn't retaliated.

Natasha must have sensed the thoughts behind his question because she quickly turned and faced him.

"If you're asking if he hit me back, he didn't. I think my reaction caught him off guard as well. A few words were exchanged and then he left. That's all."

Malik lifted his hand to her face, caressing her cheek. "And you're okay with not seeing him again?"

She nodded. "It's time I moved on."

They stood staring at one another, each in their own thoughts. Part of Malik wanted to say 'move on with me' but the words didn't form, and he didn't force them. He'd let whatever this was between them play out naturally.

"Stan told me about the reporters at the house." He led Natasha back over to the sofa. "So how are you holding up?" he asked.

"I'm all right, but I can't do the bodyguard thing." She placed her hand on his thigh. "I appreciate you looking out for me, having the alarm installed and all, but I can't handle someone following me around. Stan is nice, but I don't need a bodyguard."

Malik sat back on the sofa and stretched his long legs out in front of him, crossing them at the ankle. "It's better to take precautions and nothing happen, than for something to happen and not be prepared. I ... we don't know exactly what Dr. Halsey was involved in or who he was involved with. The other night was no accident. Whoever took him out was a skilled killer and he's still out there. Until they find him, you're stuck with either me, Stan, or Victoria."

Natasha tilted her head. "Victoria?"

Malik nodded and grinned. "She's our secret weapon. Looking at her, no one would ever know that she's a trained killer."

Natasha's mouth dropped open. "I never would've guessed. She seems ..." Natasha shook her head. "No. No, Malik. No bodyguards. I've taken care of myself all of these years, I don't want someone shadowing me. Besides, what about at work? How's it going to look for some big, muscular guy like Stan or even Victoria following me around?"

Malik sat up straight and brought his knees in. "Tasha, I don't give a da– I mean, I don't care how it looks. My only concern is that you're safe."

"I have a better idea. What if you taught me self-defense, then I can take care of myself."

"Do you know how to use a gun?"

She shivered at the question and shook her head. "No, I don't."

"Are you willing to learn how to use one?"

Natasha sighed and dropped her head before lifting it again and meeting Malik's eyes. "Can't I learn self-defense without learning how to use a gun? You do realize I'm in the business of saving lives, not taking them, don't you?"

"And you do realize that I'm in the business of protecting folks, by any means necessary?"

Natasha bolted from her seat. "We're not getting anywhere like this."

"How is it that Alandra is a third-degree black belt and you haven't taken any self-defense classes?"

Natasha shrugged. "It wasn't my thing. Most of the time I had my head in a book. I never had a need to learn self-defense to that degree."

Malik thought it wouldn't be a bad idea for her to take some classes, but that didn't mean he was going to relieve Stan of his duties of sticking close to her. Stan was one of the best. If Malik couldn't shadow her, then Stan would be his next choice.

"Malik?" Victoria's voice came over the intercom.

"Yeah, Vicky."

"Sorry to bother you, but your three o'clock is here."

"Thanks. Set them up in the small conference room and I'll be there shortly."

He returned his attention to Natasha. "What are your plans for this evening?" He moved back to his desk, and placed the file from Wiz into his top drawer.

"I just have to make some calls. Since it's my day off, I was planning to do some grocery shopping."

Malik's hand stilled and he glanced at her. "You go grocery shopping looking like that?"

She frowned. "What's the matter with what I have on? Lately, it seems I rarely get a day off, and when I do, I like to dress up a little. You don't like it?"

"Yeah, baby, I like it. You look good."

"Then what's the problem?" she asked innocently.

The corner of Malik's lip lifted into a smile. "No problem. No problem at all." She apparently had no idea how hot she was. Yet, he had no doubt that any red-blooded man walking passed her, would take a second or third look.

Malik glanced down at the documents that Victoria had left earlier for him to sign. Scribbling his name in the appropriate areas, he knew the meeting he was going into wouldn't be very productive. Natasha had him so turned on, there was no way he'd be able to talk business knowing she was in his office looking the way she did. Besides, the bulge inside his pants ....

Malik looked over his shoulder when he heard the lock on the office door click. A slow, piercing whistle slipped through his lips and he laid his ink pen down. *Hot damn!*

Rising to his full height, he took in the beautiful vision standing across the room. Natasha in an orange lace bra, with matching barely there panties and her high heeled sandals. Her dress tossed to the sofa.

He stood in front of his desk, his gaze taking in her perfect body and the sway of her full hips as she approached him. When she dropped her bra to the floor, he sucked in a breath attempting to throttle the dizzying current racing through him. *Good Lord.* Her breasts bounced in rhythm with each step she took. Being a breast man, he couldn't wait to taste them.

"Have a seat," she said when she stopped in front of him. He did as she instructed.

When she straddled his lap, her twin peaks brushed against his lips. Malik had a feeling the act was no accident, but who was he to complain? He snaked his tongue around her perky nipple and licked her. *Oh yeah. I can definitely get used to interruptions like this.* He buried his face between her breast and the scent of her perfume hypnotized him to her wanton ways.

He gripped her butt to reposition her and groaned when he felt her bare ass within his hands. Like most men, he was help-less against a woman whose breasts were in his face and who wore a thong.

Malik was powerless to resist. He reached for the telephone on his desk and pushed the intercom button.

"Yes?" Victoria answered.

"Vicky, let Arnold know that I'll be delayed for fifteen

minutes." He heard the tightness in his own voice, his shaft throbbing inside his pants as Natasha undid his belt buckle.

"Will do."

Malik dug for his wallet and quickly removed a condom. The erratic beat of his pulse hammered in his ears and he could not wait to get inside of her.

Natasha eased off of him and removed her panties. Malik dropped his pants, along with his briefs and reclaimed his seat. He didn't bother stepping out of the garments, letting them puddled around his ankle.

"Normally I like to take my time and explore this luscious body of yours, but maybe later. Right now I need to be inside you." He entered her in one smooth thrust, her heat surrounding him like a blanket on a cold winter's night, transferring warmth to every part of his body.

Her muscles tightened around him and Malik cursed under his breath. Yeah this was going to be a quickie, but he didn't want it to be too quick. Yet, the way she felt and the way she slid up and down his shaft, he'd do good to make it five minutes.

The leather chair squeaked beneath their weight, but he didn't care. Their bodies fused together and moved to a tempo that only they could feel. No other woman would ever be able to satisfy him the way this woman did. He claimed her mouth, his tongue thrusting in and out as his hands explored her naked body.

He grabbed her thighs, her arms wrapped tightly around his neck as he lifted her up and down, moving in and out of her. Waves of ecstasy throbbed through him. There was no way in hell he would ever share her. If she wasn't over her ex, Malik would just have to convince him to bow out gracefully.

"Malik," Natasha moaned against his neck, her movements more jerky, and her release teetering on the brink. She rocked wildly on top of him, her interior walls clenching and unclenching. There was no way he could hold on much longer with the way her muscles contracted around his length.

He gripped her hips, no longer able to hang on. With one final thrust, he sent her over the edge and he followed right behind her.

They collapsed against each other, their breaths coming in short spurts as Malik cradled her limp body against his.

"If that was makeup sex, I'm going to start a fight with you every day."

She released a soft laugh, her breath warm against his skin. He kissed her cheek. He loved having her in his arms, and hated that he had to cut their impromptu rendezvous short. If this wasn't a meeting that could cost him thousands, he'd have Victoria send Arnold home.

"I would love to sit here, holding you forever, but I'm going to have to go," he whispered against her ear, wondering if she'd fallen asleep since she was so still. "If you can hold off on shopping, I'll go with you after my meeting. In the meantime, why don't you hang out in here and wait for me. Then later tonight, we can pick up where we left off."

She lifted her head slightly and graced him with a smile. "I'd like that."

"Are you sure it's all right that I'm tagging along with you?" Natasha asked Malik. They were standing outside of Wiz and Olivia's house.

"Of course." Malik pulled her close and kissed her on top of her head. "They invited us both to dinner."

When Natasha went to Malik's office earlier that day, she had no idea that she would end up spending the whole day with him, enjoying every minute of their time together. During one of their conversations, Malik had questioned her feelings for her ex-husband, asking if she was still in love with Martin. Not only was she not in love with him, but the more time she spent with Malik, she wondered whether she had ever been in love with Martin.

"Hey you guys," Olivia greeted when she swung open the door, her short bob haircut bouncing around with every move she made. "Come in. I'm glad you could make it over." She hugged Natasha, pulling her farther into the foyer.

"Hey Ollie." Malik wrapped his long arms around her in a bear hug. "What's for dinner?"

"If you call me Ollie again," she said, her hands on her hips, "you won't be having anything but water."

They bantered back and forth, as Natasha's gaze traveled around the cozy space. She had always loved Tudor style homes, and the interior of their home was as lovely as the exterior. The architectural detail caught her attention at every turn, from the dark wood trim, to the wrought iron railing leading up to the second floor. Natasha's gaze landed on the dark timber ceiling beams and she was in love. The home reminded her of the time her parents took them to England for vacation one year.

"Wiz is in his office," Olivia said to Malik. "Come on back, Natasha. I'm finishing up dinner."

"Your home is beautiful," Natasha followed Olivia into the kitchen, "did you decorate it yourself?"

"I did, but technically it's not my home." She smirked at the confused look on Natasha's face. "My actual residence is in D.C. After our divorce, Cameron and I remained friends. I travel so much that I'm rarely in D.C and when I'm in Chicago, which is often, I stay here. It's a long story."

Natasha waved her off. "Trust me, I understand. Until recently, no one would've known my ex and I were divorced considering the amount of time we spent together. We knew each other since grade school. So though we were divorced, I still considered him a friend." Natasha hadn't heard from Martin since their argument, not that she had expected to.

"That's how Cameron and I are. I've been in love with him since high school. We married before he joined the military, but when he became a SEAL, things changed. He'd get calls in the middle of the night saying that he had to leave for parts unknown and I couldn't take it."

"Did you think he was cheating on you?"

"Oh no. That never crossed my mind. I believed him when he'd say they were going wheels up, going on a mission. The part I couldn't handle was not knowing where he was going or whether or not he'd return in one piece. I don't know why I thought divorcing him and moving to a different state would make me worry about him any less." She gave a humorless chuckle. "The life of a SEAL's wife is not for the weak at heart. Even now, I still worry. With Cameron being a P.I., I never know if he's going to stumble across a situation that will pose a threat to his life."

Natasha couldn't imagine what it must have been like for her. Being around Wiz and Malik, one would forget that they were just men, not super heroes able to fix and handle any situation.

"Okay, enough about me. I haven't seen you since our time in L.A. Have you been doing all right?"

Natasha nodded. "Yes, for the most part. Missing Alandra, but finally coming to terms that she and Quinn probably were right to disappear. She called the other night, so that helped. I really miss her, especially lately."

"I'm sure. I have a sister who I haven't spoken to in over ten years," Olivia said as she took the pan of lasagna out of the oven. "We had a falling out and haven't made amends, though I think about her often."

"Mmm, it smells good in here. Is dinner almost ready?" Wiz asked when he walked into the kitchen followed by Malik.

"Yep, you're right on time. Everything's done." She accepted the kiss he planted on her cheek. "I'm thinking we'll eat in the dining room."

They all helped carry the food into the dining room. They talked, joked, and laughed like old friends. While married, Natasha and Martin socialized some, but with her work schedule, she remembered having to cancel often. Eating and laughing with Malik's friends made her realize what she'd been missing. She vowed at that moment to be more intentional about hanging out with friends—old and new.

Wiz tapped his fork lightly against his water glass. "May I have your attention?" he said in all seriousness, as if he were addressing more than three people. "Olivia and I have an announcement to make." He looked at her lovingly. "I asked her to marry me ... again, and she said yes."

"Well it's about damn time," Malik blurted out and pushed back his chair. Wiz stood as well and they embraced, Malik pounding him on his back. He then went to Olivia. "Ollie, I don't know why you've been torturing my guy all this time, but I'm glad you finally came to your senses."

She punched him in the arm. "Whatever. And what'd I tell you about calling me Ollie? You know I hate that name," she fussed, but accepted his hug and a kiss on the cheek.

"You know I only call you that because you hate it," Malik teased.

Natasha congratulated them. "So when is the big day?"

"Well, I'm heading out of town on a redeye tonight and will be traveling for a couple of weeks before I take a break," Olivia said. "We're going to try and nail down a date once I return."

"If it were left up to me, we'd be getting married today." Wiz wrapped his arm around her waist and placed a kiss against her temple.

"I know," Olivia said, staring up at him, adoration in her eyes, "but I want us to have a few of our family and friends attend." She turned to Malik and Natasha. "Whatever we plan won't be big, but the wedding will be big enough to still require some planning. So, Tasha, I hope you don't mind if I pull you into the madness."

Warmth spread through Natasha at their developing friendship. Her career kept her from making many friends and she looked forward to getting to know Olivia better. "Bring on the madness."

They talked more about some of their wedding ideas and Natasha wondered if she'd ever have an opportunity to plan a wedding for herself. She and Martin didn't have much money when they married, and had a small ceremony in her parent's backyard. Though her wedding was beautiful, next time, assuming there would be a next time, she would love to have a church wedding. Then again, if she found the right man, she glanced at Malik, she would be willing to go along with anything he wanted.

"I hate to cut this short," Olivia said, "but I need to finish packing. You guys are welcome to stay as long as you'd like, but please forgive me for bailing out." She hugged both Natasha and Malik before heading up the stairs.

"We probably should get going, too," Malik stated as they all stood around the dining room table. "Are we still on for tomorrow morning?" he asked Wiz.

"Yep, but before you guys leave, let's go to my office. I might've found something regarding the case."

Malik grabbed hold of Natasha's hand and kissed the back of it before they followed Wiz. Meeting his gaze, she gave him a small smile, appreciating the little things he did for her. Big and powerful on one hand, sweet and gentle on the other. Natasha knew when she couldn't stop thinking about Malik, the other day, that she was a goner.

"Come in and have a seat."

Wow, Natasha thought when she stepped into his office, which could have doubled as a command center. She didn't know what she had expected, but a room full of computers and wall mounted monitors wasn't it at all.

Malik led her to the leather sofa in the middle of the room and sat next to her while Wiz took the seat across from them.

"It appears that the adoption agencies that the hospital is affiliated with are legit."

Thank goodness. Natasha didn't know what would happen to the hospital if word got out about what Dr. Halsey had done. But the idea that the hospital dealt with underground adoption agencies, where babies were stolen and then sold, scared Natasha to death.

"Now, Tasha, let me preface the rest of this conversation by saying that I get my data by any means necessary. With that said, many people could lose their jobs if it were found out how I came by the information I'm going to share with you."

"Oookay." She didn't know how else to respond and part of her was afraid of what he had uncovered.

"Some of the babies from your hospital, who were taken by the state, did not all arrive into the state's custody."

Natasha sat stunned, sickened by the meaning behind his words. She didn't know how long she sat there without speaking. It wasn't until Malik put his hand on her thigh that she was jarred out of her trance.

"The person who signed out some of the babies in the last two months worked for the state, but was terminated three years ago."

"I don't understand. How could they sign the babies out if

...” Natasha's hand hovered near her mouth, tears filling her eyes. “Someone walked out of the hospital with the babies and no one questioned their credentials? How could that happen?” She fought back the tears that were threatening to fall.

“The lawyer that gave Dr. Halsey a new identity and a medical license could have easily found a way to duplicate IDs to resemble the one social workers carry. I'm not sure how it was done, but I might have found the social worker involved.”

“Really? How?” she asked, but neither Wiz nor Malik answered. Natasha remembered reviewing the sign-out sheets for the babies and the signature was impossible to make out.

“Malik and I are going to pay the social worker a visit.”

“I want to go with you guys.”

“Oh, hell no!” Malik roared and stood. Until then he'd been quiet and Natasha wondered if he already knew about the information Wiz was sharing. “That is definitely out of the question.”

“Why not?” Natasha argued. “This is the hospital's problem. I should definitely be a part of any conversation that you're planning to have with someone who stole babies from the hospital! I'm going.”

“The hell you are.” Malik paced near the sofa while Wiz sat back in his seat as if knowing a battle was coming. “We don't know who or what we're dealing with. It's not safe,” Malik stated when he stopped next to her.

Natasha closed her eyes. Her fingers massaged her temples. She knew he was right about not knowing who they were dealing with, but this was not their problem.

Malik reclaimed his seat next to her and minutes ticked by without any of them speaking.

Natasha dropped her hands to her lap. “I appreciate the work that you both are doing regarding this case,” she looked from Wiz to Malik, “but this is the hospital's business. I don't think it's a good idea for you to be this involved." When neither of them spoke, only stared at her, she figured she was wasting her time. They were used to doing whatever they wanted to do. She folded her arms over her chest. "I'm starting to think that this goes deeper than you trying to find out if foul play was involved in your friend's death," Natasha said to Malik. "Who was she to you? I assume someone very special."

"A friend," he said without missing a beat. "So yeah, she was special. The other reason we're digging for answers is because Rosalyn, her sister, couldn't get answers from the hospital or the state. She wants to know what happened to her sister's baby."

Natasha sensed there was more to it than what he was sharing, but if she were Rosalyn, she'd want answers, too. Thankfully, Rosalyn hadn't gone to the media with her concerns, and now Natasha was thinking maybe it was good that Wiz and Malik were looking into the situation.

Malik sat back against the sofa, stretching his long legs out in front of him. "Tasha, maybe it's not a good idea for Wiz to keep you in the loop. You're legally bound to the hospital and have to share what you know."

"What are you saying, Malik?"

"I'm saying that because we don't know who all of the players are. The more you learn, the more your life can be in danger." He looked at Wiz. "I think going forward we should give her info on an as needed basis."

"That's not acceptable," Natasha snapped. "I want to be kept in the loop even if it means I don't share everything with the hospital. Right now, I want answers and I want to make sure that whatever Dr. Halsey and Tessa were involved in has stopped."

"I think she's right," Wiz chimed in, and Natasha was glad that he was on her side. "Just in case others at the hospital are involved, I think it would be better for her to have some knowledge of what we've found. Hopefully, we can get to the bottom of all of this soon."

Sighing, Malik ran his hand over his mouth and down his goatee. "I don't know. After what happened the other night at the Coffee House, I don't want Natasha in the line of fire again. Besides, if she goes back to the hospital with answers, somebody is going to wonder where she's getting her information. And they'll wonder if she knows more."

"I'll be fine." She squeezed Malik's hand, appreciating his concern. "Wiz, please keep me in the loop and just let me know when I can share information and when I should hold off." Malik kept a hold of her hand, but didn't say anything. She felt she knew him well enough to know that the subject wasn't over, but in the meantime, she wanted to know everything Wiz knew. Yet she had a feeling they probably wouldn't share everything. "Did you find out anything else?"

"Yeah," Wiz said slowly, tension in his voice. "I have a short list of underground adoption agencies." Wiz pulled a sheet of paper from a file folder on the table. "Do any of these names ring a bell: Angel Love Adoption Agency, My Child Adoption Agency, Sweet Haven Adopt—"

"Oh my God ... the second one." Her hand flew to her mouth, and relief spread through her body. She had lost hours of sleep trying to remember the name of the agency, knowing that information was key to finding who was behind Dr. Halsey's death. "How in the world did you find *underground* agencies?"

Wiz stared at her, the expression on his face serious enough to make her wonder if he would answer her question.

"I know people in low places."

Chapter Sixteen

"If Natasha means anything to you, you need to tell her about the baby," Wiz said when they stepped onto the elevator, heading down to the underground parking garage at Malik's agency. "You don't want her to find out from someone else."

Malik narrowed his eyes. "How many times do I have to tell you that I'm not the father? If she finds out about this kid, it's going to be because your ass keeps bringing that shit up!"

Wiz chuckled and they climbed into his Land Rover. They were on their way to pay Rosalyn a visit to see if she knew anything about Susan planning to put her baby up for adoption. Wiz also wanted to go through her bedroom and most recent journals to see if he could find anything that might help with the case.

"Seriously, man, when you two were over the other night and she asked why we were working so hard to find these missing babies. I thought for sure you were going to come clean."

"There's nothing to come clean about. The kid ain't mine! Why don't you just drop it?"

"Fine. I'll let it go, but secrets have a way of coming back to bite you in the ass."

"So are you talking from personal experience? Is that what this is all about? You have a kid out there that you haven't told us about and you're transferring your fears onto me?"

"You know good and damn well I don't have any kids out here. I don't know how you came up with that nonsense. Unlike you, who has been with more women than you can count, there is only one woman in this world who will ever be able to claim me as the father of her child."

Wiz was right about one thing, a number of women could claim Malik as the father of their kids, but none would be able to prove it. He'd made plenty of mistakes in his day, but not one included making babies. It was definitely time for him to change his ways and stick with one woman.

Malik was not looking forward to seeing Rosalyn again. She reminded him too much of Susan, and he was ready to put Susan and all the others behind him. But first he needed to find her child and prove that it wasn't his.

"Man, thanks for all of your work with this situation," Malik said to Wiz as they climbed out of Wiz's truck. "This whole thing is turning into more than I had expected."

"No problem, man. Once you get my bill, you probably won't be thanking me," he cracked.

Malik lifted a blue recycle bin that blocked the walkway and set it next to the building. Despite the poor condition of the exterior, the flowers along the pathway looked as if they had recently been planted.

Seconds after Malik pushed the intercom, the door buzzed for them to enter. They climbed the stairs to the second floor, skirting around kids playing cards on the step. When they reached Rosalyn's door, it swung open.

"Hello," she greeted, her curly hair hanging loose around

her shoulders. Today she seemed more pulled together than when Malik had first met her weeks ago. "Please come in." She stepped away from the door to let them pass.

"Rosalyn, this is the private investigator I told you about, Cameron Miller. He's going to ask a few more questions to see if he can assist you in your search for the truth."

"Don't you mean our search? Yes, I want to find out whether or not foul play had anything to do with my sister's death, but if her baby ... *your* baby is alive, I would think you'd want to know."

Malik exchanged a look with Wiz, not missing the smirk on his friend's face. His first thought was to tell her to quit calling it his kid, but out of respect, he kept his mouth shut.

"Can I get you gentlemen anything to drink? Water? Soda?"

They both declined and she directed them into the small living room. Rosalyn sat on the sofa and Wiz sat across from her with his notepad in his hand. Malik opted to stand, feeling a little too anxious to sit still. The sooner they found Susan's child and proved it wasn't his, the better.

"Why don't we go ahead and get started. Rosalyn, I understand you found other journals your sister kept. May I see them?" Wiz asked.

"Of course. Let me get them."

She returned with a small open-top box that had several cloth books sticking out of the top and handed it to Wiz.

"Prior to your sister's death, when was the last time you spoke with her?"

She sighed and thought for a moment. Her gaze settled on the floor before she returned her attention to Wiz. "Unfortunately, my sister and I weren't very close. With my missionary work, I was away more than I was here and that created the divide between us. I hadn't talk to her in at least eight months.

"Did she tell you then that she was pregnant?"

Rosalyn shook her head. "No. Actually, we didn't talk long. She told me about her job, and how much she enjoyed it initially, but how things had changed. She was having trouble with her supervisor and thought he was trying to get her fired."

"Where did she work?" Wiz asked. "And do you know the name of her supervisor or anyone she might've worked with?"

"She was a paralegal for a large downtown law firm. Kent, Schuster & Black. I'm not sure who her supervisor was, but I did find a business card from the firm." She sifted through a stack of papers on the glass dining room table. "Excuse the mess. I had no idea how much stuff Sue had, nor that it would take this long to go through."

Malik glanced around the tight space while Wiz questioned Rosalyn. Based on his calculations of the last time he was with Susan, the timing fit where he could be the father. He shook his head at the thought. He'd always been careful. No slip-ups. *I am not the father.*

"Since you've been going through your sister's belongings, have you found anything about an adoption agency?" Malik heard Wiz ask. Not only was Wiz good with people, he had never taken on a case he couldn't solve.

"No. Sue wasn't the neatest person in the world. After reading some of her journals, I ... um, it's been hard. She was the only family I had left and going through her belongings has been harder than I thought it would be." She composed herself and studied Wiz and Malik. "You think she was thinking about putting her baby up for adoption?" She shook her head and grabbed a floral journal from the box that sat on the floor near Wiz's foot. "I don't believe that. Look at what she wrote."

She pulled a red floral journal from the box and opened it before handing it to Wiz. Malik moved closer and read the entry over his shoulder.

Today was a rough day. Work was awful and Lawyer Man

won't back off. He won't take no for an answer, even when I told him the father wouldn't want me to give up the baby. I've been trying to reach Malik, but his phone goes directly to voice-mail and he hasn't called me back. That's okay, though. I'm looking forward to raising my baby, with or without him. He still hasn't returned my calls, but maybe he's out of town. He travels a lot. I'm excited and scared at the same time. Malik and I have always gotten along good, but I'm not sure how he's going to feel about being a father. Maybe since it's a boy, he'll warm up to the idea. Either way, I'm going to love this baby and take care of him the best I can, and I don't need Lawyer Man's money.

Malik didn't bother reading anything more. He needed to find the truth as soon as possible and deal with the consequences, no matter what they were.

"Would you mind if we took a look through her bedroom?"

"Of course. Follow me."

They walked down the short hall that led to the two bedrooms and a bathroom. Malik remembered her bedroom being on the left, but Rosalyn directed them to the one on the right. When they stepped into the room, Malik's gaze went directly to the baby bed near the only window in the room. The blue sheet set with a blanket, a teddy bear in the corner of the bed, and the multi-color mobile hanging above the bed, was a good indication that she indeed was expecting a boy.

"Does this look like a space of a woman who was thinking about giving up her child?" Rosalyn asked, looking pointedly at Malik before leaving the room.

"You all right, man?" Wiz asked when Rosalyn left them alone. He sifted through a few of the journals from the box Susan's sister had given him. Malik hadn't noticed he'd brought it to the room with him.

"Fine." Malik stood near the queen-sized bed, surveying the

contents on the bedside table. "Let's just hurry up and get the hell out of here."

"It looks as if Susan's journal entries got shorter and shorter the closer she got to her due date. Some entries are random. Here's something interesting." Wiz moved closer to the bed. "One of her friends, Candy, gave her child up for adoption. Made ten grand on the deal."

Malik listened as he continued searching around the bed. He wasn't sure what exactly he was looking for, but knew he'd know it when he found it.

"It doesn't say which adoption agency, but I'd be willing to bet it has something to do with the Lawyer Man that Susan mentioned in her other entry."

"Probably," Malik said absently. He glanced behind the bedside table, but didn't see anything, and pulled the headboard away from the wall to look behind it. "I might have something here." There was a small piece of paper taped to the back of the headboard.

"What is it?"

"A parking garage receipt." He turned it over and noticed the writing on the bottom. *If something should happen to me, give the police this name: Alonso Black.*

"Malik, I'm serious this time. I'm for real going to the gym." Natasha rolled her eyes at the laughter that came through the phone line. She could understand his doubt considering she'd gotten her membership over a month ago and this would be only the second time she actually used it.

She grabbed her briefcase and switched off the desk lamp before picking up her keys from the top of the desk.

"Baby, you've said that twice this week. I'll believe it when I see it."

"Well, the only way you're going to know for sure is if you go with me."

"If I wasn't on my way to an appointment, I would meet you there. I guess I'm going to have to just take your word that you're going."

"Okay," she said a little disappointed. They'd been spending a lot of time together and the more time they spent together, the more time she wanted with him. She felt like she had a social life now. "So are you still planning to come by tonight?"

"I'll be there. I'm thinking about bringing dinner. Do you have a taste for anything in particular?"

Only you was on the tip of her tongue, and she was shocked the thought even popped into her head. Since they started dating her thoughts had become more wanton, almost downright freaky.

"Tasha?"

"Yeah, I'm here." She walked down the stairs toward the parking lot. "Why don't you surprise me?"

"I thought you didn't like surprises."

"I like good surprises."

"Okay, that's good to know. So have you left the hospital yet?" He had finally agreed to her not having a bodyguard, as long as she checked in regularly.

"I know you don't think I'm going to the gym, but I'm heading to the parking lot as we speak."

He chuckled. "All right, I guess you might actually make it today."

"Whatever." She smiled loving their banter. "You just be ready to give me a massage if my muscles are screaming by the time I get home."

"Even if your muscles aren't screaming, it will be my pleasure to massage that sexy body of yours."

"Ooh, I love it when you talk like that."

"There's more where that came from, but right now I have to get going. Drive safe and I'll see you tonight."

"Okay. I'm looking forward to it."

"Oh, and shoot me a text when you get to the gym."

"Will do." He was a little overprotective, but it felt good to have someone care about her well-being.

She hurried to her car, still finding it hard to believe that she was leaving the hospital before six. After tossing her briefcase in the trunk, she climbed into the driver's seat. The moment she put her handbag in the backseat, her cell rang.

She shook her head and smiled before grabbing her phone. "Malik, I promise. I will text or call you when I get there."

With no response, she glanced at the phone screen.

Martin.

"Hello."

"Hello, Tasha. I guess things are getting pretty serious with your new boyfriend," Martin said. His tone wasn't as belittling as it was when they argued at her place, but there was still an edge in his voice.

"What do you want, Martin?" She drummed her fingers against the steering wheel.

"We need to talk."

"I think we said all we needed to say to each other. I've moved on, and you should, too."

"I can't move on without you, Tasha! Don't you understand that? I will always love you and that man will never love you the way I do."

Natasha sighed, frustrated with the way the conversation was going. "Marty, Malik is a good man. He treats me like ... like I'm the most important person in the world. You have constantly judged him and you don't even know him." She felt herself getting angry.

"I know all I need to know about him and he's no good for you. You were almost killed because of him."

"That's not true!" She slammed her hand against the steering wheel. "Are you intentionally trying to hurt me? Because if you are—"

"Tasha, I would never hurt you, nor will I let anyone else hurt you! Baby, I love you and you're making a big mistake. You need to stay away from him!"

"I've had enough of this," she mumbled more to herself. "Good-bye, Martin." She pushed the power button and stared at her phone before tossing it in the passenger seat.

He doesn't know what he's talking about and I'm not going to let him get to me. I'm going to the gym and I'm going to have a great workout.

She turned the key, but nothing happened.

"Oh come on. Really?" The car was barely a year old, there was no way it wasn't starting. She tried again. Nothing. "Urgh! I finally get a chance to make it to the gym and now this." She sat for a few minutes, debating on whether to call Malik back. If she called, he would skip his appointment in order to pick her up and she didn't want that. She grabbed her handbag and ...

"Aarghhh!" she screamed, and practically jumped out of her seat when someone knocked on the window. She covered her heart with her hand as if that were going to make her heart rate go back to normal.

After a few seconds, she recognized her visitor and opened the door.

"Ray, you scared me half to death. I didn't even see you walk up to the car. Where'd you come from?"

"I was heading to my van and heard you trying to start your car." He walked to the front of the car. "Pop the hood and let's see what's going on."

Natasha stood next to him as he checked hoses and a few

other things that she couldn't identify. Each time he moved, his fresh scent tantalized her senses. He smelled so good. A woodsy fragrance with a hint of vanilla. It was unique.

"So what do you think?"

"I think you're going to have to get a mechanic to look at it." He closed the hood and wiped his hands on the napkin Natasha handed him. "The battery looks pretty new. I'd offer to give you a jump, but my cables are in my other vehicle."

Natasha sighed. *So much for going to the gym.*

"Can I give you a ride somewhere?"

She twisted her mouth in thought. "Well, I was on my way to the gym, but I don't want to take you out of your way."

"Actually, I was heading to the gym myself."

"Are you serious? This is too perfect." She snatched her handbag from the backseat and retrieved her gym bag from the trunk. "Every time I plan to go work out, something always comes up. You're a godsend."

He reached for her gym bag to carry it for her. "Well, I'm glad I can help. I'm right over here." He pointed to the dark blue Ford. "It's not a BMW, so hopefully you won't be too uncomfortable."

Natasha waved him off. "Oh please, as long as it runs, I'm good. I really appreciate this." He opened the van door and helped her climb in.

While he walked around to the driver's side, Natasha glanced at her car. She had no idea what could be wrong with it and figured she'd see if Malik knew someone who could take a look at it.

Ray pulled out of the parking lot and headed south, the opposite direction of the gym.

"Um ... the gym is that way." She pointed with her thumb behind them.

"I know. I'm sorry. I should have told you that I needed to

drop by my mother's house first. It's less than a mile away." He stopped at a red light. "I go by there every day between jobs to make sure she's taken her medication. Otherwise, she conveniently forgets." He must have noticed the wariness on her face. "I promise. It'll only take ten minutes, tops."

"Okay." She held her handbag close to her body, mentally kicking herself for getting into a vehicle with a man she barely knew. *For a person who is supposed to be so smart, this has to be the dumbest thing I've ever done.*

"So, did you always want to be a doctor?" he asked.

"Yes." She thought back on what seemed to be a lifetime ago. "When I was eight, a baby bird fell out of a tree in our backyard and broke his wing. Before my parents could call the wildlife people, I had already gone into *save my bird* mode." She laughed at the memory. "Since it was in our yard, I claimed it as my own. I found a shoe box and did a little research on how to take care of a bird and fix its wing."

"So, did you fix it?" Ray asked, appearing genuinely interested.

"I did. It was a little crooked and we did end up turning the bird over to a wildlife rehabilitator organization. They said I had done an excellent job." She relaxed some. "From that moment on, I knew I wanted to be a doctor."

"That's cool," he said, his voice wistful. "I wanted to be a cop. My uncle was a police officer and the coolest guy I knew. I wanted to grow up and be just like him."

"What happened? Since you're working at the hospital, I assume you changed your mind about becoming a police officer."

"Yeah. My uncle was killed during my senior year of high school. He responded to a domestic violence call and the husband had a gun. Shot him in the chest."

"Oh no."

"Since my father was never around, my uncle was ... well, he taught me everything. When he died, I finished school, barely, and left Chicago."

"Where'd you go?"

He glanced at her, but she couldn't read his expression, and he returned his attention to driving. "I traveled the world," he finally said. "Not the whole world, but a few places like Germany, Bolivia, South America, where ever I was needed...to help people."

"Like the Peace Corp or something?"

"Something like that."

Natasha found herself relaxing listening as he told her about some of his previous jobs, including his new handy man business that he was trying to get off the ground. They shared a laugh when they talked about their siblings and some of the challenges of being the oldest child. She never would have guessed that he was thirty. Her respect for him grew when he told her his mother had recently had a stroke and he and his aunt shared the responsibility of taking care of her.

Ray slowed and turned into a long, narrow alley. The dilapidated garages on each side and the pungent stench of trash and cigarettes made Natasha's nervous meter rise a hundred percent. She remained quiet while Ray eased down the alley, dodging potholes and driving around a group of men huddled together shooting dice. She raised her window up not caring that it was in the mid-seventies outside and Ray's air conditioner wasn't working.

He pulled over to the left, alongside a two-car garage that was in desperate need of a paint job.

"I'll be back in a minute." He turned off the van and jumped out before she could respond.

Natasha hurried and locked the doors, watching as Ray disappeared into the yard. When he was out of sight, she glanced around. Except for what she'd seen on the news, she wasn't familiar with the Englewood neighborhood. From what she remembered, it wasn't a place to be just hanging out in a parked vehicle

I need to text Malik. She reached in the side pocket of her handbag, expecting to put her hands on her cell phone. When she didn't, she peeked inside and checked the zippered part of the bag. *What the heck did I do with my phone?* She thought back to the last time she had it, which was after she talked to Martin. It suddenly dawned on her that her cell could have fallen out of her bag when she tossed it in the backseat.

Natasha looked up to see two old men stumbling up the alley, talking loudly. She scooted down in the seat, praying they wouldn't stop. *Stupid, stupid, stupid.* Getting into the vehicle with Ray was her first mistake, and not insisting that he drop her off at the gym before going to his mother's house was her second mistake.

"Hey sweet thang," one of the drunks stammered. "Wha–what's a pr–pretty lil—"

"Get the fuck away from the van," a voice laced with steel growled out of nowhere.

Natasha turned her head, shocked to see Ray standing near the front bumper. The deadly scowl on his face made him look like a different person. He eased toward them and they stumbled back, their hands up.

"We ... we don't wa–want no trou–trouble." They hurried away from the vehicle.

Ray stood there for a moment before climbing into the van. "Sorry about that." He started the ignition and looked at her when she didn't respond. "Are you okay? Did they do something to you?" he growled, turning fully in his seat to face her. "Did they?" He moved a lock of hair from her face and Natasha jerked back.

"No. No ... they just caught me by surprised." Natasha's pulse pounded in her ear, anxiety jumbling her thoughts. "Uh, we should probably get going. It's getting late."

"You're right. Sorry about the detour. Since my aunt doesn't usually get here until late, I didn't want to take a chance on my mom not taking her medication." He pulled away from the garage. "Are you sure you're okay?" He patted her knee. "You still look a little spooked."

Natasha tried to relax, but she was wound tighter than a drum and now she just wanted to get to the gym. "I'm all right."

"I guess you're probably still a little jumpy from when Dr. Halsey was killed, huh?" He rubbed her thigh as if that would comfort her. She eased her leg away, placing her handbag between her and the center console. "Well, you don't have to worry, love. I would never let anyone hurt you."

Chapter Seventeen

"So this guy is all that, huh?" Travis asked, staring down at the photo of Brandon Walsh, better known as Street. Since Wiz was on an undercover assignment and Stan was on a special project, Malik decided to use the newbie, Travis, to make a run with him.

"If anyone knows about any underground operations, it would be Street." Malik glanced at his cell phone again, wondering why Natasha hadn't texted him. He had agreed to back off with the bodyguards if she agreed to stay in contact at all times. The morning and nights were covered since most of those times she was with him. It was everything else in between that made him leery about not having eyes on her.

"So this guy has it like that? He knows everything about everything?"

"Pretty much."

They were sitting outside one of Street's hangouts. The law office Susan worked for came back clean, but one of the partner's names stood out.

Malik pulled out his cell phone, checking to see if Natasha

had texted him as agreed. When he saw that there was still no text, he called Victoria.

"Hey Malik. Did you forget something?"

"No, but I need a favor."

"Shoot."

"I'm not sure how long it'll take me and Travis to take care of some business, so I'm forwarding my calls to you. Also, use that app Wiz created and check my text messages in about ten minutes."

"I take it that you're expecting an important call or message."

"Yeah, I should have heard from Tasha by now. She was supposed to text me when she got to the gym, but I'm assuming she forgot. If she doesn't text or call my number in the next ten minutes, I need you to find her."

"Really, Malik? You don't think that's a little obsessive?" she asked. Had the question come from anyone other than her or Wiz, he might've snapped. He and Victoria had a sister-brother-like relationship and she could get way with things that others couldn't.

"Vicky, just do it?"

"I'll do it, but she's going to eventually get pissed that you're checking up on her all the time and you know it."

"Yeah, but she'll get over it. Until we find the guy who killed that doctor a couple of weeks ago, Tasha is stuck with my over-protectiveness, if that's even a word."

"There he is." Travis pointed at the tall, thin man talking on a cell phone, his slow gait coming toward them.

"Okay, Vicky, I gotta go."

Malik shoved his cell phone into his jean's pocket and they exited the car. Street didn't see them right away, but when he did, the smile that was on his face fell. He looked left, then right, and Malik cursed under his breath knowing what was coming next.

"He's going to run," Malik murmured. The moment the words left his mouth, Street took off; Malik and Travis were right behind him.

I'm getting too old for this shit.

Malik waved his hand and pointed, giving Travis the signal to go around the opposite way. Malik chased Street down Wentworth Avenue and through an alleyway, following him through a yard. What Malik didn't understand was why Street was running. He knew Malik wasn't a cop, so something else was going on.

Malik leapt over a fence and cut across a vacant lot to cut Street off. He was glad he had changed into street clothes, opting for a T-shirt, jeans, and a pair of black Timberlands. Had he been in one of his suits and Stacy Adams chasing Street down, he would've kicked the kid's ass once he caught up to him.

Malik and Travis ended up in the same area just as Street flew around the corner.

"Where yo ass going?" Malik barked and snatched him by the collar, yanking him into a doorway, concrete blocks on the side and a green awning overhang. "Keep watch," Malik told Travis.

Street struggled against him. "Let me go, Tree. You tryin' to get me killed or something?"

"Hey! Hey," Malik said, shoving him against the wall. "What the hell is up with you? Why'd you run?"

"I'm not talking."

Malik stared at the man who had helped him out plenty of times with information. Street always hooked him up, and Malik always looked out for him. So whatever ... or whoever had him scared had power, or something on him.

"Street, you know me, man. Don't I always have yo back? You help me, I help you. Isn't that how it usually works?"

"Yeah, Tree ... but this is different."

"What's different? You don't even know why I'm here. So what has you rattled?"

"Lawyer Man."

There's that name again. Malik didn't have a clue to who he was talking about, but if he played along, he'd have a better chance of getting answers.

"What about him?"

"He was talkin' with ... to your girl."

Natasha was the first person to come to mind, but there was no way he was talking about her. "What girl?"

"You know, man. The tall, skinny, light-skinned chick you used to hang out with at that club on Eerie."

Susan.

"He helped her get a job at a law firm and then when you knocked ... uh, when she got pregnant, he was telling her about this adoption agency. Some underground shit. Um ... um, My Child somethin'."

"Why? Why was he telling her about the agency?"

Street shrugged. "He wanted her kid. Prob since she was fine as hell. Was gon' pay big money, too." Malik loosened his grip on Street. "She said the kid was yours and she wasn't giving it away."

Frustration gnawed away at Malik's patience. *Why the hell would she tell people he was the father?* He didn't care what her journal said, or what her sister said, Susan knew he was not the father of her kid.

"So why did you run?" Malik asked. The urine smell mixed with trash was starting to get to him, especially since they were in close quarters.

"'Cause, man, I thought you ... you know, I thought you were gon' start taking out folks since what happen to her."

"What happened to her?"

"You don't know?" He looked at Malik suspiciously. "They killed her, man! Had some doctor take her out *and* they took the kid."

"I need a name, Street."

"All I know is, he go by Lawyer Man."

"He working with anyone?"

"He's got this guy that do work for him. Used to be military or some shit. A bad ass. Looks innocent, but will shoot a man dead without blinking an eye. I know. I saw him do it. T-dog was looking for his sister a couple of months ago and mentioned Lawyer Man. Next thang I know, this soldier-like dude, dressed in all black, showed up on sixty-fifth and shot T-dog right between the eyes."

"Street, I'm going to need you to take a ride with me," Malik said, still trying to process everything, but knowing Street was telling the truth.

"Nah, man. I'm already dead by telling you that much." Street shook his head and tried to pull away from Malik.

"Street, you know I got you, but I need more info from you, man. And I gotta know where you are if I'm going to look out for you."

"I don't know, Tree." He shook his head. "I'm not try—"

"I have a place where you can lay low, and by the looks of you, you could probably use something to eat. You're wasting away to nothing, dude." Malik needed more information. He could force Street to ride with him, but he preferred him to go willingly. "If that's not enough to convince you, maybe that little hottie I hooked you up with before can—"

"Let's go, but if I get gunned down, it's gon' be on you."

Malik set Travis and Street up at one of the agency's safe

houses. He kept replaying in his mind all that Street had shared, still unable to wrap his brain around the part about Susan. His relationship with her, if anyone could really call it that, was casual. If it had gotten out that he and she were an item, it was because she made people believe they were together. When in reality they weren't, at least not the way she made it out to be.

The moment Malik climbed back into his truck, he deactivated his call-forward and the phone rang.

"Yeah?"

"Malik, you need to get to Natasha," Victoria said in a rush.

"What? Where is she?" His chest tightened. All types of thoughts ran through his mind, unsure of what Victoria was going to say, but knowing he wasn't going to like it.

"I never reached her on her cell, so I called the gym and pretended I was her assistant calling from the hospital. She wasn't there, Malik. She wasn't at the gym."

"What?" Malik increased his grip on the steering wheel. "What do you mean she wasn't at the gym? She should've fuckin' been there an hour ago," he roared.

"Would you calm down and let me finish? Dang, you got it bad! She's there now." He started his truck and took off in the direction of the gym. "When she arrived at the gym, they had her call me back. She lost her cell phone, which is why she couldn't text you."

"Why the hell didn't you just say that in the first place, instead of almost giving me a heart attack?" His heart still pounded erratically against the inside of his chest.

"Well, don't freak out, but there's more. She didn't sound right. She said she was fine, but her voice sounded strained. Something's up with her."

"Did you tell her to stay there?"

"Yeah. Her car wouldn't start and it's still at the hospital. So she's going to need a ride anyway."

Malik frowned. "So how'd she get to the gym?"

"She didn't say, but she did say, 'I need Malik to pick me up as soon as possible'. Those were her exact words."

Silence fell between them and Malik knew Victoria was thinking the same thing he was thinking. Something was definitely up. Natasha had fought him daily about him wanting her to have a bodyguard and she hated that he was so protective. She claimed that she was independent before he came a long and now he made her feel too needy. She vowed to never ask him for anything unless it was an emergency.

"I'm on my way."

Natasha dragged herself to the women's locker room, her body screaming in pain. The spinning class she'd taken was much more intense than she had expected, but she needed to work off her anxiousness. Thinking about her ride to the gym, she had probably overreacted. Malik's fears about her being in danger had transferred over to her, causing her irrational reaction to Ray's little detour.

Malik.

Natasha knew he was going to be pissed. Not only had she not contacted him as agreed, but considering the number of times Victoria asked if she was okay, Natasha was sure she had picked up on her anxiety. And if she had, she probably told Malik.

After a quick shower, Natasha left the women's locker room more than ready to go home. For the past couple of weeks, her emotions had been all over the place and it felt like they were coming to a head. She just wanted to go home with Malik, and curl up in front of the television. First, she had to tell Ray that she didn't need a ride home.

She spotted him at the end of the hall, walking toward her.

Broad shoulders, a lean midsection, and legs that went on forever, he definitely had a presence about him. The confidence in his stride added to his strong, powerful presence. Unlike Malik, there wasn't a dangerous air about him, except for when he yelled at the drunks who were hanging around his van. Ray seemed like a nice guy, edged with a little street. Or, at least that's how her friend Layla would describe him. Natasha smiled at the thought.

"How was your workout?" Ray fell in step with her as they walked up the stairs toward the entrance. "I looked around for you and figured you must have taken one of the classes since I didn't see you in the cardio or weight rooms."

"Yeah, I took the spinning class. I was a little late, but got in on enough of it to make me realize how out of shape I am."

His seductive gaze swept the length of her body, as if photographing her with his eyes. "Well, if you're out of shape, you make it look damn good."

Natasha looked away, not wanting to encourage his advances. She definitely had to keep her distance from him. She knew now that it was a mistake to ride to the gym with him and the last thing she wanted was for him to get the wrong idea.

She set her gym bag and purse in one of the chairs near a bank of windows and tied her shoe.

"Why don't we stop and get a quick bite to eat?" he said. "I know this great place not too far from here. What do you say?"

"I'd say you need to find yourself another date. She already has plans."

Natasha's breath caught when she turned to find Malik standing behind them, all six feet eight inches of smooth dark chocolate. Words escaped her as her gaze worked its way down his powerful body. The fitted black T-shirt, which stretched across his wide chest, showed off solid pecs, and arms that both of her hands together couldn't fit around. He was one of the sexiest men she'd ever met and she could easily look at him all day. Her gaze strolled down to his dark jeans hanging low on his hips and partially tucked into a pair of black Timberlands. If he was going for the rugged, bad-boy look, he had nailed it.

Natasha thought back to her conversation with Victoria, remembering the anxiousness in her own voice. Though she was happy to see Malik, she hated knowing she was turning into one of those needy type of women. One of those women who always needed a man around. The only redeeming quality of her neediness, was that what she felt for Malik was so much more than that. It was love. Somehow, she had fallen in love with this giant of a man who cursed too much, who was possessive, and by the scowl he wore, was the jealous type.

"Hi," she finally said, the word coming out breathless. She couldn't see his eyes due to his dark aviator glasses. Yet, with the firm set of his jaw and the down turn of his lips, reminding her of Morpheus in the Matrix movie, it was safe to say he wasn't happy.

Malik extended his hand to Natasha, but kept his gaze on Ray. He wanted her away from this man. Normally he wasn't the jealous type, but when it came to Natasha, nothing about his behavior was normal. One minute she made him feel as if he could leap tall buildings, and other times, she made him want to lock her in a tower and protect her from the rest of the world. But right now, all he wanted to do was wipe the stupid smirk off of Ray's face. The guy irked the hell out of Malik, and it bugged him that he couldn't figure out why.

"I'm glad to see you," Natasha murmured when she stepped into Malik's embrace, kissing him on the lips, her words loud enough for only him to hear. She wrapped her arms around his waist and he gazed into her eyes. Victoria was right, something was up.

"You all right?" he asked, and she nodded in reply.

Malik ran his hands slowly up and down her back, loving the feel of her softness molded against his body. If she was trying to take his mind off the fact that she'd been hanging out with another man, it wasn't working. Although, some of the agitation gripping his body earlier did lift ... somewhat, when she batted those big brown eyes up at him and smiled. It was weird that she had this type of power over him. He'd stared down some of the most dangerous men in the world without yielding, but this woman comes along and bats her long eyelashes and he turns to mush.

"Thanks for the ride," she said to Ray. "Because of you, I finally followed through on getting a work out in, so that a certain somebody can stop teasing me."

Hold the hell up! He brought her to the gym?

She smiled up at Malik, who didn't return the smile. Instead, he said, "Let's go."

She stepped out of his arms and walked over to where her bag sat on a chair, and Malik took that moment to talk to Ray.

"Stay the fuck away from her," he growled, his voice low and menacing.

"And if I don't?"

"You'll wish you had."

Chapter Eighteen

Malik and Natasha rode in silence. They had just left the hospital parking lot, trying to get her car to start. When it didn't, Malik contacted his mechanic to have it towed. While taking items from her vehicle and putting them into his truck, Natasha found her cell phone in the front seat.

Malik had yet to question her about the past couple of hours, but thoughts of her being with Ray kept popping into his head. He wasn't totally sure why he was so pissed that the guy had driven her to the gym, and didn't want to know whether Ray had seen her in some little skimpy workout gear. It was that nagging feeling he got whenever the guy was around that had him on edge.

"So are you going to give me the silent treatment for the rest of the night?" Natasha asked. He glanced at her, the streetlights shining into the window just enough for him to see her exasperated expression.

"I don't do the silent treatment," he stated simply. Until she'd said something, he hadn't realized that they hadn't spoken since climbing into the truck.

"I didn't think so since you're not the silent, quiet type, but what else should I think? You haven't said two words to me. Are you upset because I was out with Ray, or would you be like this about any man?"

Malik debated on how to answer her questions. She made it sound like her and Ray went on a date or spent more time together than just hanging out at the gym.

"Both," he finally said. "I don't like you hanging out with the motha—" He stopped himself. "I don't trust him. I can't put my finger on it, and I know I said it before ... there is something about him that doesn't sit right with me."

"Malik, he was kind enough to give me a ride. I might not know him well, but I know a few things about him."

"Like what? Tell me what you know about this man. Do you know where he lives? Do you know his favorite foods?"

"I know enough." Natasha sighed. "I know he's really nice to me."

"You're a beautiful woman, of course he's nice to you," Malik said. She gaped at him. "Don't look so shocked. There's not a man on this earth that would see a woman who looks like you and not come to her rescue any chance they got."

Natasha turned her head and stared out the front window. "He grew up in Chicago. He has a sister who lives in Detroit and a brother who just moved to Texas. These days he's working a few jobs and he looks after his mom, who is recovering from a stroke."

"What else?"

"I don't want to talk about this anymore. Let's just go back to you giving me the silent treatment."

"You asked me whether or not I was upset because you were out with Ray, or if I would be like this with any man you were with. My answer is yes. I can't stand that punk, and I don't like the idea of you going out with anyone who isn't me."

"Malik."

"And since we're on the subject," Malik divided his attention between her and the road, "it's only a ten damn minute ride from the hospital to the gym. Why'd it take so long for you to get there?" He'd told himself that he wasn't going to bring up what Victoria told him, but his concern for Natasha's safety and his wariness of Ray wouldn't let him keep it inside. From the moment Victoria expressed concern for Natasha, he'd been worried sick about her and that was before he knew who'd taken her to the gym.

She sat back in her seat and scratched her head. "He stopped by his mother's house first."

"Wait. Let me make sure I understand," he said, trying like hell to keep the frustration mixed with anger, out of his voice. "You got into a vehicle with a man you don't know, thinking that you guys were going to the gym, but instead he took you to his mother's house."

"Malik, it wasn't like that," she said defensively.

"Then how the hell was it?"

"I told you, his mother recently had a stroke. He's one of her caregivers and needed to stop by to make sure she'd taken her medication."

"Did he tell you this before or after you were in his car?"

Her silence was his answer. She wrapped her arms around her midsection and turned her head toward the passenger window. It was safe to say he wasn't getting anymore answers.

Malik turned into the parking lot of the Italian restaurant they had visited weeks ago. His plan was for them to grab a bite to eat before heading to her house, but instead he'd get something to go. Her reaction to his questions, as well as what Victoria said about her sounding upset on the telephone, made him want to know everything that happened.

He shut off the engine and debated on his next words. As

far as he was concerned, if this Ray was on the up and up, he would have been forthcoming about having to make a stop before going to the gym. And Malik wanted to believe that Natasha wouldn't have climbed into his car had she'd known he wasn't going straight there.

"Natasha." When she didn't turn or respond, he rubbed her arm. Being gentle wasn't his nature. Yet the feelings he had for her, the feelings that pulled at his heart strings whenever he looked or thought of her, made him want to be gentle. "Tasha, I need you to look at me."

She turned slowly to face him, and when she lifted her gaze to meet his, the sadness in her eyes nearly broke his heart. "Baby, why are you so upset?" He cupped her cheek, the pad of his thumb caressing her soft skin.

She accepted his comfort for a moment, but quickly pulled away. "Because I feel so stupid. During my career, I have treated rape victims, women who'd been beaten by men, and I have seen women who have been emotionally traumatized by an experience. The thought that I could easily be one of them didn't come to mind until I was sitting in a filthy alley, waiting for Ray to return to his van."

Malik's mood veered sharply to disbelief, and he gripped the top of her headrest and the dashboard to keep from exploding. Anger seared the corners of his control, thinking of her sitting in this man's vehicle, alone and in an alley. Alarm rippled through his body imagining the type of danger she could have been in.

"I was scared, but mostly disappointed in myself," she continued, shaking her head as if she couldn't believe what she'd done. "Ray was a perfect gentleman, but I'm smart enough to know that the situation could have easily turned bad."

Malik released a breath he didn't realize he was holding. Part of him wanted to shake her and scream 'what were you thinking?' The other part wanted to hold her in his arms and never let go.

"Where were you?"

"What do you mean?"

"Where did he take you? What part of town?"

She hesitated, lowering her eyes before looking at him again. "Englewood, near 65th."

Malik just stared at her. Not because he was in the same area probably around the same time, but because he knew the crime rate in that neighborhood was one of the highest in the country.

"Do you have any idea how dangerous it is for you, a woman, to sit in a car alone, especially in that neighborhood?" His voice was low and controlled, but his insides were a jumbled mess. "Even I'm slow to hang out in a parked car down there and I always have my piece on me."

She sighed and rested her head against the headrest. "I know. It won't happen again."

He dropped back against his seat. "You're damn right it won't happen again, because I'm not letting you out of my sight."

A soft laugh came from her. "So what you gon' do? Follow me around like a shadow?"

"If I have to."

She reached over and laced her fingers with his. Staring down at their joined hands, the contrast of their skin tone jumping out at him, he brought her hand to his lips and kissed the back of it.

"I want you to get to the point where, if you're caught in a jam, need someone, or just want to talk, you call me. If I'm not available, you call one of my people, people I trust and count on." He leaned across the center console, meeting her gaze. "People you can trust and count on."

Malik placed his hand at the back of her head and pulled her toward him. His mouth covered hers and he kissed her slowly, wanting the message from his lips to reveal just how much he cared for her. His tongue traced the fullness of her lips before slipping inside her mouth and tangling with her tongue. Though he loved kissing her, it wasn't enough. Tonight he wanted all of her. Every soft, curvaceous, luscious part of her.

He held her face between his hands. "Come home with me tonight," he said against her mouth before lifting his head.

She batted those big brown eyes of hers and the corner of her mouth lifted into a smile. "Okay ... but can we get something to eat first? I can smell their garlic bread all the way out here and I'm starving."

He laughed and placed a kiss on her nose. "Yeah, I guess the least I can do is feed you."

"Good. We can get it to go, and then swing by my house so that I can pick up some clothes."

Malik chuckled and released her. "I thought you were hungry. Add stopping by your house to the mix and it'll be at least an hour and a half before you eat."

"I can eat in the truck while you drive."

He shook his head and couldn't help smiling when she wiggled her eyebrows at him. "I see you have it all figured out."

Thirty minutes later, Malik pulled up to her house, surprised to see there were no lights on except for the floodlights along the walkway.

"Why's the house so dark?" he asked as they undid their seatbelts. "I thought the lamp in the living room was on a timer."

"It is, but the light bulb might've blown."

Malik's cell phone rang just as he took the key out of the ignition. It was Wiz.

"What's up, man?"

"Did you talk to Sheldon today?"

"Nope, but he might've called when I was away from my phone." Malik lifted his finger, silently asking Natasha to wait a minute when she opened her door to climb out. "I haven't checked my voicemail in the last few hours. I take it he had some news."

"Yeah, he did. The social worker you and I planned to see tomorrow is dead."

Malik cursed under his breath. Wiz had wanted to visit her earlier in the day, but by the time Malik received his message, he and Travis were sitting in front of Street's apartment.

"Even if we would've paid her a visit ..."

Malik glanced at Natasha when she touched his arm.

"I'm going in to grab some clothes," she whispered, "give me five minutes." Malik nodded and watched as she jogged up to the house.

"I'm not sure if we would've gotten much information out of her anyway. If this lawyer guy is overseeing this baby stealing organization, he has deep pockets and a long reach."

"When did they find her?" Malik asked, rubbing his forehead. He was frustrated that each time they got close to getting answers, something happened.

"A few hours ago at her home in Englewood. Her throat was slashed."

Natasha used her remote to unlock the front door of her house and deactivate the new alarm system, finding the handheld device convenient. She told Malik she'd be five minutes and this time she wanted to be ready by the time he finished his call. According to him, her five minutes were more like twenty, but tonight she intended to prove him wrong.

She walked into the semi-darkness and out of habit, dropped her handbag into the living room chair. She hated entering a dark house, hence the timer on the living room lamp, but she could get through the house with her eyes closed.

She went toward the hall that led to the bedrooms, managing to bump into only one of the large floor pillows along the way. She flipped the hallway light switch, but nothing happened. Repeating the gesture, she had the same result.

"That's weird," she murmured, surprised that both the lamp and the hall light weren't working. *Crap, something must have tripped the circuit breaker*. She normally didn't have that problem unless she had too many appliances going at one time. She debated on whether to go down the basement to the circuit breaker or grab the flashlight in her bedroom.

Not wanting to keep Malik waiting, she headed down the hallway that led to the three bedrooms. She'd get him to run downstairs and turn everything back on. Yet another nice thing about having a man around. Since he'd come into her life, she hadn't had to take out the trash, put gas in her car, and rarely had to cook. Add those qualities to his sense of humor, take-charge attitude, and his strong, hot body, she had the perfect man. She smiled at the thought. In such a short period, he'd made himself at home in her life and she liked it.

She hurried down the hall, but slowed when she walked past the bathroom door, noticing it was closed. Unless she had guests or someone was using the bathroom, the door was always open. She backed up and reached for the knob, but the door swung open. Before she could react, someone lunged at her. The side of her head hit the wall and she stumbled. Stars floated in front of her eyes and a hand slapped over her mouth.

Oh God, oh God. Her heart pounded loudly in her ears, her eyes blurring from the throbbing in her head. She tried to break free. Struggling against the hard body, she kicked her legs, which connected with the hallway table and sent the glass vase tumbling to the carpeted floor.

"Stop fighting me," he said in a low rumble, his voice deep and his heated breath brushing against the back of her neck. The front of his body rubbing against her butt sent a different type of fear through her. *God, please don't let him rape me.* A whimper escaped her lips and she fought to get free, but his grip grew tighter around her waist. "Damn you feel good. It's no wonder that boyfriend of yours is so protective."

Her heart thumped violently inside her chest. She wanted to scream for Malik, but the hand covering her mouth was too tight; she could barely breathe.

"I have a message for you, love." Despite her struggling against him, he dragged her backwards down the hall and around the corner toward the kitchen. "Tell your boyfriend to stop asking questions, otherwise he's going to be sorry. Now nod if you understand."

She gave a jerky nod, her head feeling as if an explosion had gone off inside of it, her eyes blurred by tears.

"If he doesn't back off he'll be a witness ... to your death. And then I'll kill him."

"No, please ... don't hurt him," she said against his hand, her words sounding like gibberish as she kicked her legs frantically to get free. "Please ..." Tears filled her eyes and tumbled down her cheeks, her sobs growing louder.

"Shut up!" he growled in her ear, the hand he had over her mouth gripping her face harder.

A beeping sound came from the alarm keypad near the back door and her assailant jerked toward it.

"Times up." He dragged her closer to the back door and Natasha dug her heels into the floor, fighting to keep him from taking her out of the house. "Stop fighting me!" He lifted her effortlessly, carrying her to the back door, but stopped at the edge of her kitchen counter. "Remember what I said. Get your boyfriend to back off. And so that he knows that I'm serious ..."

He released her suddenly, and Natasha's only thought was to run. Before she could take a step forward, a searing pain ripped through the back of her skull, raced down her spine, and left her immobile. Her knees buckled as a deep black cloud settled, spinning her in slow motion into a bottomless abyss.

"Sheldon agreed to meet with us in the morning," Wiz said.

"Good. I think it's time for us to compare notes. I don't ..." Malik's other line beeped. "Wiz, that's my other line, hold on a sec."

"Actually, I have to get going. Hit me up later or I'll see you tomorrow."

Malik clicked over. "Yeah."

"Malik, something's going on at Natasha's house," Victoria said.

"Something like what?" He glanced at the house, surprised to see it was still dark.

"Reuben set up the system for her to get in and out of the house with a handheld. About twenty minutes ago, the keypad near the back door was deactivated. About ten minutes ago, the system shows that the handheld was used and someone entered through the front door. It might be nothing, but ..."

Malik tuned out the rest of her words. He had specifically chosen the system Natasha had because of its ninety-nine percent fail proof rating. To date, Quinn had been the only person to penetrate the state-of-the-art circuitry.

Malik's chest tightened. There was no way someone had hacked her security system, but the slight prickling at the back of his neck told him otherwise. His eyes zoned in on the house and he reached for his 9mm Glock in the glove box.

"Vicky, let me call you back."

Seconds later, Malik nudged the front door. It opened

easily. He stepped into the semi-dark entrance, a sliver of moon-light shining through the window blinds. His eyes eventually adjusted and he gave the room a once over before easing farther into the space.

He listened, only hearing the ticking of a clock in the distance and a soft beeping coming from the back of the house, the kitchen. Other than that, it was quiet. Too damn quiet.

Malik tried to control the erratic beating of his heart as he silently went from room to room, but with every minute that ticked by the feeling of dread intensified. He turned the corner that led to the kitchen and eased toward the opened back door, adrenaline racing through his veins. There was no way Natasha would leave the house without letting him know. When he reached the end of her center island, his heart stuttered. Panic spread throughout his body and came to rest in the pit of his stomach.

"Tasha." Her name came out in a whisper, but inside he was screaming her name at the top of his lungs. He collapsed at the side of her body, her face against the travertine tile. "Tasha. Oh God. Tasha!" Gently pushing her hair away from her face, he saw the blood. Terror gripped him and a throbbing knot formed in his gut. He checked for a pulse. With shaking hands, he pulled his iPhone from his pocket and his trembling fingers dialed.

"911, what is your emergency?"

"I need ... I need an ambulance."

Chapter Nineteen

"They're not going to let you back into the hospital until you calm the hell down!" Wiz yelled. "You shouting, threatening the doctors and the nurses is not going to get you anywhere. I get that you're mad, but don't you want to be in there when Natasha wakes up?"

Malik didn't bother responding. Like a caged animal, he paced back and forth outside of the hospital's entrance. The waiting was killing him. Two hours and they still hadn't told him anything about Natasha's condition. He had to admit, now that he was out in the night air, he at least felt like he could breathe. Whereas moments ago, the walls were closing in around him. He ran his hand over his head, his gut twisting in agony.

"I talked with her friend Layla." Wiz leaned against a concrete block separating the hospital from the parking lot. "The moment she knows anything, she'll come out *here* and get you. But, man, you were like ... like crazy waiting to happen in there! I don't know if I have ever seen you this out of control. And mind you I've seen you at your worst."

"Wiz, I should have been in that house with her. I should

have been there, dammit!" Malik wanted to hit something or somebody. The rage roaring through his body was about ready to explode, and Lord help the person in his way when it did. "I fucked up. I can't believe—"

"Tree, you're going to have to stop blaming yourself. There's no way you could have known that someone was in that house. Instead of you beating yourself up, save it for the bastard who did this."

"Yeah, this shit just got personal."

Wiz stood and stuffed his hands into his pockets. "That leads me to the other reason we're out here. It's time we got to the bottom of whatever the hell is going on, and end it."

Wiz's tone held Malik's attention. The wicked I'm-going-to-fuck-you-up tone that he only used when anger was brewing inside him. The tone he only used when he was staring down an enemy, and the tone he only used when he was ready to fight.

"I'm listening."

"Between the information I dug up and the ramblings from our boy Street, I found Alonso Black, a.k.a Lawyer Man. The mastermind behind My Child Adoption Agency. With the help of your woman, we're going to find the missing babies. Then, we're going to make *Lawyer Man* pay for the lives he's ruined."

"For what Natasha has been through these last few weeks, I will do anything I have to do to make the person responsible … pay."

"So I guess it finally happened."

"What?" Malik asked.

"You fell in love."

Malik lifted his hands to the top of his head and released an exhausted breath. He wasn't going to deny it … hell, he couldn't. "I don't know how or when. All I know is that when I saw her lying on that floor unconscious … I couldn't breathe. It was as if something huge was standing on my chest, squeezing my heart."

He lowered his arms and bent at the waist, his hands on his knees as that suffocating feeling draped over him again. "I *cannot* lose her." Seconds passed. Malik stood upright, finally able to catch his breath. He swiped at his eyes, forcing himself to breathe in ... and out. In ... and out.

"Well ... *damn*." Wiz stood near him, wonder covering his features. "I never thought I'd see the day."

They turned to see Layla running out of the building. "You need to get in here quick. Natasha's awake and she's pitching a fit, asking for you." Malik and Wiz rushed behind her into the hospital.

They turned a corner and traveled down another long hallway.

"Natasha has a concussion," Layla finally said. "When you see her, don't freak out. The side of her head looks worse than it is. Thankfully, she has no broken bones and no internal bleeding. The nasty gash in the back of her head is going to take some time to heal, though."

Malik heard what she said, but the overwhelming need to see Natasha, to be near her, was drowning out Layla's words.

His steps slowed as they approached a door where Stan was standing guard. However, what snatched his attention were the sobs filtering into the hallway. Natasha's sobs.

"What the hell!" he roared, ready to knock the door down if he had to. "What are they doing to her?"

Wiz and Layla grabbed hold of him before he could plow through the door.

"Hold up, man. You can't go in there like this," Wiz said.

"He's right. If you're calm, she'll calm down," Layla added. "And if you can't get her to relax, we're going to have to sedate her. Natasha hates taking medication. Actually, considering she's been out of control since she opened her eyes, they've probably already given her something."

Malik drew in a slow breath, trying to release some of the tension battling inside him. It wasn't working. Nothing was going to help until he saw Natasha with his own eyes.

"You guys can release me now," he said in a low grumble. "I just need to see her."

"One more thing," Layla said, still holding on to his arm and trying to pull him closer. He met her eyes and they stepped away from the door. "Malik, whoever did this scared her pretty bad. She's terrified that someone is trying to kill you."

"Where is he?" Natasha cried. The blood pressure machine beeped like crazy. Her head felt so heavy, as if it would roll off her shoulders and crash to the floor. She never had a migraine that hurt this much. "P–please, I need to ... to see him." She wanted to scream the words, but they barely came out.

"Dr. Lockham, you have to calm down. He's here, we're trying to locate him," the attending nurse said, speaking softly and trying to keep Natasha from climbing out of bed.

I'll kill him. The words of her assailant rang loudly inside her head. She had to see Malik, had to make sure he was okay. It was all her fault someone was after him. All he was trying to do was find the babies and get answers regarding Halsey's death ... for her.

The door crashed open, and though her eyesight was a little blurry, she knew it was him. "Malik." Tears of pain and relief worked their way down her cheeks. Sobs gripped her body and her shoulders shook uncontrollably. Her whole body ached, but as long as he was there, as long as he was alive, she knew she'd be okay.

He stood at the foot of the bed for the longest time. Through the tears and the throbbing in her head, she noticed the worry lines etched across his forehead and his clenched jaw, a sure sign that he was trying to control his emotions.

She tried to sit up, but she couldn't. The frustration ignited more tears. "I can't—" she cried, and as if suddenly being shaken out of his trance, Malik hurried to the side of the bed.

"Hey baby." Malik cupped her cheek and kissed her lips. "I know they say doctors make the worst patients, but damn, girl, you might be taking it to the extremes. Relax. I'm right here and I'm not going anywhere."

She would've laughed, but she didn't have the energy. She had to tell him what her attacker said. "Malik," she murmured, struggling to speak.

"Shh, I'm right here. Don't try to talk. Get some rest."

"He ... he's going to kill me ... you." Her eyes drifted closed and she fought against the darkness trying to consume her. "You have ... to stop. No more ... questions."

A short while later, Malik slowly processed Natasha's words. Someone wanted them to stop asking questions about the adoption agency. Meaning Malik was getting close to the truth.

Layla walked back into Natasha's room. "She finally settled down?"

Malik didn't answer.

Layla checked the monitors near the bed, now beeping at a balanced rhythm; a nice change from when he had first walked in. Being near her, watching the steady rise and fall of her chest, the peacefulness on her face, was all that mattered to him at the moment.

"I can tell you really care for her," Layla said, standing next to him, both of them staring down at a sleeping Natasha.

"I would give my life for her," he heard himself say. Aside from his mother, he had never spoken those words, or felt that way about another woman. And there had never been a woman who totally consumed his heart.

"She deserves some happiness. I have a feeling you both do." Layla touched his arm and left the room.

Malik pulled the chair that was sitting near the window closer to the bed. He wasn't sure how long they planned to keep Natasha in the hospital, but he had every intention of being there as long as she was there.

He sat in the chair and reached for her hand, squeezing it gently. "I'm going to get whoever did this to you," he whispered, kissing the inside of her wrist. "They will pay."

Malik, slumped forward in his seat, rested his forehead on the bed and closed his eyes, still caressing Natasha's hand. *If only I hadn't let you go into the house alone.* He would never forgive himself for not being there for her.

Malik lifted his head when he heard a soft knock and the door swung open. Wiz walked in.

"How is she?"

Malik sat back in his seat, stretched his arms to the ceiling, and yawned. He'd been up almost twenty-four hours with no foreseeable sleep in the near future.

"I still haven't seen the doctor, but based on what Layla told us, she's going to be fine."

"Were you able to talk to her, ask her any questions about the attack?" Wiz leaned on the narrow, rolling table at the foot of the bed, looking as tired as Malik felt.

"She said someone is going to kill her and me if I keep asking questions."

Wiz stood up straight. "Hmm, I guess we've rattled some-body's cage."

"I didn't get a chance to ask you earlier, but did you or Sheldon find anything at the house? Fingerprints? Anything?"

Malik rubbed his hand over his head, exhaustion slowly settling in.

"We're thinking that the perp hadn't planned on being in the house when Natasha arrived home."

Malik tilted his head. "Why do you say that?"

"There were messages for her on both bathroom mirrors."

Malik's body stiffened. "What type of messages?"

"Pretty much the same thing she said." Wiz moved over to the window and stared out into the darkness. "You either back off or she dies. You both die."

Malik gripped the arms of the chair, his teeth clenched in an effort to remain calm. "You already know I'm not backing off, and whether Natasha likes it or not, she's going to have around the clock protection. We are going to find this asshole and whoever else is involved, and make them pay."

"We need to talk about the next steps regarding Lawyer Man, but are you sure you want to have this conversation in here?" They both looked at Natasha.

"I can't leave her, man. I don't know how to explain it, but I need to be wherever she is."

"You don't have to explain it to me. I'd feel the same way if Olivia was the one lying in that bed. Grab that chair."

He pointed to the seat Malik had just vacated and they went to the small round table in the corner of the room. Malik assumed being chief of staff had its perks, considering the room was almost twice the size of a regular hospital room. The soft butter color on the walls and the tranquil landscape paintings strategically placed around the space made it one of the better hospital rooms he'd ever been in.

"I have a plan, but to get things started, we're going to need your protégé, Travis."

"Travis?" Malik cast a doubtful look at his friend. Travis was a sharp kid, but the operative word was kid. "Why? No, hold up.

I have him watching Street. You're going to have to use someone else."

"When you hear what I have to say, you won't mind that I already had Stan pull Travis off that assignment, and replaced him with someone else."

Malik folded his arms across his chest. He trusted Wiz with his life and knew that if he made changes at Supreme Security without letting him know, he had to have a good reason. The team knew that Wiz, Victoria, or Stan were the go-to people if ever he wasn't around.

"So what's your plan for Travis?" he finally asked.

"Lawyer Man, Alonso Black, is one of the partners at Kent, Schuster & Black. When I looked into the law office as a whole, it checked out fine. No illegal dealings from what I could tell. So I did a little digging. What I found on Black is going to trip you out."

Malik leaned forward, his elbows on the table. No matter how often he worked with Wiz, his ability to dig up a person's deepest secrets never ceased to amaze him.

"He's a widow. His wife died years ago and Black was devastated. From what I understand, he worshiped this woman who was ten years his junior." Wiz stretched his long legs, ran his hand over his low cut hair, and sighed. "Now ask me how she died."

"Man, just tell me."

"Giving birth. She died giving birth."

Malik's mouth gaped open. "Get the hell outta here."

Wiz nodded. "I'm not kiddin'. They had a daughter. Rumor has it that Black gave the baby up for adoption when he found out his wife cheated on him. The baby wasn't his, and supposedly, it was never determined who the baby's father was."

"Oh damn," Malik murmured, shaking his head. He couldn't imagine that type of hurt, betrayal.

"I couldn't find any record of the kid or the adoption. Though I have found information that leads me to believe the underground adoption agency kicked off around that same time."

"We still need proof that he's behind this baby stealing operation."

"That's where Travis comes in at." Wiz leaned forward. "Stan was right about him. He does remind me of you about fifteen years ago."

Malik wasn't in the mood. Almost daily one of his people said something along the same line. He himself had already agreed that there were some similarities.

"He has a way with women."

Malik narrowed his eyes and frowned. "What does that have to do with Black?"

Wiz grinned, which was something he didn't do too often. Between the two of them, Wiz was the nice one, yet more intense and slower to smile.

"Black has been ill for the last few months and spends most of his time on his estate in Schaumburg. He happens to have a *hot* live-in personal assistant who is around Travis's age."

Wiz laid out his plan to have Travis get friendly with the assistant, while obtaining information. All they needed to know was where Black kept his files.

Malik shook his head and chuckled. He'd seen Travis in action a few months ago when he took him to Vegas on a case. Based on what Malik witnessed from his protégé, Wiz's plan might actually work.

"How much does Travis know?"

"Only what he needs to." Wiz stood and stretched. "I have some other things in the works, but I assure you, we're getting close to all the answers."

"Good, because I'm not going to rest until someone pays for what they've done."

Natasha squinted against the stream of light shining through the window. It felt like she'd been laid up for days when in actuality it had only been hours, or at least she thought it had only been hours.

Her gaze slid to Malik, who was sitting in the chair next to the bed. His head rested on her mattress, his light snoring filling the otherwise quiet in the room. She wondered why he'd slept in the chair when someone had brought in a cot for him, or at least it looked like a cot. Still battling with blurriness, she wasn't positive.

Natasha lifted her hand to touch Malik, needing to feel him, wanting to kiss him. Her hand stopped mid-air, remembering the night he pulled a gun on her. Now she could smile at the memory, whereas then, he'd scared her half to death.

She laid her hand on his baldhead, caressing the smoothness of his skin. She loved him so much it felt as if her heart would explode inside of her chest.

He moaned and then jerked awake, grabbing her hand with the speed of light. She gasped. Optimal reflexes probably were a requirement for being a SEAL, but he always caught her off guard.

The corners of his lips lifted, revealing the sexy grin that always turned her on, and he kissed the back of her hand.

"Hey," he murmured, his sleep-filled voice sounding sexy, his intensely dark eyes appearing exhausted. He stood and his lips pressed against hers, gently covering her mouth. After thoroughly greeting her with a kiss, he lifted his head.

"Hi," she said on a sigh. There was a time she would've been hesitant to kiss him before brushing her teeth, but now all she wanted to do was to taste those sweet lips of his. "You didn't have to spend the night."

"Yeah, actually I did," he kissed her again, "because you're here."

When he said things like that, a warmth flowed through her body and straight to her heart. He always came across so rough and tough, but he was the sweetest, gentlest man she'd ever met.

He stood and lifted his long arms above his head, his muscles bulging with each move. He leaned against the side of the bed, his hand cupping her cheek. "How do you feel?"

She felt like she'd been run down by a truck and dragged a block, but instead of telling him that, she said, "I'm all right. Maybe I'll be able to leave today." She squinted up at him, the ache in her head growing stronger by the minute.

He shook his head. "No, you're not. Your doctor wants to keep you under observation for another day. And though I would love to take you home ... with me, I have to agree with him." His fingers caressed her cheeks and kissed her forehead. "I will never forgive myself for letting you go into the house alone."

"Malik, it's not your fault." She curled up on her side and reached for his hand, holding it close to her chest. Having him near relaxed her, similar to cuddling up with a teddy bear. She could tell by the unconvinced expression on his face that no matter what she said, he'd still blame himself.

"What happened when you went into the house?"

Natasha told him how the lights wouldn't work, and her surprise at the bathroom door being closed. The more she talked, the more intense he became, anger bouncing off of him in waves.

"He shoved me into the wall and before I could react he ... he ..." She swallowed, remembering how he'd rubbed up against her backside, his erection evident.

"He what?" Malik growled. The low guttural noise sounded

more like an animal in wait than the gentle giant she'd fallen in love with. "What the fuck did he do?"

She glared at him, giving him one of the looks her mother used to give them when they had done something she didn't approve of. "Don't curse at me."

He withdrew from her grasp and backed away from the bed, running his hand over his head.

"I'm sorry, but every time I think about you in there alone with some fu—" He stopped and slowly released a breath. "Finish telling me."

"Not if it's going to make you upset."

"Natasha ... please. I have to know what happened."

She closed her eyes against the sudden queasiness attacking her body. "He dragged me into the kitchen." Her still-closed eyes fought her increasing discomfort. "He said he would kill me, and then he'd kill you if you didn't stop asking questions."

Too tired to reopen her eyes, she could hear Malik pacing next to the bed. She didn't want him to blame himself, and she also wanted him to stop with his investigation.

"I don't feel so good."

He bent down next to the bed and brushed her hair away from her face. "Why don't you try to get some rest?"

The tenderness of his touch near her ear made her close her eyes. If he were trying to put her back to sleep, it was working, but she didn't want to go to sleep yet.

"Baby, you need your rest. Why are you fighting sleep?" he asked when she reopened her eyes. "It's clear that you're tired. Besides, the doctor said that you need mental and physical rest. So close those beautiful brown eyes and get some sleep."

"I want you and Wiz to drop your investigation," she said softly, ignoring his comment. "Finding answers regarding the missing babies and Dr. Halsey's death is the hospital's responsibility. Let our team continue with their own investigation."

She thought he would explode or release a string of curse words, but he didn't. Instead, he just stared at her, still caressing her cheek.

"When you were attacked last night, this turned personal." His baritone voice held an edge she hadn't heard before. She didn't want him in danger, but she had a feeling that he wouldn't be the one hurt.

"You're not at war in some mid-eastern country. We're in Chicago. Going vigilante on someone or people can get you put in jail, or worse ... the morgue. I couldn't handle either of those scenarios. I don't," a sharp pain stabbed through her head, "I don't ... want to live without you." Natasha slammed her eyes shut, her hands fisting the sheets at her side as she tried to control the pounding in her head.

"Natasha. Tasha?"

Malik called her name several times, but the pain was too great. She couldn't respond. Instead of pushing the button for the nurse, Natasha felt him leave her side and then heard him go out into the hallway.

It was taking everything she had not to cry out. Tears welled up behind her eyelids and slowly slid down her cheeks. Bile rose to her throat and she found her voice.

"Malik." The words came out in a ragged whisper. "Oh God, I'm going to be sick." Her voice was so low she could barely hear herself.

"I'm right here." He miraculously appeared with an emesis basin in his hand.

"Mal—" She grabbed her mid-section and gagged, quickly turning to the side to empty her stomach. She moaned, feeling as if she was upchucking all of her insides, her head too heavy to hold up.

Malik handed her some tissue just as the nurse rushed in.

Natasha heard them talking, but it seemed their voices were getting further and further away.

"We're going to have to hook her up to an IV. She's lost too much fluid in the past four hours. I don't want to risk her getting dehydrated."

"Is she going to be okay?" Natasha heard Malik ask before she slowly slipped back into darkness.

Chapter Twenty

Malik sat in the same chair that he'd fallen asleep in, still keeping vigil over Natasha. He wanted nothing more than for her to get the rest she needed, but it didn't seem as if she were getting any better. She was hooked up to an IV and hadn't thrown up in the past few hours, but she still looked pale. The dreams, or maybe nightmares, had her jerking and whimpering in her sleep. It was killing him seeing her like this.

He stood when someone knocked on the door and it slid opened. "Can I come in?" Wiz asked.

Malik waved him in. Natasha was jerking in her sleep, mumbling something he couldn't understand, and just when he started to wake her, she stopped. He hoped she wasn't reliving the attack because every time he imagined what she must've gone through, his stomach clenched into a tight knot.

"How she doing?"

"About the same," Malik replied, noticing the bags in his friend's hands. He had asked Wiz to swing by his house and pick up a few items. It also looked as if he'd brought something from the bakery up the street, as well as coffee.

"You look like shit," Wiz said, handing Malik the overnight bag.

"Thanks. I feel like shit." Malik carried his overnight bag into the attached bathroom to freshen up and change. Fifteen minutes later, he walked out feeling better.

"By the way, Vicky has Tank and she said to not worry about the office. Everything is under control."

"That's good to hear. I'll give her a call a little later."

"Oh, and before I forget. Remember that guy you asked me to look in to, Ray Newton?"

Malik had just lifted his cup of coffee to his lips, but set it down. "Yeah, what about him?"

"Who is he?"

"What do you mean who is he? He's the person I wanted you to do some research on. He works here at the hospital and he's been hanging around Natasha a little more than I'd prefer. Besides that, there's something about him that doesn't sit right with me." Wiz looked at him strangely. "What?"

"I did some preliminary research on him, and it's as if the guy doesn't exist. I found a driver's license for him, but nothing else."

"Nothing?"

Wiz shook his head. "My first thought was that maybe he was a part of witness protection, but even then I'd be able to find a social security number, birth certificate, something."

Malik took a sip of the steaming hot coffee, tossing different scenarios around in his head of why nothing came up for Ray. Even when Wiz did preliminary searches, he always came back with some information. This news only made Malik more suspicious of the guy.

"Get off of me!" someone yelled on the other side of the door.

"What the ..." Malik looked over at Natasha, glad to see whoever was in the hallway pitching a fit hadn't awakened her.

He and Wiz hurried out of the room to find Stan holding Martin by his lapels up against the wall.

"Get off me. Let me go!" Martin yelled, fighting against Stan who happened to be fifty pounds heavier and towered over Martin by at least six inches.

Two nurses along with security headed in their direction.

"You handle this and I'll take care of them," Wiz said of the nurses and hospital security.

"Stan, let him go," Malik instructed. "Lockham, why are you here?"

Martin shook out of Stan's grasp. "I want to see her." He charged toward Natasha's door, but Malik blocked his way. "I'm not leaving until I see Tasha and you have no right to keep me away from her!"

"Oh, I have every right." Malik's voice was low and menacing as he felt his patience slipping. "You're not going anywhere near her unless I decide—"

"I'm sick of this crap!" Martin jabbed his finger at Malik. "First your guy yesterday, and now you ... no, I'm not putting up with this."

"Hold up. What guy from yesterday?" Malik asked.

"Oh don't play dumb with me," Martin huffed, putting his hands on his waist as he paced in front of Malik, who was still blocking Natasha's door. "The man you had working at her house yesterday. I went over, expecting Natasha to be there, and—"

"Wait. You saw someone at her house yesterday?" Malik signaled for Wiz to come over.

"Yeah, he was working on her alarm system. Told me that if I didn't leave her alone, he'd put a bullet in my head. So is that what you promote at your company? Violence?"

Malik scrubbed his hand down his face, grateful there was a witness to what the guy looked like, yet a little pissed that they didn't know about this yesterday.

"He wasn't one of my guys. He might've been the man who attacked Natasha last night."

"What?"

Malik gave him a condensed version of the night before, thinking Martin might be their only lead in catching the guy.

"Would you be willing to talk to the police and work with a sketch artist, describing to them the man you saw?" Wiz asked.

"Of course, but ... I need to know, how is she?"

"She's banged up a little, but they say she's going to be fine."

"I'd like to see her." Malik started to speak, but stopped when Martin lifted his hand. "She's made it very clear that she and I are over, but I'm not going to lie to you. I still care about her. I just want to see that she's okay and to make things right between her and I. If you let me talk to her, I promise neither of you will hear from me again."

Malik studied the man who had once been the divide between him getting to know Natasha. He had to admit that if he were in Martin's shoes, he'd probably be the same way—not wanting to let her go.

Malik and Natasha rode in the back of a town car as Stan maneuvered through the streets of Evanston, Illinois, where Malik lived. Malik felt as if he hadn't been home in weeks, versus the two days spent in the hospital with Natasha.

He kissed the top of Natasha's head, which was resting against his chest.

She snuggled closer, and her arms tightened around his waist. "Why are you so tense?" She raised her gaze to meet his.

Her eyes still weren't as bright as usual, but he did see a little color returning to her cheeks.

"I thought you were asleep." He ran his hand up and down the side of her body, glad to have her in his arms again.

"I think I dozed off for a minute, but the anxiety bouncing off of you is making me a little uneasy. What's on your mind?"

Retaliation was on his mind. For the last couple of days, all he could think about was finding the person who put her in the hospital and beating the hell out of him. However, he wouldn't tell her that. He also had no intention of telling her that before the night was over, Alonso Black was going to regret the day he decided to kill innocent women and sell their babies.

"Well?" Natasha straightened and pulled away from him.

"I have a lot on my mind and some things to work out."

They drove into the garage. The moment felt like déjà vu to Malik. He couldn't help remembering the first time he'd brought Natasha to his home. Like then, he felt as if he had failed her. Each incident could've been prevented.

Stan opened the back door. "Thanks, man, we'll meet you inside," Malik said before turning to Natasha. "Do you need me to carry you?"

Her head rested against the backseat. Although she smiled at him, her drooping eyes showed her exhaustion, a clear sign that she still wasn't a hundred percent. "I'm starting to think that you just like carrying me around." She grabbed hold of his hand, but didn't make a move to leave the car.

"I do, but you don't seem to like it."

"It's not that I don't like being carried, it's just that I don't want to feel so needy and helpless."

"Baby, nobody would ever accuse you of being needy and helpless. Besides I like it when you need me." And he did. She didn't ask much of him, but when she did, he'd stick his chest out feeling good that he could make his woman happy. He'd never wanted to do for a woman as much as he wanted to do for Natasha, and couldn't explain the overwhelming desire to protect and care for her. Sure, he might've been a little possessive at times, but only because she meant the world to him.

She leaned forward in the seat and squeezed his hand. "Okay ... will you carry me?" she asked quietly and looked up at him with shy eyes. "Not because I need you to, but because I love it when you carry me."

He kissed her and lifted her carefully in his arms. In only two days, she felt as if she'd lost weight, and as far as he was concerned, he preferred her with a little meat on her bones.

He carried her into the house, Tank tight on his heels, and headed for the stairs. She stopped him before he hit the first step.

"I've been cooped up in a hospital for two days. I'd prefer to stay down here in the family room for a while."

The moment he set her on the sofa, Tank was right by her side, excited to see her.

"Hey boy," Natasha cooed, hugging the big dog, his drool catching the side of her face. "I've missed you too." Malik was surprised at how quickly the two had bonded, and since he planned on never letting her go, it was a good thing.

Malik rubbed the dog's strong back and didn't feel slighted that Tank was showering all of his attention on Natasha.

"All right, Tank, look after her," he said and Tank barked as if he understood. To Natasha Malik said, "I'll be downstairs if you need me." He was about to walk away when she grabbed hold of his hand.

"Are you sure you don't want to talk about what's bothering you?"

He kissed her lips. "Not right now, but maybe later." Right now he needed a release, and since sex was out of the question, he headed to his workout room.

"When Wiz gets here, let him know I'm in the dungeon," Malik said to Stan, who was sitting at the kitchen counter eating.

"Will do."

Stick and move. Stick and move, Malik chanted an hour later as he threw punch after punch at the boxing bag hanging in his workout room. Sweat dripped from his body like perspiration on a cold beer bottle. He shuffled his feet, landing a straight right, then an uppercut with his left. *Stick and move. Stick and move.*

"You gon' stay down here and continue beating the hell out that bag or are you ready to expend some of that energy beating the hell out of Alonso Black? Or as Street insists on calling him, Lawyer Man?"

Malik stopped and wrapped his arms around the bag, partly to stop it from moving and partly to help him catch his breath. "Just say when. I still have a lot of pent-up energy to get rid of." According to the clock on the wall, he'd been in the basement for over an hour. With every punch to the boxing bag, came more thoughts and concerns about the case, Natasha's safety, and their relationship.

"Your woman is worried about you. Should she be?"

Malik grabbed the towel that he had tossed on a nearby weight bench and wiped his face. "I'm good." Dropping the towel, he slipped into a black T-shirt.

"Are you? Because you don't look like you're good."

"Wiz, don't start this shit." Malik pulled a bottle of water from the refrigerator behind the bar in the game room. "Just let me know what time to be ready to pay Black a visit."

Wiz sat on one of the barstools and opened a file. "Your guys didn't find anything on his underground operation when they dropped by his downtown Chicago penthouse. I'm thinking he keeps everything at his estate outside of Schaumburg." They looked over the home's blueprints and discussed how many people they'd need to infiltrate the property. "I'm thinking we go in tonight."

"Tonight, huh?" Schaumburg was only forty-five minutes from Malik's home in Evanston, but he didn't like the idea of leaving Natasha so soon after her release from the hospital.

"I'm not sure when we'll get another chance, but if you'd prefer, Stan and I can oversee everything. I also thought about letting Sheldon know what we've found—"

"No. Don't tell Sheldon yet. He'll be pissed, but I want to pay *Lawyer Man* a visit first. Not only for what he did to Susan, but I need to know who his enforcer is. If Sheldon and his men get to Black first, they may screw things up and this enforcer guy might disappear. Assuming he hasn't already."

Wiz closed the file and scratched his head. "We initially started all of this to get answers about Susan and the baby. Yet this case has clearly evolved to more than I think either of us expected. Maybe you should tell me what you have in mind for Black. Just so I'll know whether I need to remind you of what country we're in. That mess with Quinn and Alandra a few months ago could have put all of our asses in jail. I don't want a repeat. I promised Olivia a drama free life going forward and I intend to make good on my promise."

Malik hadn't made those types of promises, but now that Natasha was in his life, it was probably time for him to make some changes. Especially if he wanted to keep her in his life.

"Malik?"

Malik's head shot up at the sound of Natasha's voice. And as usual, his body reacted immediately to the sight of her. Even with the sexy bed-head thing going on, black yoga pants, and an old fitted T-shirt, he was still drawn to her. She stood at the bottom of the steps, looking unsure whether or not she'd be welcome down in his dungeon. And of course, Tank was right by her side.

"Hey baby." He placed his water bottle down and went to her. "You probably should have some shoes on down here," he said. "This floor is too cold to walk around barefoot."

"Oh." She glanced down. "Well, when you come upstairs, can we talk?"

"Actually, feel free to talk now. I'm outta here," Wiz said, grabbing the folder and tucking it under his arm. "Tree, I'll work out the details and hit you up later. Tasha, sweetheart," he kissed her on the cheek, "I hope you're feeling better soon."

"Thanks, Cameron."

After Wiz left the basement, Malik swooped Natasha into his arms. "Before you say anything, I'm carrying you so that you don't have to walk on this cold floor." He carried her to the other side of the basement to his media room. He sat in one of the leather recliners and held her on his lap. "Are you feeling okay? You still look a little tired."

She gave a slight shrug. "I feel all right." She snuggled against him. "I wasn't sure when you were coming back upstairs, so I figured I'd come down for a minute. I hope you don't mind."

"Of course I don't mind." He nuzzled her neck, enjoying the way she squirmed against him. "You're sitting on my lap. Can't you tell how happy I am to see you?" he asked close to her ear, moving his hips beneath her.

She laughed and wrapped one of her arms around his neck. "Yeah, I thought something was going on down there." She sighed and turned serious. "Malik, I want to know what's bothering you. I felt the change in your mood yesterday morning and I can't help but wonder if it has something to do with me. Does it bother you that I'm staying here for a while?"

Malik's brows drew together. "No, not at all. Why would you even say that?"

"Because I feel as if you've been avoiding me."

Malik laid his head back against the seat and pinched the bridge of his nose. These types of conversations were why he didn't do relationships. Women always wanted to talk. Always wanted to know what you were thinking. He wasn't a big talker, and he sure as hell didn't want to share his thoughts. But then Natasha laid her head against his chest, her small hand caressing his torso, stoking the sensual flames already stirring inside him.

This is how they get you.

"There's something I need to tell you." He felt her stiffen in his arms, but Wiz was right the other week when he said that if Natasha meant anything to Malik, he needed to be straight with her.

"The friend I told you about, Susan, one of Halsey's victims, claimed that I'm the father of her child."

"What?" Natasha tried to pull away, but he wouldn't let her. Instead, he told her about his visit from Rosalyn the day he had showed up at the hospital. He also told her about Rosalyn's insistence that he was the father of Susan's baby.

"So you have a baby out there?" This time when she tried to get up, he helped her stand. She had wanted to know what was on his mind, but had no idea that he would tell her something like this. "I knew there had to be another reason you were so invested in this case." She suddenly felt more tired than she had only moments ago. With the ache in her head and the weariness flowing through her body, instead of looking for him in the basement, she should have opted for taking a nap.

Malik walked up behind her. When he wrapped his arms around her waist, and pulled her against his body, she didn't pull away.

"The baby is not mine."

She turned in his arms. "How can you be so sure?"

"This is not a conversation I ever thought I'd have with a woman, especially you, but I don't want any secrets between us." His large hands slid up and down her back. It was as if he had the magic touch, knowing how to relax her. She leaned into him, appreciating his strength in holding her up. "For one, I haven't had any slip-ups. Susan and I had a casual relationship, nothing serious."

"Malik!" She pushed away again. "That doesn't mean that you didn't make a baby with her." She spat the words. She didn't know why she was making such a big deal over the news. No, actually she did know why. She was in love with Malik and if anyone was going to have his baby, she wanted it to be her.

"You know what, Tasha?" Malik said in a low growl. "I didn't want to tell you about this. At least not until I knew for sure, but you wanted to know what was on my mind." He turned her around to face him. "So there you have it. Oh, and there's another reason why I don't believe the kid is mine." He was almost yelling. "I think Susan threw my name in the mix, thinking that if certain people knew I was the father of her unborn child, it would protect them both."

"What? Why?"

"Alonso Black, the lawyer behind the underground adoption agency, wanted her to give her child up for adoption. She knew he would go to great lengths to get her child."

"I don't understand. Why'd she give your name? Why not claim someone else as being the father? Why you?"

"Because I have a reputation of protecting what's mine ... by any means necessary."

Chapter Twenty-One

Malik, Wiz, and Travis drove through the plush neighborhood outside of Chicago, with its million dollar homes sitting on large lots, ready to take down Attorney Alonso Black. If it wasn't for the fact that Black had to be stopped, there was no way Malik would have left Natasha's side so soon after her release from the hospital. Even if she was a little pissed at him. Part of him was glad he'd told her about Susan's child, whereas the other part of him was thinking he should've waited.

They pulled onto Alonso Black's block and slowed. The grand estates stood out like twinkling stars against the black of night.

"We're going to need to get a little closer," Wiz said, punching something into his handheld. "The signal's not strong enough." Malik pulled the SUV over to the side of the road. Wiz was working his magic using an app that he'd created to jam the home's security system, including the cameras. With a thunderstorm rolling in, Black's team would assume it was bad weather effecting their system.

They all slipped on their gloves and double-checked their

communication system. Travis had reported that the lawyer had a security team of four people on site, one at the front gate, and three at the house. The house staff and Black's assistant had the evening off. By their calculation, the home invasion should go smooth.

Thunder rumbled and a light rain began to fall. It was early June, and already the average temperature of the season was seventy-nine degrees, and for the last couple of days it included rain.

"Okay, we're all set. Let's move," Wiz directed.

Travis exited the truck and headed to the gate to handle that guard. Malik and Wiz would take care of the others. Wiz would handle the guard at the rear of the house. Then he'd enter through the basement, find the alarm system's main control panel, and deactivate it indefinitely. He was also tasked with obtaining the file regarding the adoption agency.

Malik ran ahead. Easing up to the front of the house, he caught a guard from behind. Hitting him on the side of the head with the butt of his gun, the man fell with a solid thump like a tree cut down in the forest. He then took care of the guard who was smoking on the side of the house.

"Clear," Travis said in Malik's ear.

"Roger that."

"First floor is clear," Wiz announced. Malik ran to the side of the house where Wiz let him in through the sliding glass doors off the kitchen. Malik nodded and headed for the stairs. The adrenaline running through his veins reminded him of his military days, when he and his team invaded enemy camps. He blew out a breath to steady his pounding heart.

They had already agreed that Wiz would venture to Black's office and Malik would find Black himself. If their specs were correct, Black's bedroom was on the second floor at the end of the hall. Malik checked every room on the second floor, just in case. He saved Black's room for last.

"Wiz, I need a status," Malik said.

"No sign of Black below, but looks as if he's been doing some shredding. I'm downloading his hard drive and pulling files. We're right on schedule."

"Roger that."

Malik had already agreed that he wouldn't cause any physical harm to Black, unless he had to. Yet, he wanted to make sure Black knew who he was dealing with, and tonight would be his last night of freedom.

This is too easy, Malik thought as he eased around a corner and checked a bathroom on the second floor. He and Wiz hadn't expected to have much trouble getting in, but this was almost an uncomfortable easy. Either Black was arrogant enough to believe that no one would have the balls to infiltrate his property, or he wasn't as smart as Malik thought.

A crackle of lightning, followed by a roar of thunder, shook the house and snagged Malik's attention. He couldn't have asked for better weather. The energy in the air, mixed with the adrenaline rushing through his body, created a magnetic vitality that he couldn't explain.

"One of our sleepers is stirring," Travis's voice sounded in Malik's ear. "We're running out of time."

"Take care of it, Travis," Wiz said.

"Roger that."

Travis was right. They needed to hurry things along. Malik had left a sleeping Natasha with Stan a couple of hours ago, and had hoped to be back before she awakened. No chance of that since he'd gotten a text from Stan almost an hour ago saying that she was asking about his whereabouts.

A bolt of lightning shone through the tall hallway window, followed by another loud crash of thunder clapping overhead.

Malik had checked every room on that floor, including the elevator. The only one left was Black's suite. He leaned against the door, listening for any movement. When he didn't hear anything, he tried the doorknob, not surprised the door wasn't locked. *This is definitely too easy.* It was as if someone had been expecting them. But how?

Malik raised his gun and pushed the door open, hugging the side as he entered the semi-dark room. A quick scan just inside the bedroom revealed an unmade bed and a lamp on the side table emitting a small amount of light. Malik moved in farther. He knew someone was there, he could hear them breathing.

The bedroom was as big as the great room on the lower level and ...

"I had a feeling you'd be visiting soon," came a voice from the other side of the room. Malik aimed his gun, despite being barely able to make out the figure. However, with his training, he knew he could shoot him with his eyes closed.

"Malik Lewis," Black said as if they'd met before. The lawyer moved into the path of light, giving Malik a better view of him. "If you've made it upstairs to my suite that means you're as good as the rumors I've heard."

What surprised Malik more than anything was the man, the almighty Lawyer Man, was sitting in a wheelchair.

"She warned me that if I did anything to harm her, or your kid, that you would come after me." He shrugged. "I called her bluff, but here you are."

"So you're admitting to having Susan killed and stealing her baby?" Malik asked, repulsed by Black's arrogance and itching to pull the trigger.

"Yes. I'm admitting to having over a hundred and forty women killed in the last seven years, all over the country. And that includes my deceased wife. It's been a long run. I'm tired," Black said with little emotion. He adjusted the folded blanket across his lap, which is when Malik noticed that his left hand was deformed. It looked as if he'd been asleep; his scraggly gray hair was flattened on the right side and his pajamas were wrinkled. His startling gray eyes looked like glass marbles as he met Malik's gaze. "If you're going to shoot me, go ahead. The doctors are only giving me three months anyway."

"That would be too easy. I'd rather beat the hell out of you."

Black chuckled. "You wouldn't beat a man who's in a wheelchair, would you?"

"Well, if you don't think I will, you obviously haven't heard all of the rumors about me. I'm more than willing and able to take out anyone who murders innocent women and then steals their babies."

"I see." Black's right leg shook uncontrollably until the old man gripped his pajama-encased leg with his right hand.

"What I don't understand," Malik started, "is why'd you do it? Why did you have innocent women killed?"

"Why does anybody do anything? Money. Those women had something I wanted. When they didn't accept my generous financial offer, I figured I'd take what I wanted." He let out a rough, smoker's cough, before continuing. "Do you have any idea how much money I've made over the years selling babies?" He acted as though stealing babies was something to brag about.

"You sick bastard," Malik mumbled, unable to say more due to the way his stomach knotted in disgust.

"I also wanted revenge," Black continued as if Malik hadn't spoken. "I was robbed of a child that I wanted more than anything in this world. A child who had *my* blood pumping through their veins. That whoring wife of mine got knocked up. I wasn't raising someone else's bastard kid. The closer she got to her due date, the closer I got to laying out a plan for My Child Adoption Agency."

The longer Malik stood there, the madder he got. He

couldn't believe someone could live with themselves day after day doing what he had done.

"So go ahead and kill me." Black laid his wrinkled, pale hands on the arms of his chair, as if preparing to meet his maker. "I deserve to die and you're the best person for the job. It's perfect revenge, especially since I sold your son to the highest bidder."

Malik knew he was trying to goad him into shooting him, but he wasn't going to do it. He wasn't going to dirty his hands for this sick sonofabitch. "Nah, I'm going to let you go to jail. I'm sure when word gets out of what you've done, one of your cell-mates will probably take your ass out."

"Do it!" Black yelled. "Pull the damn trigger!" His pale skin now held a reddish tint to it.

"I have another question for you. Who is the Enforcer?"

Black laughed that same cough-infested chortle that came out more like a rumble. "Ah, yes, the Enforcer. He came to see me a few years back when he was dishonorably discharged from the military. All he knows is how to kill. In exchange for a new life, including a new identity and cash in his pocket, he takes care of those who get in my way." The smug look of satisfaction on his face only angered Malik more.

"Tree ... we have a problem," Wiz said through Malik's earpiece. "I know who took out Halsey, Tessa ... and the social worker."

There was a pause. Wiz pausing was a bad sign. A very bad sign. Either he was in trouble and couldn't speak, or the infor-mation to come was something Malik wasn't ready to hear.

"You were right. Ray Newton is not a records technician. His real name is Eric Van and he's our killer, and not just any killer. He's a former marine sniper."

Malik felt as if he'd been punched in the stomach. A rage so deep clutched his soul. It took every ounce of control he had not to pull the trigger on Black and end the life of this worthless piece of shit. *Black's enforcer was Ray.* The same man who had been alone with Natasha. The same man who had his hands on her. The same man who attacked her.

Malik cocked his gun. His internal battle was getting the best of him. Should he put a bullet in this guy's head the way Ray did to the doctor? Or should he let Black suffer in jail for the rest of his miserable life?

"Do it ... go ahead and do it!" Alonso Black taunted. "Shoot me!"

He could easily put a bullet between Black's eyes and not feel an ounce of remorse. But then he would be just like him and Ray Newton ... killers.

He lowered his gun and spoke into the small mic attached to his shirt. "Travis, in three minutes, make the call."

"Roger that, boss."

"Just pull the damn trigger!" Black yelled, his chair rocking from the force of his anger. "Do it!" He fell into a coughing fit, sounding as if he had been a three pack a day smoker and was about to cough up a lung.

Malik couldn't believe he was actually going to walk away from the opportunity to kill the sick bastard. Instead, he'd turn him over to the authorities.

"Where's Ray Newton?" Malik asked, his voice raspy with emotion.

Black glared at him, his eyes shone like crystal glass. "You want to know where Newton is?" he spat out. "I'll tell you where he is. He's probably wherever your woman is."

Malik's heart leapt into his throat and he bolted for the door. Tearing out of the room, he ran down the hall, but before he could make it to the stairs, he heard a single gunshot come from Alonso Black's bedroom.

Rest in hell.

Chapter Twenty-Two

"Are you going to tell me where Malik is?" Natasha asked Stan. She sat at the breakfast bar sipping a cup of tea as Stan watched her. "It's after ten o'clock at night and he hasn't called, nor is he answering his cell. That's not like him." This was her second time asking in the last three hours about Malik's whereabouts. Malik probably thought she was mad about his news, but she wasn't. Disappointed, yes. Mad, no.

"I'm sure he'll be back soon."

"That's what you said three hours ago." She had awakened from a nap to find Tank sleeping on the floor next to the bed and a note from Malik lying on the pillow next to her.

Have to take care of something. Be back soon. Love Malik.

Love. It was the first time he'd said anything about love, although he showed it in everything he did for her. In the way he treated her, his protectiveness, and even the way he looked at her.

She glanced at the clock on the microwave again. She knew he was doing something she wouldn't approve of. No doubt it had something to do with that underground adoption agency.

She should've known there was more to his covert investigation than he was letting on. The thought of him having a child out there was a little disappointing. Yet, the thought of his child being stolen and sold by some ruthless person was even more troubling. He insisted the child wasn't his, but Natasha knew there was a chance. A good chance.

"Do you know how to use a gun?" Stan asked out of the blue, still standing in the same spot near the door that led to the garage.

"I don't like guns, but Malik insisted on showing me the basic operation of his 9mm."

"You don't have to like them, but it's a good idea to know how to use one, just in case."

"Yeah, that's what he said." Natasha noticed that Stan kept peeking at his cell phone. Apparently, she wasn't the only one worried. Although Stan hid his concern well, he suddenly seemed on edge. "So where is this coming from? Why'd you ask me whether or not I knew how to use a gun?" He didn't answer right away, and Natasha knew for sure that something was wrong. "Should I be worried that I haven't heard from Malik? Has something happened to him and you're not telling me?" Her insides twisted in a knot.

Stan shook his head and pushed away from the wall. "No. No, nothing like that. I'm sure he's fine, but ..." The lights flickered and another boom of thunder erupted.

"You're scaring me, Stan." Trying to get information out of Malik was sometimes impossible, and now here she was going through the same thing with Stan. "Just be honest with me. For the last few hours, you've been hovering around me. I assume that's because of instructions from Malik. But in the last hour, I've noticed a shift in your behavior. You've checked the doors, the windows, and your cell phone several times. Tell me what's going on."

A slight smile tilted the corner of his lips. "You're very observant."

"More like paranoid from spending so much time with Malik."

"I guess I am, too," he chuckled. "He's always talking about these gut feelings he has. Quinn and Wiz used to be like that. Suddenly I'm having them as well."

Since the incident with Dr. Halsey, Natasha had started trusting Malik's gut feelings. "What is your gut telling you?"

"That we should head downstairs."

Natasha tilted her head. "Why? Besides the game room and weight room, what's downstairs?"

"I'm not sure if Malik showed you this." He went down a short hall toward the back of the house and Natasha followed, surprised at how large the basement actually was. "Malik has a storm shelter. Well, it's a little more than a storm shelter."

He opened the door and a light flickered on when they stepped inside the room. Water, canned goods, and a host of other survival items lined the walls. There were also spiders; Natasha hated spiders.

"You said that this is not just any storm shelter. What did you mean?"

They went a little deeper into the room, Stan knocking down cobwebs along the way. Tank stayed close to Natasha's side.

"This room leads to a tunnel that Malik had constructed a few years ago and goes almost to the end of his property line. It exits near the neighbor's yard, concealed by a couple of trees and bushes."

Natasha's nerves were getting the best of her. She didn't like tight spaces, but what bothered her more was that Stan was telling her about this secret hide out.

"Why are you showing me this?"

"Because if something should happen, you need to know it exists, and use it if you have to." He looked at her pointedly, and she suddenly felt like crying. Something was going on. "Let's turn back."

"Stan, you're really scaring me now." Prior to Dr. Halsey's murder, Natasha couldn't ever remember being afraid of anything. There were things that made her uncomfortable, like spiders and amusement park rides, but lately everything seemed to freak her out.

They re-entered the game room and Natasha felt like she could breathe again.

Tank trotted to the stairs and looked up, his low, rumbling growl catching her attention. She still hadn't learned all of his sounds, or signs, but she'd never heard him growl before.

Apparently, Stan had. "I need you to stay down here."

Natasha gasped when the lights went out.

"Stan ..."

"Natasha, give me your hand." She did as he said, and he guided her across the room. She didn't know what he was doing, but suddenly there were lights along the perimeter of the wall and near the stairs. That was when she noticed that Tank hadn't moved from the stairs, his growl deeper and more threatening.

"I need you to stay down here." Stan pulled a gun from the back of his waistband. Before she could protest, he shoved it into her hands. "Just in case."

Thoughts of the attack from the other night at her house flooded through her mind. "Please don't leave me down here." Her body shook and she had no idea where to put the gun. What she wanted to do was crawl into a hole somewhere and never come out.

"Let me check things out and I'll come back down." He removed another gun from his ankle holster. When Tank made a move to follow him, Stan stopped him. "Take care of Tasha."

He pointed to Natasha; Tank turned his head to look at her, and then trotted to her side.

Glancing at the gun in her hand, Natasha looked around the room to see what she could do with it. She placed it on a shelf behind the bar just as another roar of thunder shook the house. She rubbed Tank's back wondering what was taking Stan so long.

There was a sound of shuffling over their heads, and then it sounded like Stan was running.

"Maybe we should go up and check on him." Tank looked up at her and then trotted over to the stairs and growled. "What's up with the growling? Is it the stor—"

"Run, Tasha!" Stan yelled and Natasha startled.

"Wha ..." Her heart pounded and her feet finally moved. She hurried to the stairs. "Come on, Tank!" She pulled on his collar but he wouldn't budge. "Come on!"

Two gunshots rang out, but before Natasha could react, the door at the top of the stairs swung open and Stan appeared.

"Run, Tash—" He grunted, blood shooting out of his mouth.

Oh dear God!

"Stan!" She ran up the first three stairs, freezing when another gunshot rang out. "Stan!" His eyes rolled to the back of his head and he fell forward, barely giving her enough time to get out of the way. "Oh my God!" She cupped his cheek and then checked his pulse, which was thready. Tank was barking uncontrollably. "Hold on Sta—"

"Step away from him!" A loud voice boomed from the top of the stairs.

Natasha jerked her head up, regretting the sudden move when she swayed, but gripped the railing.

Ray?

Tank charged up the stairs toward him. When Ray lifted his gun, Natasha screamed.

"*No!*" She fell up the stairs grabbing at Tank's collar, not caring about the pain shooting through her knee. "Please, oh God please, don't shoot him!"

"Well get him away from me!"

"Okay, okay, just let me put him in a room." At first, she couldn't budge Tank. He stood firm, growling at Ray. Natasha's heart was pounding so loud, she thought for sure Ray could hear it. "Come on, Tank. Please." Tears suddenly bloomed in her eyes, blurring her vision. *What am I going to do?* Her mind raced as she continued to fight against Tank's strength.

"Hurry it up. Otherwise, I will put a bullet in him.

"No, no, please, don't. Just stay there so I can get him to calm down."

She practically had to drag Tank away. "Come on, boy." He finally settled down and went with her toward the shelter.

"And don't try any funny stuff or you both will die!"

"Okay, give me a minute to put him in this room." There was no way they'd be able to get far without Ray coming after them. She was going to have to leave Tank, praying that he would be okay. Then she needed to come up with another plan.

When they got to the shelter, Natasha knelt down and held Tank's large head between her hands. Her body trembling in fear. "All right, I need you to be a good boy and stay here." He barked and she hugged him. "God, I wish you could go and find Malik." He barked again. She heard movement in the other room and hurried to back out of the space, Tank following. "Stay here, boy, and I'll be right back," she said for Ray's benefit. This time Tank's vicious bark scared even her.

Natasha closed the door, and went around the corner. Ray was walking toward her.

"I'm sorry it took so long. I couldn't get him to settle down." Her voice shook despite her efforts to stay calm. She moved around Ray and tried not to look at Stan, but she couldn't miss all of the blood painting the tiled floor. She also noticed blood staining Stan's pant leg, a few drops dripped onto the floor.

"It's good to see you again, love," Ray said, his voice deeper than usual.

Natasha stared at him. *That voice ... I've heard that ...* She swallowed hard. "It was you. You broke into my house. You ..." Her words trailed off. She couldn't believe her attacker was Ray. "Why are you doing this?"

"As a trained killer, I'm all about removing obstacles. I was hired to do a job." He shrugged. "I did what I had to do, but for you, I have big plans for you."

She inched back, trying to do it discreetly, but her whole body was shaking. "Well, Malik is going to be here soon. So I suggest you leave while you can."

He released a ruthless laugh and slowly approached her, shoving his gun into the back of his waistband.

"I'm not worried about your boyfriend. In fact, I have a feeling he won't be returning for a long time. A very long time."

For every step he took forward, Natasha took a step back until she bumped into the pool table. "Ray, you're making me very uncomfortable."

"I don't mean to, love. I just want us to get to know each other better. That's all I've wanted for the past month, but you never gave me a chance."

He grabbed her arm before she could react, and pulled her against the hardness of his body.

"Let me go!" She pounded on his chest, her efforts useless. The smirk on his face scared her even more.

"Fighting me is pointless. I know you would've given me a chance had it not been for Malik Lewis. Now that he's out of the way—"

"What have you done to him?" she screamed. A burst of adrenaline shot through her and she took out all of her fear and frustration on him, hitting him with everything she had. She even kicked at his injured leg, but he blocked her efforts.

"Stop it!" he yelled, dodging a fist to his face before he locked his arms around her. His lips twisted into a wicked grin. "I never pictured you as a fighter, *Natasha*, but I like that." He pressed his nasty mouth against her neck, despite her struggle to get away from him. "It's just you and me now, love."

"No!" She kept squirming and he loosened his grip. "There is no you and me! I love Malik and no matter what you say or what you've done, that will never change!"

He grabbed her by her hair. "Don't say that!" he growled, the look in his eyes deadly.

"Stop it. You're hurting me." Tears rolled down her cheeks. She didn't know what he'd done to Malik, but it literally felt as if her heart was crumbling inside her chest. "Pl–please don't hu–hurt me," she sobbed.

"If you don't fight me, I won't hurt you." He released her hair. His arms tightened around her upper body, making it impossible for her to move her arms as he backed her against a card table, his pelvis grinding against her. "I won't hurt you. All I want to do is love you."

Her sobs grew louder and bile rose to her throat as he placed kisses along her neck.

"You smell so good," he mumbled against her skin, his grip loosening as he went lower.

"No!" Natasha lifted her knee, connecting with his groin, panic rioting inside her. She ran toward the shelter, but he grabbed her ankle. A glass-shattering scream started at the pit of her stomach and flew out of her mouth just before she crashed to the floor. Dizziness overtook her. She lay dazed against the cold, ceramic tile. Natasha heard Tank barking frantically, but she couldn't get to him. The room wouldn't stop spinning.

"I see you like it rough." Ray climbed on top of her.

"Get off of me!" She pounded against him with fisted hands, connecting with his chin.

"Why you ..." He slapped her, then pinned her to the floor. He held both her hands above her head and ripped her shirt as she screamed and wiggled beneath him.

"Get off of me!"

A loud crash sounded in the distance, and before Natasha could process what was happening, Ray was yanked off her. She scrambled to the bar area and watched as Malik slammed Ray to the ground, punching him over and over again like a prize fighter.

Ray growled, kicked up his legs, and jerked Malik off him.

Ray whipped out his gun. "Move and you die!"

"I have waited a long time for this moment," Ray said to Malik, his tone deadly. He had Malik pinned to the floor, the barrel of his gun resting on the bridge of Malik's nose.

This wasn't the first time Malik had stared down a barrel of a gun, but it was the first time he'd had to stare down one with the woman he loved in the room. He had hoped she would run when he got Ray off her, but he knew she was still here. He felt her presence.

Malik had entered the house through the tunnel, thanks to Tank's incessant barking. Fear of what he'd find once he arrived overwhelmed him. However, when he'd heard Natasha screaming and saw Ray on top of her, terror like nothing he'd ever experienced washed over him. He'd charged in without thinking. Fury drove his every move and he tackled Ray, his fists moving on their own accord, punching him in the face repeatedly.

Ray now hovered above him, his bloody nose dripping onto Malik's shirt. "I told her that if you didn't stop asking questions and butting into things that were none of your business, I would let you watch me kill her," Ray said, his breaths coming in short spurts after their wrestling match. "Now I've changed my mind. I'm going to let her watch me kill you."

"No!" Natasha screamed. Malik cursed under his breath. He could handle Ray, but not with her in the room. "Please don't shoot him. I'll do whatever you want. We can leave, Ray. Just you and me," she pleaded.

"Ahh, isn't this sweet, she's trying to save you. Too bad it's too late." Ray turned and pointed the gun at Natasha. Malik roared and caught Ray by the throat, throwing him to the side. The gun went off and slid from Ray's grasp. Malik couldn't stop pounding him. He wanted him dead. Malik punched him in the side of the head with everything he had, and Ray stopped moving, but he wasn't dead. Malik jumped up and grabbed the gun that he had lost when he first tackled Ray.

He aimed the gun at Ray, whose eyes were barely opened. "Now, *your* ass is going to die."

"Move, Malik!" Natasha's frantic voice came from behind him. He glanced back and his heart leapt into his throat. He swallowed hard.

Where the hell did she get a gun?

Natasha stood ten feet away, a gun in her trembling hands, tears flowing down her cheeks. *Oh damn.* He shoved Ray's gun into the back of his waistband, knowing that Ray wasn't going anywhere. Malik eased away from him, his hands lifted half-mast.

"Natasha, what are you doing?" He moved slowly, not wanting to scare her into pulling the trigger accidently.

"He's going to pay for what he did." The anguish in her voice tugged on Malik's heart.

"I know, baby, and he will, but not like this." If she shot and killed Ray, Malik knew she would never recover from taking a life. "Remember our conversation about guns? What did you tell me?" She cried harder. Her shoulders shook and the gun bobbed up and down as he inched toward her. "You told me that you're about saving lives, not taking them."

"He deserves to die … the way … the way the others died. I couldn't save Stan. He ki–killed him!" Her eyes conveyed the fury inside of her. "He hurt me," she sobbed.

"Ahh, baby …" Sorrow seared Malik's heart. "I swear to you. I won't let anyone hurt you again. Just give me the gun." Malik held out his hand.

"I ca–can't." She cried harder. "I can't let him get away."

"He's not going anywhere, and he'll never be able to hurt anyone again."

Her sobs came loud and hard, her body shaking violently. Malik eased the gun out of her hands and set it on the bar, just as he saw Wiz and Detective Sheldon near Stan.

"Come here." He pulled Natasha into his arms, kissing the side of her head and holding her tight. "Baby, I love you so damn much," Malik said into her hair, his own emotions getting the best of him. Tonight he could have lost her. "God, I love you. I swear I will spend the rest of my life showing you just how much I love you."

Epilogue

Three Months Later

Malik stood at the podium, in the small banquet room, with a glass of champagne in his hand talking to Cameron's father. Natasha admired how good Malik looked. His dark Armani suit draped over his broad shoulders and across his wide chest made him look like a GQ model. He had such a powerful presence, garnering attention no matter where he went. It wasn't just his physical size that turned heads. Malik exuded confidence. Wearing a fearless and commanding persona like a Medal of Honor. Natasha couldn't think of anyone else she'd rather spend the rest of her life with.

"I'll be right back," Layla, who was sitting next to Natasha said. "I see someone I know."

"Okay."

Layla turned to Stan and kissed him on the lips. "Be back in a sec."

Joy bubbled inside Natasha every time she saw them together. Considering the pints of blood he had lost, no one thought Stan would survive his injuries from the gun battle in Malik's basement. He suffered a gunshot to the stomach, barely missing some vital organs, and another shot that shattered his leg. Despite still walking with a cane, Stan claimed that Layla had nursed him back to health.

Malik tapped the microphone. "Excuse me. May I have everyone's attention?" His deep voice boomed around the room, and Natasha smiled when he met her gaze and winked. He still had the ability to make her blush, and she fell in love with him more and more each day.

"Just in case you haven't figured it out," Malik said, "the rumors are true. Cameron "Wiz" Miller and Olivia, *Ollie* to me, are engaged to be married ... again." Cheers and whistles went up around the room.

"Please lift your glasses." Malik waited. "Congratulations to two of the most important people in my life. Wiz, Ollie, I wish you both a lifetime of happiness and if you ever need me, I will always be here for you both. I love you, guys. Cheers." Everyone sipped from their glasses and then clapped. "Oh, and Ollie." Olivia glared at him, wagging her finger. "Oops, I mean Olivia, you're getting a helluva man. You're not only marrying my best friend, my brother, but you're marrying a man who loves you above all else. I know this because he and I can't have a simple conversation without him mentioning you." Laughter filled the room and Malik stepped away from the mic.

Natasha watched him walk toward her. His gaze held hers and everything else around them disappeared. The past couple of months had been some of the most heart-wrenching days of her life, but also some of the most amazing. Her and Malik's relationship was growing stronger by the day. She never thought she'd experience such happiness.

When Stan almost died trying to protect her, and Ray tried to kill her, she thought she would never recover. The fear, guilt, and anger dominated a huge part of who she was. Even more so, when she found out that the day she rode with Ray to his mother's house, they were actually at the social worker's house. He killed her and Natasha hadn't had a clue. She still shivered at the thought. For a while, she wouldn't go anywhere without Malik, or someone from his security team, and the guilt of Stan's injuries had her seeking professional help.

The anger Natasha harbored toward Ray was even harder to deal with. He was charged for murdering Halsey, Tessa and the social worker. It wasn't until he was sentenced to life in prison that she could release some of the hurt and pain. It also helped that with the assistance of Malik and Wiz, her hospital had located all of the babies that had been taken. There was still an ongoing investigation to find the others, taken from hospitals in other parts of the country.

Natasha knew she still had some healing to do, but her faith, therapy, and the love of her man helped her survive the most traumatic season of her life.

"Hey, baby. You okay?" She nodded, and Malik cupped her face between his large hands and kissed her. The firmness of his lips against hers was like medicine for her soul. She felt so much peace whenever he touched her. Held her. Loved her.

Whenever Malik held Natasha in his arms, all was well in the world. The past few months had him on a serious emotional rollercoaster. He had almost lost one of his best friends, Stan, and Natasha, who he couldn't imagine living without. As a soldier, he was prepared to give his life for this nation. A couple of months ago, he was prepared to give his life to save Natasha.

He kissed her with every emotion inside him. He was never going to take for granted that she'd always be there. If the situation with Ray Newton and Alonso Black taught him anything, it was that life was precious and not to be taken for granted.

"Mmm, you taste good." Malik lowered his hands to

Natasha's waist and pulled her closer. Their kiss was like heat from a soldering iron, joining metals together, hot, and binding. He didn't think he'd ever get enough of her. He could kiss her sweet lips all day, but since they were in public, he figured he'd better stop while he could. "Dance with me," he mumbled against her mouth before he lifted his head.

Natasha flashed a smile that lit up her whole face. Weeks ago, he didn't think he would ever see that electrifying smile again—Ray had broken her spirit—but now his baby was back. Almost. She still had the occasional nightmare and didn't like going some places alone, but her sweet, gentle spirit had returned.

Malik led her to the middle of the dance floor and pulled her into his arms, holding her close as they swayed to the song "Reunited" by Peaches and Herb. Each time he stared into her beautiful brown eyes, his heart beat double time at the realization she was his.

He would never forget the moment he knew without a doubt Natasha was the one. It was the day he received the paternity test results regarding Susan's baby. He had always insisted the child wasn't his, even when the baby boy was found. Before he opened the letter containing the results of the test, he wasn't so sure. Natasha had sat on his lap, put her arms around his neck, and told him it didn't matter. She wasn't going anywhere. It was then that he knew she was the one for him. When he finally read the report, and saw that there was zero possibility of him being the father he had made a decision. He wanted to be a father, but only if Natasha was the mother. For the first time in his life, he wanted to be a father, and a husband.

Screw this.

"I know you don't like me cursing," he stopped dancing and reached for Natasha's hand, "but I love you so damn much sometimes I feel as if my fuckin' heart is going to explode. I know we agreed to live together and let our love blossom naturally. Your words, not mine, but baby I need more."

He released her hand and pulled the small velvet box from the pocket inside of his jacket. If anyone had told him a few months ago he would be proposing marriage to the woman of his dreams, he would've laughed them out of the room. Yet, here he was, about to do the one thing he vowed he'd never do.

Right there in the middle of the dance floor, he dropped down on one knee.

Natasha's hands hovered near her mouth, and tears pooled inside her eyes. "Oh my God, Malik," she whispered. "What are you doing?" The dance floor parted like the red sea. Malik owned center stage.

"I could give you this long drawn out speech, but I'd probably end up tossing some curse words into the mix and I know you don't like me cursing." The crowd laughed and Malik heard Wiz say, 'It's about damn time' which caused another round of laughter.

"Tasha, I hadn't planned on doing this here, or this way, but I can't go another minute of my life without knowing if you'd be my wife. And no, I wasn't trying to rhyme." He paused and rubbed his forehead, trying to rein in the emotion clogging his throat. "I just love you so fu— much. Ah, hell ... will you marry me?"

She laughed through her tears and lunged into his arms. "Yes. Yes, I'll marry you."

***

Next book in series

T hank you for reading Truth or Consequences! I hope you enjoyed Malik and Natasha as much as I enjoyed writing about them. The next book in the Reunited Series is Operation Midnight (Wiz and Olivia's story). Be sure to pick up a copy!

If you enjoyed Truth or Consequences, consider leaving a review on retailer sites, review sites or social media outlets.

And check out the Jenkins & Sons Construction series starting with **LOVE UNDER CONTRACT!**

Join Sharon's Mailing List

To get sneak peeks of upcoming stories and to hear about
giveaways that Sharon is sponsoring,
click **here** to join her mailing list.

Other Titles By Sharon

Atlanta's Finest Series

Atlanta's Finest Series
A Passionate Kiss (book 1 - prequel)
Vindicated (book 2)
Indebted (book 3)
Accused (book 4)
Betrayed (book 5)
Hunted (book 6)
Tempted (book 7)
Committed (book 8)

Jenkins & Sons Construction Series (Contemporary Romance)
Love Under Contract (book 1)
Proposal for Love (book 2)
A Lesson on Love (book 3)
Unplanned Love (book 4)

Jenkins Family Series (Contemporary Romance)
Best Woman for the Job (Short Story Prequel)

Still the Best Woman for the Job (book 1)
All You'll Ever Need (book 2)
Tempting the Artist (book 3)
Negotiating for Love (book 4)
Seducing the Boss Lady (book 5)
Love at Last (Holiday Novella)
When Love Calls (Novella)
More Than Love (Novella)

Reunited Series (Romantic Suspense)
Blue Roses (book 1)
Secret Rendezvous (Prequel to Rendezvous with Danger)
Rendezvous with Danger (book 2)
Truth or Consequences (book 3)
Operation Midnight (book 4)
Casino Heat (book 5)

Stand Alones
Something New ("Edgy" Sweet Romance)
Legal Seduction (Harlequin Kimani – Contemporary Romance)
Sin City Temptation (Harlequin Kimani – Contemporary Romance)
A Dose of Passion (Harlequin Kimani – Contemporary Romance)
Model Attraction (Harlequin Kimani – Contemporary Romance)
Soul's Desire (Unparalleled Love series)
Show Me (Irresistible Husband series)
His to Protect (Harlequin Romantic Suspense)
His to Defend (Harlequin Romantic Suspense)
Business Not As Usual (Romantic Comedy)

About the Author

Award-winning and USA Today bestselling author Sharon C. Cooper loves anything that involves romance with a happily-ever-after, whether in books, movies, or real life. Sharon writes contemporary romance, as well as romantic suspense and enjoys rainy days, carpet picnics, and peanut butter and jelly sandwiches. She's been nominated for numerous awards and is the recipient of Romance Slam Jam Emma Awards for Author of the Year 2019, Favorite Hero 2019 (INDEBTED), Romantic Suspense of the Year 2015 (TRUTH OR CONSEQUENCES), Interracial Romance of the Year 2015 (ALL YOU'LL EVER NEED), and BRAB (Building Relationships Around Books) Award -Breakout Author of the Year 2014. When Sharon isn't writing, she's hanging out with her amazing husband, doing volunteer work or reading a good book (a romance of course). To read more about Sharon and her novels, visit www.sharoncooper.net

www.ingramcontent.com/pod-product-compliance
Lightning Source LLC
Chambersburg PA
CBHW030240200626
46816CB00002BA/441